LEAP OF FAITH

LEAP OF FAITH

Radu Herklots

Matador
Unit E2 Airfield Business Park,
Harrison Road, Market Harborough,
Leicestershire. LE16 7UL
Tel: 0116 2792299
Email: books@troubador.co.uk
Web: www.troubador.co.uk/matador
Twitter: @matadorbooks

ISBN 978 1803133 218

British Library Cataloguing in Publication Data.
A catalogue record for this book is available from the British Library.

Printed and bound in Great Britain by 4edge Limited
Typeset in 11pt Adobe Garamond Pro by Troubador Publishing Ltd, Leicester, UK

Matador is an imprint of Troubador Publishing Ltd

In memory of Einstein, beloved border terrier and the inspiration behind the character of Barker.

"There's a breathless hush in the Close tonight
Ten to make and the match to win
A bumping pitch and a blinding light
An hour to play and the last man in."

From Vitai Lampada, by Sir Henry Newbolt

ONE

Rhyminster,
August Bank Holiday Monday,
late afternoon

"Howzat!"

As soon as the bishop raised his index finger to the sky, a dejected dean began to trudge past him on his way back to the pavilion.

"I thought we were on the same team, Your Grace."

"Sorry Dan – you were plumb lbw – and haven't you got to get ready for evensong?"

"If we had ultra-edge technology, you'd have seen that I got a bat to it – what do you think, John?"

"I didn't see it," said Tedesco. "But don't worry, I'm sure the last man in can save the day."

Charles Tantum, Master of Musick at Rhyminster Cathedral and number eleven batsman for the Bishop's XI, strode out to the crease to an accompaniment of jeers from the watching choristers.

Once he had reached the wicket, he made a big deal of questioning the ability of Bishop Robert to find a suitable guard for him, before he grumpily deigned to crouch down in an elaborate crab-like stance to face the last ball of the over.

The equation was a simple one: the Bishop's XI required six to win and their ferocious opponents, the Cathedral Volunteers, needed one wicket.

As the suspiciously youthful volunteer began his run up, Tantum charged down the pitch like a raging bull, somehow managing to connect with the ball by deploying what the late John Arlott would have called an agricultural slog, but which this batsman would later describe as a beautifully executed straight drive.

Unfortunately for the Master of Musick, his bold attempt at glory ended in abject failure, as he was caught on the boundary by a sprightly tour guide: Tantum, displaying a breathtaking but entirely characteristic lack of sportsmanship, argued long and loudly that the ball had already cleared the ropes before the fielder had completed the catch.

"This is an outrage, Your Grace. Reverse your decision at once! That was a six, and we will leave the field in triumph!"

Tantum's rudeness provoked an instant reaction from the players – way too gentle and Anglican to warrant the description 'pitch-side brawl' – but it was rather more than a polite disagreement.

The portly musician was about to threaten to report the bishop and the dean and chapter to the MCC when a prolonged scream echoed around the Close.

Tedesco immediately looked up at the cathedral tower, from which a body was very clearly hurtling through the air. There was no gothic majesty to this death plunge, no romantic tinge of balletic beauty. Instead, there was an audible, dreadful thud of finality as the body reached the ground.

The private investigator whipped out his mobile phone

and called 999 just as the chief sidesman was to be seen running across to the cathedral – there would be no evensong tonight.

*

This was all they bloody needed, Tedesco reflected as he wandered across Cathedral Green, his faithful border terrier, Barker, at his side.

Nearly two years had passed since the world's media had last descended on the sleepy little city – when a body had been discovered in the Rhyme Chantry – and now this.

What had his lovely Cornish grandmother told him about some places being accursed?

The police were soon on the scene, clearing the Close. Dean Dan gravely announced from the pulpit that evensong was cancelled, and that those who were already in the building should remain in place to await instructions from the vergers and the sidesmen.

Tedesco spotted DC Matt Lovell, busy supervising the uniforms securing the crime scene.

"Here we go again, Mr Tedesco!"

"I rather fear that we do, Matt. Is it still okay if I head home through the Close? And you may want me to make a statement at some stage – I saw the body fall and kept a note of the precise time."

"I'm sure that's fine – you live on the other side, don't you?"

Tedesco's cottage in St Budeaux Place was accessed from the south gate of the Close, well away from where the body had landed, so he did, in more ways than one, dwell on the other side.

"Do we know who it is yet?"

"No, but it must have been someone on a tower tour. The last one of the day finishes half an hour before evensong."

"Well, it's a tragedy whatever caused it. I expect we will be seeing a lot of each other."

And with an ironic shrug, the detective constable turned and headed off in the direction of the West Front.

TWO

One week earlier

A grim, rain-soaked scene greeted Mike and Sue Knowles as they looked out over the seafront at Dawlish, lingering disconsolately over their cooked breakfasts.

But quite frankly, what did they expect in late August on the south coast?

This was no light shower. It was stair rods, Dylan's hard rain, or an old-fashioned hooley: cut and paste your cliché of choice.

Mike and Sue had been coming to the same establishment every August for the last thirty years, a routine that had encompassed the rock-pooling days with the children, right through the teenage years when Kelvin and Marie had wanted to visit nightclubs in Torquay rather than joining their parents on outings to see clapped-out TV comedians performing at the Palace Theatre in Paignton, and then well on into the couple's retirement.

They were a solid twosome, Mike and Sue, in every way. They spent the rest of their year in their 1930s semi in the Coundon area of Coventry, where Mike had managed to hold on to his job as a toolmaker until he retired, despite the post-Thatcher devastation suffered by Britain's equivalent of Detroit.

Sue had worked 'in the office' for various of the old motor manufacturers before retraining as a classroom assistant. She habitually betrayed her native Leicestershire by her verbal obsession with waterfowl – "How are you, me duck?" – which was how she greeted Mrs Lean as the proprietor cleared away the remains of the full English.

Hazel Lean was a fellow Midlander who had moved to Devon in the 1990s to run Seaview with her late husband: she now considered herself a fully paid-up Southerner, and visibly blanched at being referred to as Sue's pet mallard or whatever.

"I'm very well, Mrs Knowles, thank you kindly. And what are your plans for today?"

"Looking at the weather, it might be the day for Kent's Cavern," said Mike.

"We go there every time we come down here," said Sue. "I have had it up to here with stalactites," she went on. "I thought this was the year when we were going to try new things?"

Hazel Lean put her tray down and sat at the table opposite.

"I was watching *Searchlight* recently – they have been running a series on unusual days out in the south-west, and the one I saw was about the tower at Rhyminster Cathedral."

Mike's ears pricked up. "I think I caught the end of that before we went over to the bingo the other night. It looked really interesting. Come on, Sue, you're good at online and what have you, why don't we have a look at the web page or whatever it's called?"

Back in their sauna-like room, crammed with Capodimonte statuettes, Sue eventually managed to book two spaces on the final tour of the bank holiday. This triggered Mike's elaborate process of route planning, and Sue accepted that she could look forward to several days of angst about parking.

"You know what these old places are like love – they weren't designed with the motorist in mind."

*

The previous two slots on the tower tour had been nabbed by Brad and Betty Budden, a couple from Plymouth, Massachusetts, who were visiting their twin city in the UK.

They had exhausted the obvious tourist hot spots of the Hoe and the Barbican – although Plymouth native John Tedesco would gladly have suggested some more niche aspects of his home city – and were looking for something to do on the bank holiday weekend once they'd had enough of Navy Days at Devonport Dockyard.

As they rifled through the tourist leaflets in the carousel adjacent to the reception desk of their boutique hotel, Betty was taken by the offering from Rhyminster Cathedral.

"Look Brad – this is genuine – 900 years old. It looks like something out of *Harry Potter*."

The receptionist overheard them and recommended the tower tour. "There was something about it on our local TV station the other night – I quite fancy going myself."

*

Jock Barton, the chief tower guide at Rhyminster Cathedral, joined Kerry Franklin for a pot of Minster Blend Tea in the refectory.

"All the tours are booked out for Monday now – I thought we might have a space or two left on the final one, but it's going to be 'House Full' notices this time."

Kerry, a petite blonde in late middle years, had spent most of her adult life working abroad. Once she'd qualified as a physio, the world had become her oyster, and after several years and a disastrous marriage in Sweden, she'd worked in entertainments on cruise ships, then endured a brief but lucrative spell as a live-in physio for a fabulously wealthy family in Dubai. She used the money she'd made in the Middle East to start her own physiotherapy practice in Gibraltar, before eventually landing back in her hometown to look after her mother.

One of her old boyfriends used to work in the mason's yard at the cathedral and he suggested guiding to her. She had been sceptical at first, but soon discovered a previously untapped thirst for learning and sharing interesting stories about the imposing edifice that she had simply taken for granted when she was growing up.

"Here we are, Kerry," said Barton, handing her a printout of names. There were twelve in all, including hers, this being the maximum allowed by the cathedral health and safety police.

"What have we here – Mr and Mrs Budden from the States, there's always at least one Yank couple."

"Gee, it's so wunnerful, Howie, wait till we tell the folks back home."

"Then we have Mr and Mrs Knowles from Coventry, Sanjeev and Anjana from Exeter, with their children Zac and

Millie, the fun-sounding Mr Meer from faraway Ivybridge, Crispin and Arabella from across the road in the Close and finally your good self!"

"Arabella – now why does that ring a bell?"

"She's Maxwell Patrick's daughter – the MP for Somerset Central? She's moved down here from London and is eyeing up the constituency. Sir Vere has just announced that he's standing down at the next election."

Kerry's shoulders visibly slumped. "I hope she isn't going to start canvassing for votes when we reach the top – I might be tempted to heave her off!"

THREE

August bank holiday, morning

"So, what have you got planned today? I see you are on your way out again, leaving your old mother on her lonesome as usual."

Kathleen Meer despaired of her only son. Alan had made it to grammar school and could have gone to university but opted to leave school at sixteen and join the firm of Gallant, Nelson and Rickard (now just known as Gallants) as an office clerk, and there he had remained, slowly rising to the rank of legal executive in the probate department.

Both of their lives had been affected by the tragedy, but Alan stubbornly refused to move on. His friends only seemed to exist on the internet, where he spent hours playing various elaborate fantasy games with similar men – they all seemed to be men – from across the globe. The only exception to this life in cyberspace was the local astronomy club, but the other members appeared to be as detached from reality as he was.

"I thought I'd go into work today, Mum. It will be quiet, so I can catch up with some estate accounts."

This much was true. He would cycle in and do a couple

of hours of billable work. But he had other plans for the afternoon.

He'd seen *Searchlight* the other evening – he 'watched with Mother' while they were having supper – and Nicola Tedesco, who he had secretly fancied for years, was presenting an item about the tower tour at Rhyminster Cathedral, featuring an interview with a strangely familiar-looking guide.

Alan moved quickly and booked a place on the Bank Holiday Monday tour. Once he'd finished at the office, he planned to cycle to Ivybridge station and get the train over to Rhyme. It was long overdue a visit – not that he could tell his mother, of course – and who knew, the gorgeous Ms Tedesco might just be there in real life, or if the gods were aligned, that familiar-looking guide might be taking him up the narrow steps of the ancient tower.

He'd done his research. The cathedral's website contained a section called 'Meet our Volunteers' so he refined his search to 'Tower Guides'. It was her all right.

FOUR

August bank holiday, afternoon

There was a bottleneck at the visitors' entrance, and the hard-pressed desk ladies were in serious danger of losing control of the queue.

Beyond the entrance one soon became aware of the volunteer tour guides scurrying around in their crimson sashes, which looked as if they had been acquired as a job lot from a beauty pageant.

Kerry Franklin strode through the crowd with a practised confidence before raising her loud-hailer to her lips.

"Anyone with tickets for the tower tour, come straight through. It starts in fifteen minutes."

A disparate cross-section of the queuing group detached themselves from the main herd and shuffled awkwardly across to a holding pen indicated by a pull-up banner labelled 'Tower Tour Wait Here'.

"Well," said Mike Knowles, "credit where credit's due. I'd been very concerned about trying to park here, but that park and ride system is dead easy. We live near Stratford-upon-Avon – it's nigh on impossible to park there."

"We came down from Exeter on the train," said Sanjeev.

"No problem at all. They had a special offer for the kids, and the cathedral was really well signed."

"You could have just looked up, Dad. The tower is over fifty metres tall, you know," said Millie.

"That's telling you and no mistake, me duck," said Sue Knowles.

Kerry reappeared, clipboard in hand, and started to count heads. "We seem to be one short. Mr Meer? Could Alan Meer make himself known? Okay, we'll give him five minutes, but then we do need to get started."

She used the time to get to know a bit about her charges. Sanjeev and Anjana were both lecturers at Exeter University, and Brad Budden had served in the US Marines.

"Whoah, cool," said Zac, aged ten.

"Are you a Trump supporter?" asked Millie, fourteen.

Crispin and Arabella joked about how far they had come, and Kerry instantly realised that she should not have asked them so pointedly why they hadn't taken a tower tour before now. The prospective Member of Parliament glared at her then started to make polite conversation with Mike and Sue Knowles, feigning intense interest in Mike's detailed summary of his journey until she realised that he didn't live in the constituency so couldn't vote for her.

It was time for Kerry to get the show on the road. "Okay folks. I think we've given Mr Meer plenty of time, so please follow me."

Just as she made her way to the entrance to the tower, Kerry felt a sudden tap on her shoulder and turned around to face a small, crushed-looking man wearing a Dungeons and Dragons tee-shirt and carrying a plastic shopping bag. "Mr Meer, I assume?"

"Sorry I'm late. I've been waiting over there for half an hour, looking at the scale model of the cathedral."

"Oh well, you are here now," she replied, while wondering how someone could be engrossed with a scale model for a full thirty minutes, no matter how good a representation it was.

She unlocked the door leading to the first of the stairways, this one ending at a viewing platform that gave unrivalled views of the interior of the cathedral. Before they commenced their ascent Kerry gave the group a safety briefing and showed them the lockers where bags must be stored.

Alan Meer affected not to hear – or was he just today's problem tourist? He clung tightly to his Morrison's bag, seemingly struggling to extract something from it.

As she practically had to wrestle the bag off him, Kerry couldn't avoid noticing his nauseous body odour – *that's going to be popular when we get to the narrow part of the steps*, she thought to herself.

"Now people – this is your final chance – if you aren't sure about heights don't feel embarrassed if you would rather stay down here."

Brad Budden looked across at Betty, who gave him a tight little smile.

"I'll be fine, Mike," said Sue Knowles, bravely.

"Okay! Follow me please, taking care to use the ropes by the side."

Once the group had huffed and puffed their way to the viewing platform, Kerry counted heads again, noting that Alan Meer had brought up the rear.

They were invited to have a breather and then to have a good look at the view. "You have earned it."

Anjana asked if they could take photos – yes – and Betty commented that the view was "like looking down on the dining room in Hogwarts".

After allowing time for the taking and sharing of photos Kerry gave them some more safety reminders as they headed towards the narrowest of the stairs.

This proved to be harder work for some of them: it sounded like a heavy breathers' convention was in town when they all eventually emerged in the bell chamber.

While they waited for the hour of four, when the great bell, Chimin' Rhyme, would strike, Kerry gave them a brief description of the methods used in the construction of the cathedral.

Mike Knowles wanted to know about the tools that were employed – "I'm a retired toolmaker, you see," – and Zac asked if any dead bodies had been found up there.

Arabella Patrick used the wait to begin a party political broadcast, explaining how the fiscal prudence of the Conservative government had allowed for extra spending on national heritage.

"Saved by the bell!" exclaimed Kerry as the cacophony commenced. She'd made a real enemy of the prospective candidate now.

Once the four strikes had faded into quiet, she pointed out a small opening in the side of the room.

"Can anyone guess what that is used for?"

"A toilet?" suggested Millie.

"For pouring oil on enemy soldiers?" her brother put forward.

"I think I know," said Sanjeev. "I'm guessing that you need an emergency escape hatch."

"Top of the class! Once a year we arrange for a volunteer to be hoisted down the outside of the building to test it. The refectory manager, Mark Tubbs, did it last time."

"Did it work?" asked Betty Budden.

"Well, you will see for yourself if you visit the refectory later. Okay – now who wants to step outside?"

FIVE

"Is it safe for the kids?" asked Anjana, trying to mask the fact that she didn't care for heights herself, while Betty Budden had taken the merest glimpse outside and retreated to the ringing room before Brad managed to cajole her into joining the others.

"We won't get another chance, honey, and the views will be awesome."

Kerry reassured Anjana that it was fine, as long as Zac and Millie didn't climb on the walls, adding that the cathedral had a 100% safety record.

"But please don't feel that you have to step out on the roof – we want you to enjoy the day, not feel scared."

Suitably reassured, Sanjeev led his family up the final stairway and then through the narrow portal leading onto the highest viewing platform.

Arabella and Crispin were next up – "Look down there, darling, it's our house!" – followed by Mike and Sue Knowles, with Brad and Betty Budden bringing up the rear.

Kerry was about to point out the views over the city when she realised that they were one short.

"Sorry people, have a wander around and take some photos – and please don't climb on the walls. I just need to see what's happened to Mr Meer."

"There's always one," tutted Sue Knowles.

Arabella spotted that Brad had the most expensive-looking camera, so she commandeered him to take several photos of her and then some with Crispin, with the Close and the water meadows as a perfect backdrop: these would come in useful when the time came to publish her election address.

Sanjeev and Anjana tried to interest Zac and Millie in the views over to Rhyminster Down, but they were more engaged in trying to spot swans on the River Rhyme.

It was Mike Knowles who heard it first: the animal response to imminent danger, the first sound of panic before the full scream comes.

"Quick! Everyone! Someone's about to jump!"

At the exact same moment Alan Meer finally clambered out onto the roof.

*

"All of you, stay where you are. I'm going to get you down."

Cometh the hour, cometh Brad Budden, who would be presented with a bravery award months later via the miracle of Zoom.

The military veteran ordered Sanjeev, who he had assessed as the calmest of the crew, to slowly descend followed by Zac and Millie, with Anjana close behind.

After a couple of minutes, which felt a whole lot longer, Sanjeev shouted, "Down!" as instructed.

Brad sent Mike Knowles back down next, followed by Sue, with Alan Meer nervously following behind her. He let Arabella wait with her husband until Meer was halfway down – she had seriously pissed off the retired marine.

Once Mike had shouted "Down!" Brad helped a distraught Betty, thus completing phase one of the rescue mission.

"Well done folks, take a breather. When you are ready, begin to descend the next staircase, use the ropes, and go easy. Same order as before. Sanjeev please!"

The business studies lecturer resisted the urge to salute and gathered his family for a group hug, before leading them safely back to terra firma.

Despite a missed step from Sue Knowles, the group eventually reassembled on the platform overlooking the nave. They all felt safer back inside the main body of the cathedral, even though there was still one more staircase to negotiate. But although the vergers had been largely successful in clearing the visitors from the building there was still a stubborn group of stragglers queuing for the emergency exits. This being the twenty-first century, some of them were taking photos or shooting videos of the rescued tour group.

A deceptively demure young woman in a black gown was issuing instructions via a loud-hailer: this was Izzie McCalliog, acting head verger.

Once she had seen that the tour group had descended as far as the interior viewing platform, she walked towards the West Door and spoke to them through the megaphone.

"Stay where you are! The police and the fire brigade will be here soon, and they will see you safely down."

Izzie reflected that it was a good job that none of the group had witnessed the looks of panic in the vestry once it had dawned on her and her terrified colleague Colin that Kerry would have locked the door to the tower behind her in accordance with protocol. She had been wearing the key around her neck so they could hardly go and take it off her dead body. And neither she nor Colin knew where any spare was kept.

This shocking oversight was due to the fact that the cathedral guides were in charge of the tower, a privilege they guarded with an almost medieval ferocity worthy of the neighbourhood guilds who organised the *Paleo* in Siena.

Izzie had persistently tried to get hold of Jock Barton, the head tower guide, but when she was finally able to track down his wife, Ann Barton reported that her husband was up in Taunton, watching county cricket.

This is going to look good, Izzie reflected, as she saw Dean Dan and Canon Wilfred Drake marching purposefully towards her.

SIX

Izzie had managed to order her thoughts by the time the dean had joined her in the vestry.

Having pleaded with DC Lovell to see if there was any way that they could use the key that was still on Kerry's person and been told very firmly that the body should not be touched, as it could contaminate the crime scene, she had been fretting that the fire brigade would struggle to get ladders into the cathedral and that any attempt at a rescue from the outside would be a logistical nightmare.

They could always open the Great West Door – the dean was on side with this – but Wilf pointed out that to do so could encourage both gawpers and the media to try and get inside, thus impeding the emergency services.

"I know," said Izzie, experiencing a lightbulb moment, "we always borrow ladders from the works department to decorate the Christmas tree. We can get them in via the cloisters."

"Good idea," said Dean Dan. "Have you got everyone out of the building yet?"

"Yes, it's just us and the tour group now."

DCI Bloomfield was less than thrilled to have been interrupted just as he was firing up his bank holiday barbecue. "That fucking cathedral again!"

His mood wasn't helped by the fact that DS Julia Tagg, his most reliable colleague, was on a midge-infested holiday in Scotland with Lynne Davey, Tedesco's sidekick and his former CID colleague.

Swinging himself over the taped-off area near where Kerry had landed, he joined the police medical officer, Nigel Brimacombe, who was dictating his findings into his ancient Grundig recorder.

"So, Nige. Did she jump or was she pushed?"

"No sign of any wounds before the impact, no signs of a struggle."

"Okay. I'm going inside to see what the dean has to say. It had better be good."

The dean, Dan Luxmoore, had visibly aged since his elevation to the deanery from his successful parish in Clifton. He increasingly questioned why God had called him to cathedral ministry just as the picture-postcard city was about to be become a byword for scandal. Or perhaps that was why he had been called?

Jimmy Bloomfield, not given to self-doubt, nevertheless looked ill at ease out of his normal 'antique dealer' work uniform comprising a three-piece suit and his trademark bow tie. Today, the DCI was wearing red chinos and a polo shirt with some sort of designer logo. While the look may have been casual, the mood of the wearer was anything but.

"I won't even pretend that it's good to see you, Dean. What can you tell me about the girl who fell?"

"I didn't really know Kerry. There are so many volunteers here it's hard to meet them all. Our HR department will be back in tomorrow, and I expect they can fill you in on her family and so on. I do know that her mother died last year – Kerry came back to Rhyme to nurse her – but I don't know about partners, brothers and sisters and so forth."

"Okay, I get it. Lovell and I are going to take statements from the tour group, once they are safely down. The fire brigade tell me that they are still stuck halfway up there. Honestly, I wouldn't believe it of anywhere else. I hope you have your story straight before the media start descending."

*

Tedesco felt frustrated at being locked out of the Close just as another massive thunderbolt had struck his idyllic world. Not only was Lynne away, but his sister, BBC *Searchlight*'s Nicola Tedesco, would also be missing out on the fun as she was absent enjoying, or maybe enduring, a corporate jolly on the River Dart, organised by her upmarket car salesman husband.

There had been no mention of the incident on the main BBC *News* nor on the brief local summary, and nothing as yet on the online version, but as there had been plenty of onlookers in the Close when it happened it wouldn't be long, surely, before the red 'Breaking News' warning appeared.

Feeling trapped outside the Close, he decided to take Barker for a walk in the opposite direction, over the little river bridge, past the paper shop and on to King George Field.

Meanwhile, Izzie's plan had worked. The fire brigade had been able to access the inside of the building by going through the mason's yard and then the cloisters and had got their ladders up to reach the viewing gallery.

Shock seemed to anaesthetise most of the group into allowing themselves to be rescued without undue alarm, with exception of Betty Budden, who seemed to be frozen to the ladder.

"Stay strong, sweetie, these guys are the experts," exhorted her husband, and the group gave her a resounding cheer as she reached the safety of the stone floor, in last place; but it wasn't a competition.

Arabella was the first to reach for her phone, followed by Meer, who was desperately trying to cobble together a plausible excuse for being late home for tea on a bank holiday.

Bloomfield called the rescued group to attention. He and Lovell would need to take statements from each of them before they could be released from the cathedral. He started by promising to arrange transport for any of them who might be stranded.

Mike and Sue Knowles offered Meer a lift home: it was a bit out of their way, but they didn't mind. Sanjeev and Anjana had already checked the trains, relieved to find that the last one left at nine, and the Buddens had come by car, so they were catered for.

"Good, that's decided then," said Bloomfield. "I suggest that we interview Mr and Mrs Bhasra first, so they and the young ones can get to the station in plenty of time."

"And when are you going to release us, officer? We have people coming for drinks in an hour."

Bloomfield, like Budden earlier, had taken an instant dislike to Arabella Patrick.

"Madam, as you live nearby, you will surely agree that it would be reasonable for you to be our final interviewees of the evening. And, unless your guests are already in the Close, they won't be able to attend your soiree tonight."

Bloomfield rather enjoyed putting the Patricks back in their box.

Arabella smiled sweetly at him, as if she had just realised that upsetting a respected local senior police officer was not, perhaps, the best career move for a putative Tory MP.

SEVEN

"Mother? It's me. Remember, your son? Alan?"

"Where have you been? You haven't been answering your calls, so I've just walked all the way to your wretched office, and there was no sign of life. What's going on, Alan?"

"Nothing to worry about. It was a good job that I called in to work. One of our clients died recently, and the executor lives in the Midlands. He phoned the office on the off chance that we might be open as he and his wife were down for the bank holiday. We had a lot of paperwork to go through, but he left his ID documents at his bed and breakfast in Dawlish of all places, can you believe it, so they drove me back there to check them as I didn't have anything else planned for this afternoon. I'm on my way home now."

From his pathetic waffling, Kathleen Meer knew straight away that her son was lying, but at least he was safe.

*

The dean suggested that Bloomfield and Lovell use two of the side chapels, dedicated to St Nonna and St Budeaux respectively, for the initial statements, and he and Izzie would act as runners between the two makeshift interview rooms.

Sanjeev and Anjana gave virtually mirror-imaged accounts of their ordeal: Kerry had left the group to take in the views while she went to look for one of her charges who hadn't joined them on the roof. Lovell asked Anjana if she had taken any photos, which she had, so he asked her to forward them to him. They could provide evidence of the time when the incident occurred.

Sanjeev told Bloomfield that the first he had known of Kerry's disappearance had been when Mike Knowles had yelled out that someone was about to jump. He had rushed to where Mike was standing, but by then it was too late.

The lecturer hadn't seen Kerry in the act of falling; she was almost at the ground by the time he saw her.

Neither he nor his wife saw Meer join the group, but the straggler was out on the roof with the others when Sanjeev had gone to find Anjana and the kids.

Brad Budden was next up. He too confirmed that Kerry had left the group to find "that odd little guy", but that he had been too busy taking photos of Arabella and Crispin to notice anything untoward until Mike Knowles had sounded the alarm. He had rushed over to where Mike was standing, but, like Sanjeev and Anjana, he was too late to see Kerry jump.

Betty was nervous, initially refusing to be interviewed without Brad before eventually agreeing, but only on condition that she was interviewed by a female officer, the instant problem being that there was none available on site.

Bloomfield, while eager to get a contemporaneous statement, was sensitive and shrewd enough not to interfere, wisely allowing the combined soothing voices of Dean

Dan and her husband to persuade Mrs Budden that she had nothing to get worried about, and so she agreed to be interviewed by the DCI.

This proved to be important, as Betty did have something new to offer.

"I'm no good with heights – I was convinced I was going to fall off that ladder – and so I didn't wander around much, but stuck close to the stairs. I must have been the last person to speak to poor Kerry. She asked me if I'd seen Alan – I hadn't – but I saw him later when he appeared at the entrance to the roof."

"Take your time, Mrs Budden. Can you remember when you saw him?"

"Why yes. I heard Mike shout that someone was about to jump, then I looked behind me and saw Alan climbing out onto the roof."

While Bloomfield was taking Betty's statement, Alan Meer was being put through his paces by Matt Lovell.

The witness was nervous – nothing unusual there – but kept glancing at his watch as if he was late for an urgent appointment.

Meer didn't offer a convincing explanation as to why he had failed to join the others on the roof, thus necessitating Kerry's search for him. Nor did it seem to occur to him that he might be in any way to blame for the incident by going AWOL.

"Did you have second thoughts about going out on the roof, Mr Meer?"

"No, not really. I was just a bit tired after all that climbing so I had a bit of a rest."

"Did it ever occur to you to let the guide know that you would be remaining behind for your 'rest', Alan?"

"No, not really."

As he wasn't getting anywhere, Lovell tried the old *Columbo* tactic.

"Just one final thing, and then you can go. You live in Ivybridge – not a million miles from Rhyminster, is it? Pretty much the next stop on the train, in fact. You could go on a tower tour at any time, so what made you choose a Bank Holiday Monday?"

"Er, I've always wanted to go up the tower since I was little, but I was ill when there was a school trip, and I have been waiting for another chance ever since."

"I see. So what finally persuaded you to make the ascent?"

"I saw an item on *Searchlight*. Nicola Tedesco was very enthusiastic about it, and that convinced me that it was time to go."

"Bit of a fan of Nicky, are you, Alan?"

*

Tedesco, as was his way when out walking, was tuning in to his internal soundtrack. Van Morrison: 'If I Ever Needed Someone.'

He was missing Lynne, he wasn't over Liz Gerrey, and he could never forget Sorcha, his one true love.

In the immediate aftermath of the earlier murder in the cathedral, his pride in tying up the loose ends of the case had been shattered by an urgent summons to Sorcha's hospice in Ireland. He dropped everything, leaving Barker to the tender care of his sister Nicky, and then he took the first available flight to Cork.

Although his heart was breaking, he somehow managed to negotiate the narrow roads to the hospice just in time, for which he would always give thanks.

He'd kept a low profile at the ecumenical funeral, which was a celebration of a life well lived. After studying English at Trinity College, Sorcha had gently rejected Tedesco's offer of a life in Devon in favour of a publishing career in New York. But they never lost touch, and his fading hopes were raised years later when she returned to the village of Schull in West Cork to start her life afresh after two failed relationships in the States, and he became both a regular visitor to her café bookshop in the village and a familiar face in the local pubs, crossing the Irish Sea whenever work allowed. He had even suggested, after a good night in Newman's bar a couple of years ago, that he could leave Rhyminster to help her run the shop.

Schull would always be a magical place to him because it was there that he first met the bewitching Sorcha Doolin, home from university, working in her uncle's hotel. But although he could dream of a future there, she was unconvinced.

"I know you think it's just like *Local Hero* over here, but don't imagine it's an easy option. The shop only just about wipes its face, the winters are long and hard. And what would you do about that stupid soccer team of yours? And wouldn't you miss the cathedral, the whole C of E thing that you love so much? Have you even consulted Barker? We've got each other for life, but we don't need to be with each other for life, do we, my love?"

He knew deep down that she had been right. Absence meant that the heart never wavered.

Having deliberately stayed away from the burial he walked out to the cemetery on the Colla Road in the late afternoon, soaked through by the rain swirling in off the Atlantic.

He found what he was searching for in a quiet corner overlooking Roaring Water Bay.

It was a simple slice of Irish slate bearing a beautifully carved inscription.

The words were from TS Eliot, who she had studied at Trinity.

"In the end is my beginning."

He knelt down and kissed the memorial. He would spend the rest of his days trying to be really strong for her.

But he couldn't switch off the internal playlist. Kate and Anna McGarrigle this time: 'Heart like a Wheel'.

*

"Hello, boss!"

It was his faithful but incredibly annoying PA, Sally Munks. Why did some people have to be so unrelentingly positive?

"Sally – what have you been up to?"

"Weren't you here earlier? You don't know what I'm talking about, do you?"

"I'm afraid not, Sally, but I fear that you are going to tell me."

"You are so funny, Mr T. It was the parish fete, St Georges. I was on the fairtrade stall. I did tell you about it."

Sally's charitable works were as legendary as her ill-advised attempts at fancy dress.

"Anyway, just as we were packing up there was terrible screaming and shouting coming from the cathedral, so I thought I'd wander over and see what was going on."

"You will have a wasted journey, I'm afraid. The Close is sealed off. I expect you will see it on the news later, but – how can I put this gently – someone has fallen from the tower."

"No! You don't think it's another murder?"

"I really don't know anything yet, Sally."

"Whatever it is, I bet the bishop will want you and Lynne to investigate."

He decided not to complicate things by trying to explain that it would be the dean who would be the source of any instructions: as the incident took place in the cathedral precincts, then this was not a diocesan matter.

"You may well be right, Sally. I think we might be about to get very busy again."

EIGHT

Arabella and Crispin paced up and down the nave, both superglued to their phones, both looking furious.

Crispin spotted the dean and marched up to him, bristling with anger.

"Look here. We can't be kept hanging around like this. We have some very important guests waiting for us. Can't you exert some influence on that awful man? You are supposed to be in charge of this place, aren't you?"

"By 'that awful man' I take it you are referring to DCI Bloomfield, over whom I have no operational control. I know this is unpleasant for you, but it does seem fair for the others to give their statements first."

"Yeah, yeah. We get persecuted because we are unfortunate enough to have worked our balls off to buy a house in the Close. Perhaps your next sermon should be about the politics of envy."

Mike and Sue Knowles were called next. Bloomfield saw Mike, while Sue was gently guided to the Chapel of St Nonna to be questioned by DC Lovell.

The retired toolmaker's statement was the one that

Bloomfield was waiting for. He had spotted Kerry just before she fell, so he at least should be able to offer some direct evidence of the fateful leap.

Having confirmed that he had seen Kerry standing between two crenelations on the edge of the roof, Mike told the DCI that he could tell that she was about to topple over, so he shouted over to the others.

"'Topple over' – that's an interesting way of describing the act of jumping, Mr Knowles, wouldn't you agree? Think carefully. You warned the others that 'Someone's about to jump', not 'Someone's about to topple over.'"

Mike Knowles furrowed his brow, as if he was comparing alternative routes on his AA Route Finder app.

"Well, officer. She was trying to balance, but it was windy up there, and she just fell."

"Mr Knowles. This is important. Did she fall backwards?"

"Yes, she did."

"I wouldn't describe the act of jumping as falling backwards, would you?"

"Now you put it like that, no. Look – it was the spur of the moment. I just said the first thing that came into my head."

"Okay, Mr Knowles, fair point. How did Kerry appear to you?"

"Shit scared, of course."

"Yes, yes. But beforehand, had she seemed distracted? From what you are saying, about how she fell, we can't rule out suicide."

Mike looked serious. "Got you, I see. No, she was fine. Lovely. I remember telling Sue that we ought to give her a good review on Trip Advisor."

Bloomfield wisely resisted the temptation to point out the inappropriateness of referring to that particular site if Kerry had, indeed, fallen off the roof by accident.

"Mr Knowles, did you actually see Kerry climb up onto the edge of the tower?"

"No, she was on it by the time I got round there. She was balancing, using her arms to try not to fall, a bit like a trapeze artist, if you get my drift."

"Did she see you?"

"Oh yes, she just looked at me, as if she wanted to say something, but couldn't get the words out. Am I making sense?"

"You are, Mr Knowles, thank you. You've been really helpful."

Sue Knowles corroborated her husband's view of the late Kerry Franklin's state of mind.

"She was lovely, dear. Not like some guides we've come across. We had a right mardy cow when we went to Kenilworth Castle. I told Mike that we should give Kerry a five-star write up on Facebook or whatever. She was so nice, so reassuring to that American lady who didn't like heights. There's just no way that Kerry was about to jump off."

Lovell let her ramble for a while, then asked her about the other members of the party. "Was there anything about their behaviour, or how they appeared, that stood out for you?"

"Well," she said, pulling herself up to her full height, "I took against that snobby couple, Crispin and Arabia. The Americans were great. Brad deserves a medal. I suppose it was his marine training that kicked in. And that young couple with the kiddies, they were so polite. I told the parents that they had a lovely family."

"That's all good, Mrs Knowles. What about Alan Meer? What did you make of him?"

"Call me Sue, me duck. I wasn't sure what to think of him – perhaps he was just shy? But hang on, I do remember something that happened when we were getting ready to climb up."

"Okay, Sue. What was it? It might be important."

"Oh, I doubt it. It was when we were putting our bags in them locker things. I had just closed mine when I looked up and saw that he, Alan, was being a bit funny about it."

"What do you mean, Sue?"

"Sorry dear, I'm not used to explaining stuff. He had a plastic bag, and Kerry told him to put it in the locker. He insisted on taking it with him, and poor Kerry almost had to force it off him. There's something else – he took something out of the bag and put it in his trouser pocket. He looked very guilty about it as well."

"Could you see what the item was, Sue?"

"Not really. I wondered if it was an inhaler or something like that. I thought this might explain why he wanted to take the bag, because he needed his meds up there."

Once they'd signed off on their statements, Alan and Sue were reunited in the nave.

"Are you all right, Mr Knowles?" asked the dean.

"He's fretting about missing the last bus back to the park and ride," Sue said, "and Alan is relying on us for a lift home."

"Don't worry. Once the last two witnesses have given their statements, I'll drive you all up there. It's the least I can do."

NINE

Just as Tedesco was about to unlock his front door, an unmistakably raucous sound shattered the tranquillity of St Budeaux Place, the little mews which nestled just outside the Cathedral Close but within its 'Ancient Liberty'.

The private investigator had grown up across the road from Home Park, Plymouth Argyle's picturesque ground, and he remained steadfastly loyal to his first love.

The Pilgrims had run out to their theme tune – Sousa's 'Semper Fidelis' march – from before he was born so, quite naturally, Tedesco had installed it as his ring tone.

Barker absolutely loathed it and made his feelings known.

"Sit, Barker. It will stop in a second. "Tedesco here. Nicky! I can guess what this is about. Can I call you back in a minute? I've just this second got home, and Barker needs his supper."

*

A couple of hundred yards from Tedesco's cosy bolthole, the final two witnesses were giving their statements.

Arabella had eventually managed to speak to her father, Maxwell Patrick, QC, MP, who had offered his usual robust advice on how to respond to questioning.

Her husband was interviewed by Matt Lovell, who gleaned nothing new from him, in fact Crispin had been aggressively unresponsive. He had not seen Kerry on the edge of the roof, and he hadn't noticed when Meer had joined the group.

"I was arranging for that American fellow to get some shots of my wife – I was concentrating on that really. She's on the short list for the seat, as you may know."

Arabella was charm personified. "If chosen for this seat, DCI Bloomfield, then I will make it my business to increase the police budget for this area. I'm very focused on law and order."

Aside from the party-political broadcast, which was wasted on Bloomfield, who tended to cast a tactical vote for the Lib Dems, she didn't offer anything else of interest.

"Thank you, madam. You are free to go now. I hope you and your guests can continue with your plans," said the DCI, his fingers firmly crossed behind his back.

*

Once he'd filled Barker's bowl, Tedesco returned his sister's call. She'd evidently been enjoying the lavish hospitality provided by Aspirational Cars.

Put more simply, she sounded a wee bit pissed.

"Bro, bro. How are you? It's getting really dangerous in the cathedral. That's two murders now!"

"Nicky, we don't know if it was a murder yet. Look, what's this really about?"

"To tell you it's going to be on the news later. I normally cover the Rhyme beat as you know, but I was on the yacht when the story broke."

"Okay, I'll make sure to tune in. Er, are you okay, sis?"

"Yeah, it's been a long day, that's all. Listen, I'll call tomorrow. And John?"

"Yes."

"Who, apart from you obvs, 'tunes in' these days?"

Tedesco ignored the jibe – he was getting weary of being teased about his 'Boomer' references. Anyway, what on earth was wrong with 'tuning in', or referring to the 'Hit Parade' instead of the 'Charts', or to 'Groups' instead of 'Bands'?

He applied his mind to the vital task of his supper as he sliced up some mouldy-looking peppers, fried them in olive oil and then jiggled them around with a bit of pasta before 'tuning in' to the local news update.

It was the third item, behind heath fires in Dorset and holiday traffic chaos throughout the region.

Searchlight had sent Duncan Chivers to cover the story. He was standing on Cathedral Green, so the police had either reopened the Close or granted the BBC special permission to film there.

Tedesco had met him once, at Nicky's fortieth a few years ago. Chivers himself was probably now only in his late forties, but he seemed to have been around for ever. The broadcaster had won Tedesco over by introducing himself as the Alan Partridge of the south-west.

He was a good bloke, Duncan. Safe pair of hands, the regional TV equivalent of the utility player: he could do sport, local politics, the lot, but tonight he was turning his hand to the second tragedy to befall the cathedral in as many years.

"The morning will bring more questions. Why did the deceased fall from the tower? Was it a tragic accident, or was there foul play? For now, this beautiful cathedral city and its frightened residents must be wondering why Rhyminster finds itself in the eye of the storm once again. This is Duncan Chivers, for BBC *Searchlight*, outside Rhyminster Cathedral."

"It will be all over the national media tomorrow, Barker. I think we'd better have an early night, don't you?"

The wise border terrier yawned, stretched, and then curled up in his basket.

TEN

As he slowly came to, Tedesco became aware of a background humming, thrumming noise, not unlike that of the funfair setting up in Central Park when he was a boy. That was the one in Plymouth, of course, not Manhattan. The proper one.

The penny eventually deigned to drop – it was the sound of the media gearing up for a day of hysterical coverage over on Cathedral Green.

Crunching through his morning toast, he heard the story featured on the *Today* programme on Radio 4.

"Here we go again, Barker. More people, more noise. Oh well, we'd better face the music."

As the terrier and his master made their way to work through the media scrum, the dean spotted them and came over.

"John, I'm so glad to see you. Can I call you later? I'm afraid that we will be relying on your good counsel, and Lynne's of course, once again."

Before he could reply, another familiar voice attracted his attention. It was Vicki Thomas.

"Mr Tedesco, fancy seeing you here! I'm going to have to whisk the dean away."

"That's right," said Dean Dan. "Victoria is about to interview me in front of the tower."

"We're going to be here all day," said Victoria Thomas.

"So *Searchlight*'s coming live from here tonight?"

"Yeah, even the weather forecast."

As he headed towards his office, neatly squirrelled away just off the far side of the Close, Tedesco remembered that Nicky had taken the whole week off. She'd be sorry to miss out on another rare scoop on her patch.

Victoria Thomas was the studio-based anchor for the local TV station, incredibly professional but quite intimidating, so he didn't envy the dean as the poor chap was dragged off for what would doubtless be the first of several media interviews.

The office of Tedesco and Davey, private investigators, was on the top floor of Minster Precincts, which he liked to refer to as a medieval office block.

In order to access 4A, a twisty staircase had to be negotiated. Lynne Davey habitually returned from her lunchtime powerwalk by taking the stairs two at a time, but Tedesco and Barker took them at a statelier pace, as befitted the surroundings.

Sally Munks had beaten her boss in to work and was fussily scrolling through Facebook and Twitter as Barker located his day bed under Tedesco's desk.

"Look at this, Mr T! There are people calling for a public enquiry, and for the dean to resign!"

"I'm sure there are, Sally, but how the dean can be held responsible for someone falling off the tower is beyond me."

No matter how hard he tried to concentrate on his bread and butter casework that morning, the cathedral was calling him like a siren, but he decided to delay his visit until mid-morning, when the guides tended to congregate in the refectory for a well-earned break between tour groups.

The cathedral website revealed that while tower tours were postponed indefinitely, it was otherwise business as usual, which meant that the guides were free to shepherd the usual gaggle of bemused visitors, stained glass window aficionados, brass rubbing weirdos, organ freaks and, if they were lucky, a few genuine pilgrims, around the vast interior of the medieval edifice.

*

A few miles away, Kathleen Meer was busy cross-examining her son over the breakfast table.

Alan had returned home very late last night, and she wanted an explanation.

"Listen, Mother. As I told you yesterday, I spent the day with clients. They drove me back here after I'd checked their ID paperwork in Dawlish, and seeing that the traffic was dreadful, we took a detour and got a bit lost."

"Why don't I believe you? I'm not senile, you know, I saw the news. It was her, wasn't it? That Kerry. What was she doing back after all this time?"

"I really have no idea, Mother, and you are making me late for work."

"You were in Rhyminster yesterday, weren't you? Don't lie!"

*

At precisely 10.30 Tedesco descended the stairs and turned into the Close. The media village had expanded since first thing, and he spotted the local press, in the voluptuous shape of Julie Stringer, busy recording vox pop interviews. She winked at him as he walked past, which he found more than slightly unnerving. He enjoyed a love-hate relationship with Julie, who was infamous locally for her 'It Makes Me Mad' column in the *Rhyminster Journal*.

Her heart was in the right place, but she boasted several Olympic golds for tactlessness.

The refectory was rammed solid. As well as the usual melange of tourists and volunteers, he noted a sizeable journalistic presence, so he would need to be careful.

There was a special corner table reserved for volunteers, and Tedesco was pleased to see that it was occupied by Jock Barton, the head tower guide, who would be as good a witness to start with as any.

Like many of the volunteers, Barton was ex-Navy, a world which Tedesco felt connected with. Aside from growing up in Plymouth, his father had been a chief petty officer.

"Mr Registrar. How good to see you!"

Tedesco was used to being addressed by his former title of diocesan registrar and had given up trying to explain that he had retired from the law.

"And you, Jock. I'm surprised to see you here, to be honest. I assumed that all the tower tours had been suspended."

"Yes, they have but I wanted to come in and see if I can be useful. There will be the inevitable internal investigation into how this happened, not to mention the police enquiry, and a lot of these volunteers are quite vulnerable themselves. This will have hit them hard."

"Good man, Jock, they'll need to see friendly faces after such a jolt. I guess some of them might be thinking about giving up?"

"That thought had crossed my mind. You know, I still can't believe it happened, and Kerry was such a vital person, she'd soon become one of our own."

A waitress came and asked Tedesco if he wanted anything, so he opted for a cappuccino, going against his normal adherence to the Italian rule that it should never be taken after ten in the morning.

Barton hesitated, and then continued, "Actually John, there's been something niggling at me all weekend, something Kerry said when I gave her the list of guests for yesterday's tour."

"Try me – you know that it won't go any further."

"Okay, it's probably nothing, but when I mentioned that Arabella Patrick was part of the tour group, and that she was looking to become our next MP, Kerry said that she hoped she wouldn't be canvassing for votes, or words to that effect."

Tedesco took off his glasses and rubbed his eyes. "I'd have said much the same. I wouldn't read anything into it."

"Yes, but it was what she said next that struck me. I remember it clearly. She said that if Ms Patrick did canvass for votes, she might have to heave her off the tower. It was the word 'heave' that stuck with me."

"Again, this just sounds like a joke, doesn't it? And it was poor Kerry who fell off, not Arabella."

"Look John, I'm the last person to give any credence to conspiracy theories, but let's suppose that Kerry wasn't

45

being entirely flippant, and that she really was thinking of heaving her off. What if something had gone wrong up there, and Kerry had been pushed off by Arabella – or maybe her husband?"

ELEVEN

While 'the registrar' was drinking his coffee his business partner was striding through the narrow, unmarked tracks leading away from Campbeltown. She and her friend Julia Tagg had a long day's walking ahead of them.

If Tedesco or Julia's boss DCI Bloomfield had been trying to update them on the sensational happenings in far-off Devon, they'd have had a job, as mobile reception was at best haphazard, and in any case, the women had deliberately set out to stay off grid for a few precious days. They hadn't seen much news, and the little they had been aware of was almost entirely Scottish in content. A tragedy in a far-off Sassenach town could never compete with the Holy Trinity of Celtic, Rangers and Nicola Sturgeon.

The two friends had commenced their Argyll and Bute adventure in Tarbert, where an old uni contact of Lynne's sister had opened a small bed and breakfast. After two days of loading up on exquisite seafood, washed down with plenty of Picpoul de Pinet, they were well into the serious hiking now.

Both of them had well-earned reputations as fitness

fanatics, and so they kept up an energetic pace as they headed ever nearer to the Mull of Kintyre.

"So, what did go wrong with John and Liz?" asked Jools.

"I thought we weren't going to mention work this week?"

"I'm not. I just wondered, that's all."

"Sorry to disappoint, there isn't any juicy gossip. It was all rather sad, actually. I was expecting to see them together at John's sister's place, but Nicky took me aside and told me that Liz had decided to move back up here."

"I thought they looked good together, and they'd both been through enough pain to get there."

Liz Gerrey, who had until recently been the glamorous public face of the cathedral volunteers, lost her husband to cardiac arrest within months of her moving from Scotland to Rhyminster and, as we have seen, Tedesco's mysterious Irish muse, Sorcha, the love of his life, had died just under a year ago.

"Working with John, I've grown to realise that he's a lovely man but a complex character. He doesn't let anyone get really close. Sorcha was the only one. I don't think he was quite ready for Liz – he may never be ready. Perhaps he prefers solitude to company?"

"Bloomfield used to wonder about you two, you know."

Lynne threw her head back and laughed. "Everyone in Rhyme thinks there's something going on. Even the bishop's wife has tried to get us together."

"So you don't think there's a chance?"

"He is *quite* a bit older than me, so his cultural references are different, and I'd have to go with him to watch Plymouth bloody Argyle! No, seriously, it works as it is. And I'd never compete with Barker, of course."

"No one else caught your eye recently?"

"I could ask you the same, girlfriend. Anyway, we'd better crack on if we want to make it to that bothy by sunset."

*

Back in the Rhyminster Cathedral refectory, Tedesco was intrigued by what he had heard from Jock Barton, but deliberately set out to make light of it.

"Does Kerry really strike you as the type of person to arrange for a little accident? I know that people like to talk about the 'Cathedral Mafia', but I didn't think they actually went to the trouble of employing female assassins."

"What about the diocesan secretary?"

"Good point, but technically Amanda isn't employed by the cathedral."

Barton sensed that the chat had run its course.

"Oh well, Mr Registrar. I'd better see how the troops are coping."

Tedesco stayed behind to finish his coffee, then wandered into the main body of the building, casually ignoring the woman behind the donations desk as he noticed that there were still plenty of tourists around; perhaps the numbers had been swelled by the ghoulish?

Colin Scopes, the deputy verger, was doing something terribly important with votive candles so Tedesco went over to him.

Poor Colin had become inadvertently involved in the earlier suspicious death at the cathedral but was gradually rebuilding his confidence.

"Hello Mr Tedesco! I suppose that you are helping with the investigations?"

"Not officially, Colin. How are you all coping?"

"Well... it's a bit different this time, isn't it? Poor Kerry just fell off while she was taking a group around. A tragic accident, you could say."

"Maybe Colin, but we still need to find out *why* it happened, don't we? Anyway, is the canon precentor in today?"

"I think I saw him heading to the Song School with the master. I don't suppose he will be long."

"Okay. If you see him in the next ten minutes, come and find me in the cloisters."

Canon Wilf Drake, the precentor, was easy to underestimate, but behind the gentle manner and the scruffy appearance there lurked a man of iron faith. As Tedesco had often remarked, anyone who could handle the Master of Musick, the bombastic Charles Tantum, was a force to be reckoned with.

Instead of busily checking his phone for messages, Tedesco was sitting alone in the cloisters, seemingly staring into space when Wilf bustled into view, cassock flapping gently in the breeze.

"Deep in thought, John?"

"Not really. I was just reflecting on how I don't really like this time of the year – the thought of a new term."

"I know just what you mean. Freedom about to be curtailed, back to anxious Sunday evenings. Colin told me that you were looking for me. I assume it's related to yesterday's little drama."

"Of course. The dean has already indicated that he will

want me to see what I can find out, so I've started by having a nose around the cathedral and the Close."

"And have you sniffed anything yet?"

"Nigel Brimacombe has already confirmed that there was no sign of a struggle, and that might suggest that Kerry either jumped, or fell over, but neither of those possibilities sits right to me."

"I agree. The tower guides have to undertake rigorous health and safety training before we let them loose on the public, so the idea that she simply dropped off the edge seems fanciful. And everyone I've spoken to in the volunteer community describes her as cheerful and outgoing. I know that you can never tell what's going on in someone's head, of course."

"Well said. There have been plenty of tragic cases of suicides taking place even when a parent or partner had no idea that this was a possibility."

"John, have you heard if there was a note?"

"No, but I haven't spoken to Bloomfield yet. I will wait for him to approach me this time."

Tedesco and Bloomfield worked well together, and had developed a strong mutual respect, but he didn't want to be seen as interfering in the early stages of a police investigation.

"Wilf, I did pick up something from one of the guides. When Kerry had been told that Arabella Patrick and her husband were going to be on her next tour, she made a joke about heaving Arabella off the roof if she tried to canvass for votes."

Before responding, the precentor waved at one of the Holy Dusters, off for a session of heavy-duty artefact polishing.

"So, what did you make of Kerry's little quip? It wasn't in the best taste, but you surely aren't reading anything into it?"

"This is going to sound far-fetched, but you know that Sir Vere Alston has announced his retirement at the next election?"

"Yes. He told me at the last meeting of the Friends of the Cathedral, but he reassured me that he would be continuing as our chairman."

"Arabella moved down here with the express purpose of nursing the seat."

"Yes, I am more than aware of that as well. Her father bought the house for her so she could polish her local credentials."

"And you will doubtless remember Barry Gulliver's role in the purchase."

Gulliver, the Bluff Yorkshireman's Bluff Yorkshireman, had managed to ingratiate his way into Rhyminster society to the extent that he was tipped to be Arabella's main rival in the battle for the Conservative nomination. Whichever candidate the party chose would be a racing certainty to become the next Member of Parliament.

"Anyway," Tedesco went on, "Barry must be feeling used, incredibly stupid, or both. He wants to be our next MP, but by securing that mansion in the Close for Sir Maxwell he's given his rival the perfect base for her campaign."

"What are you hinting at, John? That Gulliver somehow persuaded Kerry to arrange for Arabella to fall off the tower, and that instead she ended up being the one landing on Cathedral Green during the cricket match?"

"Put like that, it does sound insane, but I want to discover if Gulliver and Kerry knew each other. The battle for the seat is going to be bitter, and I wouldn't put anything past our Bazza."

TWELVE

Victoria Thomas had lined up Julie Stringer for her next interview on Cathedral Green.

She enjoyed the 'It Makes Me Mad' column and admired Julie's wit, envying her the freedom of indiscretion denied to public service broadcasters.

The dean had carefully played all of Vicki's questions with a straight bat: Julie could be relied upon to spice things up a bit.

"I'm joined outside the cathedral by local columnist Julie Stringer. I hope you won't take this the wrong way, Julie, but you've seen it all in your time here."

"Ha Ha! We veteran reporters should stick together, eh Vicki?"

Touché, bitch, thought the BBC legend, which somehow came out as "What are you hearing, Julie? Are people assuming that this was a tragic accident, or could there be more to it?"

Julie tried her best to look thoughtful. "Honestly, Victoria, the community is numb. That's how I'd describe it. We are feeling as if there is a curse on us – two suspicious deaths in the cathedral in as many years."

"And what about you, Julie? Have you picked up any insights?"

"Well, I'm not sure that this is an insight, but I have heard that Arabella Patrick was one of those on the roof of the tower when the incident happened."

"Julie, perhaps you could enlighten our viewers. Who is Arabella Patrick?"

"She is the daughter of Maxwell Patrick, the MP for Central Somerset. She has just moved into the Close. Perhaps your cameraman could point over there."

Julie was pointing at Stannary House, the magnificent listed Georgian town house that the Patrick family had acquired from the estate of the late David Helford.

"And why do you think that this might be significant, Julie?"

"I'd say more interesting than significant, Victoria. The local gossip is that Ms Patrick has moved here to take over as the MP when Sir Vere Alston stands down."

*

DCI Bloomfield and DC Lovell joined Area Commander Jacqueline Hinton and Media Liaison Officer Luke Barnard live in Truro by the wonder of Microsoft Teams.

"You need to unmute, Jimmy."

"Can you hear me now?"

"No need to shout, we're in Truro, not Tahiti. Anyway, Rhyminster Cathedral, rapidly becoming more dangerous than our most notorious estates. Where are we, Jimmy?"

"We've interviewed the tour group, ma'am, and the SOCOs have been sweeping the tower."

"Okay, let's start with the tourists. Anything of note?"

"Most of the statements were tediously predictable – didn't see anything, hadn't noticed anything out of the ordinary before she fell. The key witness was Mike Knowles, the guy who sounded the alarm. He told me that he saw Kerry standing on the tower wall with her back to the edge. He described her as balancing like a trapeze artist, and he thought she might have been trying to say something. Matt here interviewed his wife – Matt?"

"Yes sir, ma'am. Mrs Sue Knowles mentioned that she had noticed one of the other visitors, Mr Alan Meer, demonstrating a reluctance to hand in his bag before climbing up the tower. To clarify, ma'am, all visitors have to leave handbags, rucksacks and so on in lockers before they are allowed up."

"I see. And what was this man objecting to?"

"Mrs Knowles said that she saw Kerry almost having to force Mr Meer to surrender his bag and that he deliberately removed something from it before he put it in the locker: she thought it might have been an inhaler."

Bloomfield butted in. "We are going to see Mr Meer for a follow-up, ma'am, and the SOCOs have been alerted to look out for an inhaler or similar in case Meer left it up there."

"Very well, Jimmy. Was there anything else?"

"Two things. Firstly, we've not discovered any suicide note yet. The other point is about Alan Meer.

"He is a local man, and so we asked him why he hadn't visited the cathedral tower before now."

"Jimmy, I grew up in Portsmouth, and I still haven't been on board HMS *Victory*."

"Fair point, ma'am. But there was something odd about Meer. He said that he'd always meant to go up the tower, but when he saw Nicola Tedesco reporting on it for *Searchlight*, he booked as soon as he could."

"Mmm. Your friend Mr Tedesco's sister – small world you have up there. Okay, keep me posted."

Luke Barnard joined the conversation. "I have it on good authority that *Searchlight* are filming tonight's programme live from the cathedral. Victoria Thomas is even venturing out of the studio, so they are making a big deal of this."

"And it's your job, Luke, to calm things down. Jimmy, do we have enough for a press briefing?"

"I don't think so. All we can assume is a suicide, or just possibly a tragic accident. I suggest we hide behind the results of the inevitable inquest."

"Sounds like a plan. I can let you have DS Tagg when she gets back, but that's about all. I assume the family know?"

Bloomfield gestured to Lovell. "I have spoken to the neighbours, Ma'am. Kerry lived alone after her mother died. There is no sign of a partner, but she has an ex-husband in Sweden. Her only living relative is a brother near Bristol – Keynsham."

*

"Mr Tedesco! I was thinking about you yesterday. I hope you weren't caught up in the latest goings on over there. What's happening to this place?"

"I was in the Close, watching the annual cricket match between the Cathedral XI and the Volunteers. But I'm fine, Joan. How was your bank holiday? Working, I expect?"

"Afraid so. Anyway, I thought you'd be hungry, so I've saved you a pork and apple roll. How does that sound?"

"It sounds perfect, Joan. We will see you tomorrow, God willing. Come on, Barker."

Tedesco, a man of routine, had taken his lunch at Jenks Bakery, ideally situated opposite the Butter Cross, since his early days in Rhyminster. He and Joan were almost exact contemporaries.

After picking up a copy of *The Times* – *The Times* 2 crossword was an integral part of his lunchtime ritual – he and his faithful companion made their way up the familiar stairs to 4A Minster Precincts.

He was just about to finish his lunch when a scarpering Barker expressed his routine displeasure at the sound of Tedesco's mobile ringtone.

The private investigator had hoped it might be Lynne, but it was his sister.

"Nicky! What are you doing calling me on your week off?"

"Hi bro. Look, the show's coming from the cathedral tonight and I thought you might like to come and watch it here."

"I know, I saw Victoria this morning. Okay, we'll get there before it starts. 6.15?"

Tedesco put his phone down. He worried about his sister. To describe her marriage as a rollercoaster would be an insult to fairground attractions. She was probably feeling in need of support. Be good to see Jack and Ella, though.

THIRTEEN

Tedesco busied himself with a new case for a couple of hours. His former colleague Neil Sparkes had instructed the agency to track down a missing beneficiary.

He enjoyed this type of job, as it combined the bits he missed about legal work, like poring over old deeds and family trees, with his more recently acquired detective skills, and in contrast with many of his cases, there was a fair chance of a happy outcome, with the added bonus that his old firm paid well.

Just as he began to wonder about calling it a day, as he had to drive over to Nicky's place, Sally buzzed him.

"Sorry to interrupt, Mr T, it's the dean's wife."

"Okay Sally, put her through please."

"Jo, how nice to hear from you. How are you?"

"Good, plenty of clients, but since Liz left, I'm multi-tasking as Dan's unpaid personal assistant."

Jo Luxmoore taught yoga and mindfulness: Lynne Davey was one of her enthusiastic disciples.

"I had heard that you were being shamelessly exploited by your husband. I'd offer to share Sally, but I think she'd send him over the edge."

"Mr Tedesco! You've shocked me, but I will tell Dan. He could use a laugh at the moment. Anyway, in my PA role, the dean would like to see you."

Tedesco suggested that he could be free after prayers the following morning, Jo responding that this would be fine, as the dean normally returned home for breakfast after the early service.

"Why don't you and Barker meet Dan in the cathedral, and then you can all wander back here. Coffee and toast okay?"

The former registrar swiftly accepted, relieved that Jo hadn't proposed raw vegetables and a vegan smoothie.

"Come on Barker! Home time."

As dog and master walked back through the Close, Tedesco noticed that the BBC outside broadcast van was still parked near the visitor entrance, but he was pleased to see that the other signs of media interest had largely dissipated.

Barker seemed to sense that they were going on an outing as he trotted alongside his tame human, wagging his tail with anticipation.

"Wait there, old friend," the human said to the border terrier as they reached the sanctuary of St Budeaux Place. "I just need to change into my scruffs."

His idea of the scruffy look was most people's idea of smart casual – pale chinos, Crew Company top, and his prized but battered pair of Docksides.

Tedesco's Lancia was immaculately parked outside his little cottage, as if awaiting take-off, but he was appalled at what he saw on the bonnet. "Ugh! Ruddy birds! Sorry Barker, I need to clean that muck before we set off."

He let Barker into the back seat, and his faithful friend waited patiently while his master went to work with the sponge. The terrier had seen it all before.

As they left behind the ancient liberty of the Close, Tedesco noted with relief that the traffic was relatively clear and so, once he was on the Woolford road, he felt sufficiently switched off to choose a suitable track by Christine McVie: 'Red Sun'.

He didn't really like Woolford, it was too straggly, no real centre, and the village pub doubled as the HQ of the local chapter of the red trouser brigade. During his infrequent visits there with his brother-in-law, he had been put off his beer by the braying expressions of entitlement that he'd been subjected to.

As he turned into Crane House, his sister's tasteful barn conversion in the prettier end of the village, his beloved nephew and niece heard the sound of wheels scrunching up the gravel and rushed out to cuddle Barker, just as off-duty BBC reporter Nicola Tedesco appeared at the bifold doors of the kitchen diner.

"Hurry up! It starts in two minutes!"

Why Nicky couldn't have recorded it, he had no idea. He supposed that her journalistic instincts meant that she needed to see the broadcast in real time.

As Clive Myrie made the ritual handover – "And now it's time for the news where you are" – Tedesco felt patronised. It always sounded so bloody condescending: over to the news for the little people in the boondocks.

Nicky joined him on one of the massive kitchen islands, where they could stare up at the huge screen. She poured herself a large glass of Pinot Grigio, and a juice for her brother, safe in the knowledge that he morphed into a strict teetotaller when he was driving.

Victoria Thomas, looking pleased to be let out of the studio for once, opened the programme confidently.

"*Searchlight* is coming to you live from Rhyminster Cathedral this evening. Yesterday afternoon, a woman plunged to her death from the tower, right above where I am standing now.

"Earlier today, I interviewed the dean, the Very Reverend Daniel Luxmoore."

Tedesco felt proud of Dan: he came over as human, focusing on the personal tragedy and the loss that the dead person's friends and family would be feeling while at the same time managing to deflect Vicki's clever attempts to get him to speculate about the cause of death.

Once Dan had finished, Victoria handed back to the studio, where the excellent Duncan Chivers went through the other news stories of the day, including a fascinating piece about an escaped snake in Ottery St Mary, then it was back live to the outside broadcast from Rhyme.

"I recorded an interview earlier today with local reporter Julie Stringer, from the *Rhyminster Journal*," said Vicki, picking up from where she left off.

"Fasten your seatbelts," said Tedesco, while his sister shushed him.

The Tedesco siblings were aghast as they viewed the replay of Julie asking the cameraman to get Stannary House into the shot while she speculated about what Arabella Patrick was doing on the tower tour.

"Nicola," her brother said, "I sincerely hope you didn't put Julie up to this? No, don't bother answering."

"I didn't know that she was going to try and bring Arabella bloody Patrick into it!"

"Okay, resorting to solicitor mode, Julie hasn't actually accused her of anything, but I'm still surprised that your lawyers let this go out."

"Shut up bro – Julie's back!"

"Julie Stringer joins me again, live from outside the cathedral. How would you sum up the mood tonight?"

"Victoria, I just want to echo the beautiful words of Dean Dan. I know this community, I'm part of it. This is going to affect all our mental health, but we will get through this. Resilience is in our DNA."

Tedesco pretended to retch as Nicky zapped the remote.

"Julie Stringer! She makes me mad!"

"Nicky – and I will disown you if you use this – I heard from Kerry's boss at the cathedral that she had made a joke about heaving Arabella off the tower if she started to talk politics. And I mentioned this to Wilf. So how the hell did Julie get wind of any connection to Ms Patrick?"

"But Arabella wasn't thrown off the tower. Do you think Kerry was pushed by her or something? Is that what you are saying?"

"No, I'm not saying that. But I don't know, why was Julie pointing out that house when she was being interviewed, and why does the name Barry Gulliver keep spinning around in my head?"

Nicky shrugged as they joined the children, who were playing with Barker.

"Ella has just told us that she wants to be an influencer," Nicky said, rolling her eyes heavenwards.

Tedesco let his niece patiently explain the concept, then

asked if he could become a YouTube or TikTok sensation at his age. "I could influence Jenks Bakery products by showing people the correct way to eat a cheese straw."

Ella smiled indulgently. It was clearly time for Uncle John to make a graceful exit.

"Come on Barker, let's get home before it gets dark."

He hugged Nicky and made the ritual enquiry after her husband.

"He and his classy mates are having a 'Wash Up' meeting for the yacht reception. It sounds like it's going to be an all-nighter."

As he turned towards home, the interesting cloud formation suggested a Nick Drake track for his musical accompaniment: 'Northern Sky'.

As ever, it was a relief to return to the familiar surroundings of St Budeaux Place, and once Barker had retired for the night Tedesco sat at his desk overlooking the tower: it was time to open another casebook. He lovingly creased down the pale blue cover, picked up his ink pen, and carefully inscribed the title: 'The Mystery of the Tower Tour'.

FOURTEEN

It was another early start at 17 St Budeaux Place. Morning prayers began at 7.30 during the week, which meant a change to the normal routine.

"Don't worry, Barker, we will be going out for a special breakfast this morning, but we are visiting the cathedral first. You enjoy going there, don't you?"

The border terrier's expression suggested 'yeah, right', but the pair of them were soon to be seen wandering through the early morning mist in a companionable silence.

Tedesco was pleased to note the lack of any renewed media presence on the Green, the only signs of life being a pair of early morning runners, and some elderly regulars heading slowly towards the main entrance.

He imagined them as the cathedral's equivalent of the stalwart lower league football supporter, present in all weathers, even turning up for reserve games – which wasn't a bad analogy for midweek prayers, particularly as today's service was being taken by one of the many retired clergy resident in Rhyminster rather than by one of the regular first team squad.

Dean Dan waved at Barker and his master as he slipped into the chapel just as the service was about to start and sat down unobtrusively on one of the stone benches at the rear. Only the persistent whistling of a dying hearing aid could interfere with Tedesco's enjoyment of the familiar words of the liturgy – as he had often commented, who needed mindfulness when you have an ancient cathedral on your doorstep.

He and Barker hung back while the dean said some kind words to the old boy who had conducted the service, and then the three of them walked the short distance across Cathedral Green to the deanery, where Dan led them into the homely kitchen, which boasted a side-on view of the tower: far more to Tedesco's taste than Nicky's gadget-filled monstrosity.

Jo greeted her guests warmly: although the Luxmoores didn't have a pet, they'd bought some dog biscuits from the market, and Barker was soon tucking in appreciatively.

"Coffee and toast okay? One of the Holy Dusters – Gloria, do you know her, John? – she makes this lovely medlar jelly, although we've got some of the bishop's honey, if you prefer."

Tedesco smiled to himself, as in one short sentence Jo had captured the charm of life in the Close.

He opted for the medlar jelly as it was somehow redolent of Agatha Christie, or at the very least *Midsomer Murders*. Didn't someone try and poison Barnaby's daughter with it?

After ten minutes or so of relaxed chat, Jo had to leave as she was running a mindfulness session for staff at Dartmoor prison.

"So, John. It's déjà vu all over again," Dan said as he glanced up at the tower for inspiration. "I assume you saw Julie Stringer last night. Arabella Patrick's ghastly husband has been active on Twitter, trying to blame the cathedral for Julie's piece to camera, even suggesting that Arabella is being drawn into this in order to deflect attention from our alleged negligence."

"I see, but I'm not surprised. Crispin is a member of his father-in-law's chambers and fiercely ambitious for his wife. I gather that our friend Barry is a serious rival for the nomination, so all that is going on in the background."

"What an awful prospect! I don't share Sir Vere's politics, but I've grown to respect him. He's a proper constituency MP. Privileged, of course, but he's one of the old type of Tory, with a sense of *noblesse oblige*."

"I agree. Ms Patrick has her eyes on the prize. She has no real local connection and is only standing here because her father's seat is a marginal now. And as for Barry Gulliver, may heaven help us!"

"Anyway John, putting local politics to one side, I've got meetings with DCI Bloomfield and our safety officer, in that order, but I wanted your take on things first. I hope that we can rely on you to look into this, on the usual basis?"

"Of course, Dan. And I know that Lynne will want to be involved when she gets back from her break. Okay, where have I got to? I've already spoken to Jock Barton, the head tower guide. From what he tells me, Kerry was friendly, outgoing, no sign of any inner turmoil: but as you know, this doesn't rule out suicide. Then Barton let slip that Kerry had made a joke about heaving Arabella off the tower if she mentioned politics."

"Good Lord! And Julie Stringer more than hinted that Arabella might have had something to do with what happened up there. Could Julie have overheard Jock Barton, do you think?"

"I doubt it, we were well away from any eavesdroppers. I've spoken to Canon Wilf about it, and he reminded me that Barry Gulliver played a key role in acquiring Stannary House for Maxwell Patrick, so maybe that's what La Stringer was alluding to when she pointed to it."

"Which has turned out to be ironic; now that Sir Maxwell has installed his daughter there, she could prevent Barry from being selected as the candidate. It's another unholy mess, Mr Tedesco."

"I'm afraid so. I'll keep you informed, but the Patrick/Gulliver contest bothers me. I want to find out if Bazza knew Kerry. And once Lynne is back from Scotland, she can keep an eye on the official investigation."

"What would we all do without your master, Barker?"

The terrier stretched, yawned, then made his way to Tedesco's side. What a canine legend!

FIFTEEN

John Sousa's rousing march interrupted Tedesco's lone supper, a Charlie Bigham fish pie for two: the solo version wasn't filling enough for him, and he didn't want to be looked at with pity at the Waitrose checkout.

Barker leapt up and barked at the phone until his master answered it.

"Tedesco! Who is this? Are you calling from a public house?"

Lynne yelled above the noise, "It's me! And I am calling from a bar, you pompous thing! Jools and I are enjoying our last night in Tarbet."

Tedesco cut in, "It sounds like it. What are you doing interrupting my supper? Barker is very cross with you."

"Tell him I'm sorry. Look, we've been offline for the last few days, but there's an ancient TV in here and they were showing a roundup of the week's news. I couldn't hear a thing, but I saw Vicki Thomas broadcasting from outside the cathedral. What's going on?"

"Oh, you know, another day in sleepy Rhyme. One of the tour guides fell off the tower on Bank Holiday Monday."

"My God! Who was it? Was he killed?"

"It was a she – Kerry Franklin. And she's dead, I'm afraid. Dean Dan has already asked us to take an interest, so enjoy the rest of your wee break while you can."

"Kerry Franklin – why does that name ring bells? Okay, I'll let Jools know. I expect she will call Bloomfield. And we will both need a stiff whisky or two."

"Haven't you got a long drive ahead of you tomorrow?"

"Our flight from Glasgow isn't until teatime, so I think we'll be okay. And I do know about alcohol limits, actually."

"Of course you do, detective sergeant. I will see you in two days' time then."

*

As Tedesco was resuming his lonely supper, DCI Jimmy Bloomfield and DS Matt Lovell were in Ivybridge, walking up a short flight of steps leading to an unprepossessing pebble-dashed semi on what was once a small council estate. As Bloomfield correctly assumed, most of the houses had been sold to their tenants under right to buy in the 1980s, although this one might be the exception.

As the bell didn't seem to be working, Lovell rapped on the frosted glass section of the door, and after what seemed like an eternity a light went on and a dark shadow appeared, moving slowly and a trifle menacingly towards them. The shadow unhooked the security chain, revealing itself to be an elderly woman who wore an expression of instinctive suspicion.

"Who are you? I don't conduct business like this. Go away, or I'll call the police."

"Mrs Meer? We are the police. Could we come inside?" said Lovell. Despite the detective constable's courteous approach, Kathleen Meer was not going to cooperate without further proof of his bona fides.

"You could be anyone. And what are doing here? This is a respectable neighbourhood."

Bloomfield had been taking in the woman before him. She somehow contrived to be both shrew-like and on the plump side, and the blue rinse was worthy of a preservation order. Perhaps this was what Norman Bates' mum had looked like before she met her unfortunate end?

He produced his warrant card. "I am Detective Chief Inspector Bloomfield, and this is my colleague, DC Matt Lovell. Now can we come in please? It won't take a minute and it's getting quite cold out here."

She snatched the warrant card from his grasp, peered suspiciously at it, then handed it back. "It seems to be in order. I will let you in but if you put a foot wrong, I'll be straight to the press."

The CID men were ushered into a small sitting room, their eyes drawn to a ceramic fire surround housing an electric bar heater. If there had been a mural on the wall, then Kathleen Meer's front room would have been a dead ringer for Hilda Ogden's parlour in *Coronation Street* from back in the seventies.

"You can sit over there," she said, indicating two stiff-looking wooden chairs, while she purposefully sat herself down on the ancient sofa.

A cup of tea would be nice, thought Lovell, but then cancelled the idea – it would surely be made with condensed milk.

Bloomfield smiled beatifically at his hostess. "Mrs Meer. Thank you so much for your time. You must be wondering what we are doing here."

"If it's Alan you wanted, he's out at his astronomy club up on the moors. He won't be back till late."

"Let me explain, Mrs Meer. You may have seen the story in the news about the poor woman who fell from the cathedral in Rhyminster on Monday. We are talking to everyone who was on that tower tour, including your son."

She fixed them with a steely glare. Bloomfield wasn't overly concerned – here was a woman who viewed the universe with suspicion.

"My son says that he has already told you everything he knows. And he won't be back till later. So you can go now."

It was time for Lovell to employ the oldest trick in the book. "Very well, Mrs Meer, but we do need to check a few points with Alan. Sorry to be a nuisance, but could I use your loo before we drive all the way back to Rhyminster?"

"All right. The toilet is upstairs on the left."

While Lovell went to relieve himself, Bloomfield's attempts at small talk were met with brusque resistance. It was like bowling at Geoff Boycott.

Lovell located the loo, switched on the light, then got his torch out. He soon found Alan's bedroom, as the door was decorated with stickers of Marvel Comics characters, and once he had carefully pushed the door ajar and gently shone the torch on the walls, they revealed more evidence of Alan's geek-like interests, from framed tickets to *Dr Who* conventions to a *Lord of the Rings* poster.

However, it was the wall behind the headboard that drew Lovell's alarmed attention. As he focused the beam, he was

71

confronted by a series of photos and articles clipped from the local papers. They all concerned the same person. It was John Tedesco's sister.

Although he was shocked, the DC had the presence of mind to take a photo of the wall on his phone before going back across the landing to the bathroom, flushing the toilet, and washing his hands thoroughly. What he really felt like was a long hot shower, but not in this claustrophobic time warp. He hurried back down the stairs.

"Ah good, DC Lovell. We will leave you to enjoy the rest of your evening, Mrs Meer. Oh, by the way, does Alan suffer from asthma, by any chance?"

SIXTEEN

"Can you drive, boss? I'm feeling a bit shaky."

"What is it, Matt? Have HR sent you on one of those mental health awareness courses? What a waste of police time!"

"Nothing like that. That house – it creeped me out. And I need to tell you about Alan's room. He's decorated one of the walls with pictures of Nicola Tedesco."

"Jesus Christ! Okay, Matt, give me the keys."

*

Rhyminster's answer to Thelma and Louise were feeling slightly ropey as they were greeted by a steady drizzle as they forced themselves awake on their final morning in Scotland.

A combination of kippers, toast and black coffee got them moving again, but a final stroll around Tarbet's long harbour was necessary to complete the recovery.

"Jools. I kept going over her name last night."

"Kerry Franklin?"

"Yeah. I think I might have interviewed her when I was in the CID. It may have been before your time."

"She doesn't ring any bells with me. Why don't I call Matt and see if he can uncover anything useful?"

*

Back at Rhyminster, Lovell had been going over the interviews with the tourists.

The discovery of Alan's dodgy wall coverings had more than justified Bloomfield's insistence on a trip to Ivybridge, which also led to Granny Meer, which is how he thought of her, confirming that her precious son did indeed use an inhaler.

However, the overall evidence against the lonely legal executive was mixed. While Sue Knowles had witnessed Alan's reluctance to leave his bag in the locker, this may have been due to his need to always carry his inhaler with him, and Betty Budden seemed to have given him an alibi by spotting him struggling up the steps to the tower just as Kerry was about to take the plunge.

But what about Alan Meer's pictures of Nicky Tedesco: was it just an innocent fixation?

He didn't think so, and nor did Bloomfield, who was on his way to the BBC in Plymouth.

The DCI was a familiar interviewee on *Searchlight*, and so he was on automatic pilot as he drove to the studios in the leafy Mannamead area of the city.

Nicky was expecting him, and she was quickly summoned from the newsroom.

"Jimmy! Is this about the tower?"

Bloomfield, a walking definition of the word dapper in his three-piece suit, matching tie and pocket handkerchief, asked if there was somewhere private where he could explain things.

Nicky found an unoccupied office and offered him some plastic instant coffee in a BBC mug.

She knew that she was taking a risk, as he was renowned for his caffeine snobbery, but he seemed happy to chance it.

"Nicky, I wanted to see you in person, at the earliest opportunity."

She threw her head back and laughed. "I'm flattered, DCI Bloomfield, but I'm a married woman."

"Sorry, Nicky, this isn't a laughing matter. One of the tourists who was on the tower when Kerry Franklin died told us that he booked the tour after seeing you reporting from there."

"Jimmy, it was a puff piece. The whole point of it was to advertise the cathedral. It was part of a series designed to show our lovely visitors that there's more to tourism down here than birds, booze and beaches."

"Granted. But this bloke is a nailed-on weirdo. Still lives with his mum in his forties, no girlfriend. And when we tried to see him yesterday, Matt Lovell found a shrine in his bedroom dedicated to you."

Nicky, clearly rattled, tried to make light of it.

"He sounds harmless enough. Look, I used to get fan mail from lonely old chaps when I first started out reading the local news, but these days, apart from the odd request for a selfie when I open the village fete, I'm left alone. Probably too mumsy to attract the oddballs."

Bloomfield couldn't have disagreed more: he'd always thought that Nicky's husband had been 'punching', as his son would say.

"Nicky, it's a different world now. Social media makes any public figure vulnerable to all sorts of abuse and threats. And Meer is a concern, as his profile fits a standard type. Matt Lovell found just about every image of you from the local press over the years on Meer's wall. He is clearly obsessed."

"Jimmy, I get it. But I'm a grown-up. I can handle someone like Alan. He sounds too shy to actually contact me."

"Okay. But take particular care when you are out and about. And I'd go off Twitter and Facebook for a while. You know that you can speak to me any time."

"Jimmy? Do you think Meer is involved in Kerry's death in some way?"

"Always the reporter, Ms Tedesco. You know I can't discuss the case with you."

"Okay, but worth a try. Should I keep this to myself?"

Bloomfield took a gulp of BBC instant before giving his considered response.

"What you tell your husband is up to you. I know you will want to share it with John, and you know what, I don't think it would be such a bad idea. I expect that the bishop and the dean are already asking him to keep an eye on things."

Sadly, she agreed with him. John would understand. Her car-dealer husband was the last person she could discuss this with. He'd be rounding up a posse of overweight vigilantes and heading over to Ivybridge at the drop of an ignition key.

*

As the little plane flew south out of Glasgow, Lynne peered out of the window and looked at the impressive collection of wind turbines arising out of the North Sea like Ray Harryhausen's skeletons in *Jason and the Argonauts*.

DS Julia Tagg was concentrating on her PC, switched onto flight mode.

"Lynne, I've been getting up to speed on the tower. It looks like a tragic accident, at least that's how the press are playing it."

"Anything from Matt?"

"I was coming to that. You did interview Kerry Franklin. And it was just before you left to set up the agency with John, so I would have been around. Kerry had only recently returned to the UK to look after her mother. She thought that she was being followed by a man who had bothered her when she worked on the cruise ships. He'd obviously gone to some lengths to track her down, so I could understand why she wanted to report it.

"We gave the usual advice, sent a patrol car round. As we hadn't heard from her for a while, I followed it up – you'd left us by then – and she said that the man had disappeared into thin air, so we closed the file on it."

"Did she describe him?"

"Oh yes. Big, brash, northern accent…"

SEVENTEEN

Before setting off for another fun-packed day of notifying banks and utility companies of the sad death of various of his firm's former clients, Alan Meer carefully peeled back the photos of BBC *Spotlight*'s Nicola Tedesco from his bedroom wall. He'd go over to Trago Mills later and get some paint. The room could do with a refresh. While he hated having to say farewell to his precious collection, he had swiftly decided to put the cuttings through the confidential waste shredder at the office after his mother had given him the hair-dryer treatment when he got back from the moors. The cops would be returning soon so he needed to stay one move ahead.

*

Over at 4A Minster Precincts, Tedesco and Barker were fully occupied. The private investigator was losing himself in Neil Sparkes' missing beneficiary case, enjoying a helpful chat about it with private client expert Gill Withers, while the border terrier busied himself in his role of office mental health tsar.

Sally Munks, acting in her unofficial capacity as Tedesco annoying champion, interrupted her boss's chain of thought.

"I've got your sister on the phone. She sounds worried."

After the usual Chuckle Brothers-style rigmarole of trying to transfer the call, Sally eventually succeeded in putting Nicky through.

"Bro! Why can't you leave your mobile on? Then at least I'm spared that living and breathing wind chime that you call your PA!"

Although Tedesco felt that the comparison was a little hard on wind chimes, he loyally sprang to Sally's defence.

"I'll take comments like that more seriously when you raise tens of thousands for the hospice, Nicola. Anyway, to what do I owe this disruption to my routine?"

"I really need to see you. I had a visit from Jimmy Bloomfield yesterday, and I can't discuss it with anyone else."

This pierced his heart. Since they were infants, cowering from their alcoholic father, he had vowed to look after his little sister.

"Where are you, sis?"

"I'm on the late news team, so I'm not due in till four. I can come over to you if you like."

"Sure. How about the cathedral refectory in half an hour?"

*

Alan Meer knocked shyly on the door of the senior partner of Gallants solicitors – he hadn't mastered any other way of knocking.

Felicity Gallant, daughter of the previous senior partner, Roger Gallant, yelled through the door, "I know it's you, Alan. Next time, knock like a man. Hurry up!"

Ms Gallant was renowned for her organisational skills, as evidenced by her desk, always clear apart from the file she was working on.

Alan had made the mistake, never since repeated, of asking her how she managed to keep her desk so tidy. "It's called being organised, Alan. An untidy desk indicates an untidy mind."

He entered the office as if he were stepping over a minefield.

"What is it? I've got a video conference with counsel in ten minutes."

Alan coughed and looked down at his shoes.

"I know it's short notice, and I wouldn't ask, but my mother has just called. She's fallen, and needs me to take her to A and E."

"Can't she call an ambulance? Oh, go on. I expect it will take ages to summon one. But you will make up the time."

Alan made a cringing exit, walking backwards. He had got on fine with Mr Gallant. But he hated his daughter. *Why can't she stay at home, like my Mum*, he thought to himself.

Workaholic Felicity, with her husband staying up in London all week, earning huge amounts in the City, was unlike any woman he had come across. He comforted himself by thinking of Nicola Tedesco. There was a 'career girl' who still found time for her husband and her children. He'd read an article about her in the South Hams lifestyle magazine in which she'd shared her love of baking with the loyal readership, while all Felicity seemed to care about, apart from billing targets, were her horses.

He cycled home, left his bike, and walked over to the bus stop. He'd better get that paint and cover up the evidence before the police came calling.

*

"I'm popping over to the cathedral, Sally, so could you take care of Barker? I won't be more than an hour."

Tedesco carefully negotiated the death-trap staircase, then turned into the Close, glanced at his watch, saw that he was early, so took himself on a circuit of the outside of the cathedral. This was normally a failsafe method of lifting his mood, a glance at the majesty of the ancient building putting his problems into the perspective of history. But today was different. Nicky was clearly rattled.

He piloted himself to his normal 'secret' corner in the refectory and had just ordered tea for two, Minster Blend of course, when he spied his sister coming through the swing door. She was wearing sunglasses. Indoors. On a cloudy day. Chag hadn't hit her, surely? He had next to no time for the guy, but never imagined him as violent.

"Nicky! You look terrible!"

"Gee, thanks brother! That's all a girl needs to hear."

"I'm sorry. Look, let me start again. Why the sunglasses?"

"It's okay. I haven't walked into a wall or been involved in a punch-up at the Salcombe Regatta. I was just, you know, a bit teary earlier."

"Come on, Nicky, you can tell your big brother."

While Tedesco had always performed the hands-on,

caring and listening role in her life, Nicky had quickly learned to accept that her husband was an empathy-free zone.

"Okay. As I told you earlier, Jimmy Bloomfield came over to see me at Seymour Road yesterday. I thought he wanted to fish for anything we'd heard about poor Kerry Franklin, but it was to warn me."

Her brother poured them both a cup of the refectory's restorative tea.

She went on, "It looks like I have a stalker, or is it a troll these days? Anyway, Jimmy took it seriously enough to drive over to Plymouth to tell me about him."

Tedesco sipped his tea, then he waved in recognition at one of the familiar cathedral guides.

"Nicky, how did Jimmy discover him? And more to the point, what is he going to do about it?"

She explained that Bloomfield and Matt Lovell had paid a visit to one of the tourists who had been on the tower tour that fateful bank holiday afternoon, as they had concerns about his general demeanour on the day. Then she told him all she had been told about Alan Meer, his job as a probate executive, how he still lived with his mother in Ivybridge, and about his bedroom wall.

He took her hand and squeezed it. "I'm glad that you told me about this. Look, this is a bit left field, but you remember Neil Sparkes?"

"Your old partner? Always looks on the verge of a coronary? Didn't he get dragged into the office party spiked-drinks case last Christmas?"

"That's him. Look, Neil spends all his time dealing with elderly folks' affairs, so he must have come across Alan Meer. He will certainly know about his firm. I'm working on something for him at the moment, so I'll take him for a pint and pick his brains."

He continued, "I'm sure that Neil will confirm that Meer is a harmless saddo who fantasises about unattainable women, but in the meantime, you will take extra care, won't you?"

"You can depend on it, John. And I've taken Jimmy's advice to take a break from social media."

*

Kathleen Meer bitterly resented being disturbed during *Countdown*, especially during the teatime teaser.

"What the hell are you doing here in the middle of the afternoon?"

"I'm owed leave, so I thought I'd give my room a fresh lick of paint."

"First time since your father was alive. What is it, want to bring someone back, do you?"

Alan Meer ignored her and went to the garage, emerging in his late father's overalls, carrying some old dust sheets. Just one coat of paint would do.

EIGHTEEN

Tedesco had returned to the office in plenty of time for his ritual lunchtime walk with Barker, so he emailed Neil Sparkes and arranged for what his erstwhile colleague referred to as a 'swift half after work'.

He knew Sparkes well enough to realise that it would be neither swift, nor a half, but as this concerned his sister, he would take the hit.

It felt quieter than normal in town as Barker trotted behind him to the usual chorus of approval from passers-by.

"What a lovely dog you have. Such an intelligent expression."

There was no queue at Jenks today and, as he needed to line his stomach in readiness for his 'swift half' with Neil, he asked Joan for two extra cheese straws with his ham and tomato on wholemeal.

He'd leave the office early, drop Barker off at home, and then walk to the Grapes in time for his rendezvous at 5.30.

As Tedesco wolfed down his lunch *al desko*, Bloomfield was planning his next moves, the first of which was a call to Kathleen Meer, who promised him that Alan would be at home that evening.

Matt Lovell popped his head around the door as arranged and was given the unwelcome news that they would be driving to Ivybridge again.

"Oh, and there's someone else who is overdue a visit."

"Who – the brother?"

"Got it in one. He's had a few days to get his head around what happened, so I'm sending Julia up to Keynsham tomorrow."

"Bit harsh, boss? She's still on her way back from Scotland."

"She likes a long drive. Right then, we'll go over to see Mr Meer at around six, if that's okay with you, DC Lovell."

The young DC was sorry to be missing his weekly five a side football session but had to concede that he was curious to see Alan Meer again.

At Minster Precincts, Barker seemed surprised to be leaving the office early. His master explained to him, as best he could, that he'd be going out that evening, and so he'd leave him a bowl of Waitrose Essential dog food.

After a quick shower Tedesco pulled on some old cords and a zip-up Gant jersey top, opting for his brown polished brogues over his deckies, then he headed out away from the Close.

The Grapes was a surprising choice of venue. He would have chosen the Kingfisher by the river, or at a pinch the Rhyminster Arms.

He assumed that Neil had chosen the sleazy boozer due to its proximity to his office, just outside what passed for the city centre of the smallest cathedral city in England.

The pub was to be found at the end of a mugger's alley, and that wasn't the only reason that it was known as 'The Gropes' by generations of Rhymesiders.

While the bar was bathed in its trademark Stygian gloom, he could still make out the recognisable form of his friend and smiled as Sparkes stood up and greeted him warmly. "I thought you said a swift half, Neil," said Tedesco, staring at his friend's pint glass.

"A half is never enough after a day at the Fun Factory. Anyway, I've left the car at the office, so I'll get a cab home. Mary will drop me back at work tomorrow."

After asking after Neil's infinitely patient wife, Tedesco spent the next five minutes listening to his former partner berating the merged firm of Easlick Creber. "You were so wise, John. You could see it coming."

Tedesco had indeed been sceptical about the merger, and so had accelerated his plans to leave the law for a new future working as a private detective with Lynne.

Noticing that Neil had drained his glass he took this as an opportunity to get him another pint of Deacon's Delight, while he opted for a half of the weaker Canon's Comfort, and to change the subject.

"So, Neil, you are probably wondering why I called. Do you know anyone at Gallants these days? I don't suppose Easlicks want to add them to their growing empire?"

"I'd be the last to hear about it if they were. Funny little firm, easy to forget that they still exist. Two partners as far as I know. Old man Rickard runs the Tavistock office with a couple of conveyancers and Flick Gallant heads up the Ivybridge branch. She's got two non-partner solicitors. One does wills, and the other helps her with litigation, mainly divorce. She's very well connected, so it's mainly high net worth stuff."

"Is Alan Meer still there?"

Sparkes chuckled. "Poor old Alan. I clean forgot about him. He's been there since he left school, poor sod. Must have done at least twenty years, and he's only about forty. Why are you interested in him, John?"

"Okay, and this is strictly between us. He was one of the tourists who did the tower tour on Bank Holiday Monday. The police have been making routine enquiries of all of them, and it turns out that Meer was prompted to visit by a piece that Nicky did on *Searchlight*."

Sparked shrugged and took an almighty slurp of his ale.

"Anyway," Tedesco went on, "Matt Lovell and Jimmy went to call on Alan, but he wasn't at home. However, his mother let them in, and Matt took the chance to sneak a quick look in his bedroom. There was a shrine to Nicky on one of the walls."

"Shit! So our Alan's a stalker."

"It looks that way. Jimmy has been to see Nicky and she's obviously worried about it. As Alan practices in your area of law, and I assume it's a small world, I just wondered what you knew about him."

"Tell you what, John, why don't you fill that up for me while I gather my thoughts?" said Sparkes, waving his empty glass in the air with flamboyant insouciance.

*

As Neil Sparkes was working his way through his third and final pint of the session, Bloomfield and Lovell found themselves awaiting admission to the Meer residence for the second time in twenty-four hours.

In stark contrast with the first occasion Mrs Meer almost skipped to the door and there was a new smell to greet them as they got over the threshold – freshly applied emulsion.

"Alan! Stop what you are doing and come downstairs. You have visitors," she yelled.

As Bloomfield and Lovell were led into the knick-knack-crammed front room again they heard a symphony of sound from above, a mixture of banging, rustling, and sweeping noises.

"Hurry up, Alan!"

In person, Meer was shorter than Lovell had remembered, but otherwise the reality coincided with the mental picture he had prepared. He was thin, his greying hair was lank and greasy and there were vast spreading sweat patches on his *Dr Who*-themed shirt, which looked as if they were about to drench the poor Dalek depicted on the front of it. "Saturate! Saturate!"

He was visibly nervous and sat down on the sofa without introducing himself, his right leg jigging to a silent metronomic beat, then he glared at his mother as Bloomfield began to speak.

"Mr Meer, as your mother would have explained to you, she told us that you would be home tonight. I gather that you were busy observing the night sky when we called yesterday?"

Alan nodded.

"You will remember my colleague, DC Lovell, here? He took your statement after the events of Bank Holiday Monday."

Meer grunted and looked anxiously towards the door.

"Mr Meer. We are continuing to investigate the circumstances of the death of Kerry Franklin, and we do have a few follow-up questions if you are happy to help with our enquiries."

His mother spoke up. "Of course he will help you, officer. He's still shaken up about it. We're a law-abiding family; Alan is a lawyer, you know."

It was Matt Lovell's turn to speak to Alan. "Mr Meer, it is up to you whether you want to help us this evening. You are free to continue with what you were doing. From the lovely smell of new paint do I assume that you are decorating?"

"Yes, I am. Upstairs. Not that this is any of your business."

"Alan! Don't be so rude. He's giving his bedroom a fresh lick of paint. I think he's got a girlfriend and he wants to impress her."

Bloomfield tried to imagine the type of girl who might want to see inside Meer's bedroom, but couldn't, so he tried his luck with some questions.

"Could you cast your mind back to the tower tour for me, Alan? Can I call you Alan?"

Meer gave a most reluctant nod of assent.

"Good. Did you carry anything with you when you visited the cathedral?"

"Yes, I think I had a Morrison's bag for my lunch."

"And did it contain anything else?"

"No, don't think so."

Bloomfield joined in the questioning.

"Alan. Do you use an inhaler?"

"Yeah, what's that got to do with it?"

"So you would have had it with you in the cathedral? If it wasn't in the bag, then where would you keep it?"

Meer glanced at his mother with a look that spoke volumes, then he suddenly established eye contact with a disconcerted Bloomfield and gave his first clear answer.

"I would have taken it out of the bag before I went up the tower. What if I had an attack up there?"

Good answer, thought Lovell. *But in that case, why did he struggle with Kerry when she told him to leave his bag in the locker?*

Bloomfield returned to the decoration project.

"What was on your bedroom wall before you painted it today? You don't have to answer but think carefully before you decide."

"I know I don't have to, and I won't. This is harassment."

"That's your choice, Alan. We will be on our way now, but before we go, DC Lovell would like to show you a picture on his phone."

Lovell showed Meer the photo of the bedroom wall, complete with the Nicola Tedesco picture gallery.

"Is this your bedroom wall, Alan?"

"No comment."

*

"Right, Neil. A pint of Deacon's Delight. So, what can you tell me about Alan Meer?"

"Well. The only time I saw him was at the STEP meetings. They were sometimes held at Gallants' office as it is quite central and on the train line."

STEP was the Society of Estate and Trusts Practitioners, a specialist group dedicated to that unglamorous branch of legal practice.

"I tried to speak to him in the coffee break a few times, but it was like getting blood out of a stone. I do remember one thing, though."

"Go on, Neil."

"It was his briefcase. It looked like he would have had it at school. It was black, but half of the leather had come off. He never seemed to open it, which I found odd, and it had a sticker on one side, as I remember."

"What was this sticker – a *Star Wars* convention or something?"

"No, it was a BBC *Searchlight* car sticker."

NINETEEN

After eventually managing to shoehorn Neil into a taxi, Tedesco didn't make it back to the sanctuary of St Budeaux Place until nine, Barker rewarding him with one of his 'And what time do you call this?' looks.

He hadn't given much thought to supper, so he heated up some tomato soup and defrosted some bread.

The net effect of the session with Sparkes was that he endured a disturbed night and was still feeling distinctly subprime the following morning when he really should have been looking forward to welcoming Lynne back from her holiday.

She had already arrived at the office by the time that Tedesco and Barker made their weary way through the Close, and was chatting animatedly with Sally when they eventually landed at Minster Precincts.

Lynne had presented the PA with some Tarbet tablet, which to Tedesco's untutored eye resembled nothing more than a lump of pure sugar.

She gave Barker some tartan-themed McWoof treats and produced a small bottle of single malt for her partner.

"I know you prefer wine but there isn't much of that in Scotland."

"It's a tragic combination of the wrong climate and the wrong terroir, Lynne. Anyway, I'm sure I will find a good home for this on my top shelf."

"And I trust that you might actually try it! Look, why don't I get settled back and then you can tell me all about Kerry Franklin."

*

DS Julia Tagg was still feeling cheesed off with her boss as she retraced her steps from the drive back from Bristol airport last night.

The traffic was building as she joined the M5 just south of Exeter, so she would be late for her meeting with Graeme Franklin. She'd text him from Taunton Deane Services.

Bloomfield was right – she did enjoy long drives, but this was taking the piss.

*

The DCI was wishing that he had volunteered to drive to Keynsham by the time he had finished his video conference call with Area Commander Jacqueline Hinton, having been summoned to the virtual meeting within minutes of Tagg exiting the car park. It was urgent, apparently.

"Jimmy, thank you for finding the time for this."

Yeah right, he thought, *like I had a choice.*

"My pleasure, ma'am," he said.

"Jimmy, as you can probably guess, this is about Kerry Franklin. There have been developments that I need to share with you as the senior investigating officer."

"There have been some developments at the sharp end as well, ma'am, and—"

Hinton spoke over him, somehow without appearing rude, as if she had been on a video conference etiquette course.

"Jimmy. I've been reviewing the evidence. Peter Gill's post-mortem confirmed Nigel Brimacombe's original findings, there is nothing to suggest either foul play or a suicide and the inquest is odds-on to deliver a misadventure verdict. So, unless you can pull a rabbit from your hat your work here is done."

"With respect, ma'am, we have been following up on Alan Meer, and—"

She cut across him again. "I know you have, Jimmy. And I had to deal with a difficult call from his solicitor this morning."

"His solicitor?"

"Yes, the senior partner of the firm he works for, Flick Gallant. To be open, I know her socially through dressage, but the allegations she made of harassment of a witness and illegal obtaining of evidence sounded all too plausible. And Maxwell Patrick has been loudly complaining that the BBC are dragging his daughter into all this. I'm sorry, Jimmy, but this was an accident, and you must accept that."

And we can't upset prominent solicitors or MPs, can we? he thought to himself.

After Hinton abruptly ended the call Bloomfield most uncharacteristically got up and kicked a filing cabinet.

Should he call Jools, tell her to turn round and come home? Should he hell.

*

Julia Tagg managed to reach Keynsham at the rearranged time, despite the heavy traffic and the sat nav getting its knickers in a twist trying to find the new development where Graeme Franklin lived with his partner and their three kids.

There had been a huge expansion of this dormitory town for Bristol in the 2010s and Franklin had managed to snag one of the larger of the executive homes in the hidden cul-de-sac.

From the outside it was mostly garage but otherwise it looked suspiciously like Bloomfield's anonymous four-bed detached in Derrington.

Graeme Franklin was a web designer and worked at home for much of the time. His partner was a teacher at the local primary, so this explained both why he was able to meet during the working week and his partner's absence.

The man that greeted Tagg at the door was tall, dark and attractive in an understated way. He was a good few years younger than Kerry, but you could see the family resemblance.

"I expect you could use a coffee after driving up from Devon," he began, then continued by suggesting that they sat in the garden as it was still warm, apologising for the state of the kitchen as they walked through.

Once the pleasantries had been concluded and Tagg had sympathised for his loss, Franklin asked if the police had any grounds for suspicion.

"It looks as if your sister fell without being pushed, but we are still interviewing witnesses. In these circumstances we haven't ruled out suicide, but no note was discovered. Her colleagues at the cathedral all felt that she was in a positive state of mind on the day in question."

"Look, DS Tagg, I didn't see much of Kerry growing up, she left home and started travelling as soon as she could, but we got on well despite hardly knowing each other. And yes, she was a really positive person. She was rescued from drowning when she was little, and I think that made her determined to grab life with both hands."

"I see. But, and I have to ask this, did she have any enemies, anyone who bore her a grudge?"

Franklin stroked his chin. "Her ex-husband Stefan is still in Sweden, but she hadn't seen him in years. There was some bitterness at the time of the split, and they soon lost contact. Kerry has moved on, as they say.

"But hang on, there was an issue when she came back to Rhyminster. I'm afraid that I let it slip my mind till you asked about enemies."

Jools drank her coffee and let him continue.

"She told me that a man had started hanging around near her house or at the garage where she filled her car. She thought he looked like someone who had pestered her when she worked on the cruise ships, one of the passengers."

This was no surprise to Jools as it chimed with what Kerry had told Lynne Davey when she reported the incident, but Kerry had obviously been worried enough to share it with her brother.

"Did Kerry describe him? Give a name? It may be significant."

"Let's think. He was a large man – I remember now! Kerry said that he'd become a bit of a player in Rhyminster. I think he owned an estate agency, and he may have sat on the council. I don't think she mentioned a name."

"That's very helpful, Mr Franklin. If anything else comes to mind, here's my card."

Before she left, DS Tagg established that there would be a small humanist ceremony once the inquest had been concluded. Graeme was the executor and would let her know once the arrangements had been finalised.

So, she thought to herself as she headed back down the M5 again, *Kerry had described her stalker as big, brash and northern. To that we can now add estate agent with an interest in local politics. Not Barry Gulliver, surely?*

She selected Radio 2 and was enjoying a pointless phone-in on the *Jeremy Vine Show* when she was interrupted by a call from an agitated-sounding DCI Bloomfield on the hands-free.

She was just about to tell him about Graeme Franklin's revelation about Kerry's mystery stalker when her boss gave her the bad news.

"Hinton's pulling the investigation. The inquest will confirm that it was death by misadventure, so it's nothing to see here folks, time to move on. Bloody ridiculous. There's no way that she just toppled off the tower by mistake."

"And her brother has just told me something very interesting about a cruise passenger who bothered his sister when she worked on the ships. Lynne was looking into it just before she left the CID to join John."

She heard Bloomfield's sigh as she approached the A30/A38 junction.

"If Tedesco and Davey are still looking at it then perhaps it's time for us to re-establish our unholy alliance."

TWENTY

"I'm glad that you enjoyed your time in the far north, Lynne. Did you manage to visit Ochil View Park by any chance?"

As well as his obsession with Plymouth Argyle, Tedesco had a favourite Scottish team, Stenhousemuir. He had been intrigued by the name whenever he heard the football results being read out every Saturday teatime at his parents' house and had even chosen 'Stenny' as his team in the Plymouth Subbuteo League. The real Stenhousemuir played their home games at Ochil View and a visit there was number two on his bucket list, number one being to see Argyle play in the Premier League.

Only half-jokingly he had asked Lynne if she and Julia Tagg could take a detour to the Central Belt and get some photos of the ground. It was the nearest he would get to the legendary stadium for the foreseeable future.

"I did have a look at the map when we were there, but it was miles out of our way. So sorry to let you down," said Lynne, with a total lack of sincerity.

"Oh well, maybe I can persuade Nigel Brimacombe to come on a Scottish road trip with me, taking in the wonders of Cowdenbeath and Brechin before ending up at Stenhousemuir."

"So, John, Kerry Franklin. What do we know?"

Tedesco recounted the gist of his conversation with the dean, focusing on the suggestion that Arabella Patrick's presence at the cathedral that day may not have been pure coincidence. He also told her about Jock Barton's revelation that Kerry had referred to shoving Arabella off the tower.

Lynne shared what she had learned from Julia Tagg about Kerry's cruise ship admirer and then Tedesco, clearly worried, went through his distressing meeting with his sister in the refectory, introducing Lynne to Alan Meer as someone who had not only been present on the tower but had demonstrated an unhealthy interest in the *Searchlight* presenter.

"What about the other people on the tour?"

"I haven't found out too much about them. Dean Dan gave me the names, of course, as well as Kerry, Meer and Arabella Patrick and her husband. The others seemed to be straight from central casting. A young couple from Exeter and their two kids, two Americans visiting Plymouth, and a Mr and Mrs Knowles from Coventry who stay in Dawlish every August."

"Okay, I expect Bloomfield will have interviewed them all. I'll see if Jools can give me anything in return for what we've got."

Sally Munks interrupted them. "DCI Bloomfield's on the phone."

Tedesco took the call. "Jimmy! To what do I owe this honour?"

"I think we need to meet up about the tower case. There's been a development and when I tell you about it you will see why I'm not a happy bunny. I assume you're taking an interest for the cathedral?"

"You may think that, DCI Bloomfield…"

"But I couldn't possibly comment. Yeah, yeah. How about your place on Saturday morning? About nine? I hate to admit it but if we don't get our heads together quickly someone's going to get away with murder."

After a lunchtime chat with Joan at Jenks Bakery, which resulted in the purchase of a new sandwich offering of crayfish salad on sourdough, Tedesco returned to Minster Precincts to a voicemail from Nicky.

She had news. Her colleague Victoria Thomas had been asked to act as chair and moderator at the upcoming meeting of the Rhyminster and Woolford Conservative Association, held for the purpose of selecting a parliamentary candidate to stand for the seat at the next general election.

The meeting was to be an open forum, so members of the public could apply for tickets on a first come, first served basis. Nicky would be going there to support Vicki and had applied for tickets for Tedesco and Lynne.

He chuckled at the thought of his fellow detective, a *Guardian* reader to her core, attending a Tory party selection hustings, before reflecting that this meeting would bring the Arabella Patrick/Barry Gulliver fight to its conclusion and thus could well have a bearing on the investigation.

He messaged his sister to say that she could count them in: he'd pick his moment before he told Lynne about her upcoming surprise treat.

After munching through his sandwich – good filling but wrong choice of bread – he finished his crossword with a flourish then wandered over to his rickety filing cabinet and extracted the 'tower' casebook.

He filled his pen with ink and began to inscribe his latest insights.

Kerry Franklin – seemingly cheerful character, popular with colleagues. Why would she leap off the tower? No suicide note.

Her comment to Barton about Arabella – surely just a joke? No one likes politicians these days. But why did Julie Stringer deliberately point out Arabella's house to the viewers when she appeared on Searchlight?

What was Alan Meer really doing on the tour? Why did Bloomfield think Meer's behaviour warranted a visit to Nicky?

Why were Maxwell Patrick and Felicity Gallant getting involved? And who facilitated the purchase of Stannary House and was now engaged in fighting Arabella for the nomination? Were all roads leading to Gulliver?

But if Kerry had been thrown off the tower, why was there no evidence of a struggle?

Should we be asking if any of the group had been on a cruise at the time when Kerry was bothered by the mystery stalker?

As Searchlight's *veteran weatherman Carl Miller would put it, 'Lots of mist and murk in the forecast'.*

Meanwhile, Lynne had been immersed in her latest project, vetting some potential recruits for a local engineering company. She was keen to expand the agency into more commercial matters as she was getting a little weary of the usual divorce and missing persons work. And the cathedral couldn't be relied upon to maintain the pipeline of high-profile murder investigations, surely?

Tedesco peered around the door of the meeting room where she had determinedly ensconced herself.

He was looking more like his old self. Perhaps it was the focus of a new case, but his subterranean lovelorn sadness was fading somehow.

"Lynne – sorry to interrupt your industrial espionage for a moment but I don't think I established if you are coming over on Saturday to meet Jimmy?"

"It clashes with my Parkrun, and as Jools is coming on the run, I thought I'd pick her brains afterwards."

"By the way," he added, failing to conceal a guilty grin, "what are you doing on Friday next week?"

TWENTY-ONE

Tedesco and Davey seemed to have reached a silent agreement to take a day off the Kerry Franklin case. It was Friday, after all, and he needed to get back to work on his missing beneficiary case, while she was happy to spend the day scrolling through the social media pages of the various potential recruits.

They couldn't entirely avoid the Franklin investigation though – Neil Sparkes had called midmorning.

"John, I know that you are taking an interest in Gallants. Anyway, one of my colleagues had a call from the fragrant Felicity yesterday."

"She's about as fragrant as own-brand disinfectant from what I remember. Anyway, what was she calling about?"

"She was canvassing support for Arabella Patrick. Flick is on the executive of the local Tories, and she's put herself in charge of drumming up support for the daughter of Fat Pat in the upcoming selection."

"How interesting. I'd have thought that Bazza had already stitched up the local professional vote."

"I'm not so sure. I've applied for a ticket to the show – it should be a laugh if nothing else. You going?"

"Nicky has applied for me. It's a week today, isn't it?"

*

As Lynne and Jools were setting off on their regular 5k Parkrun, Bloomfield was awkwardly squeezing himself into Tedesco's tiny kitchen at St Budeaux Place, Barker taking the arrival of the lanky policeman as his cue to sniff around the garden.

Bloomfield accepted the offer of coffee, but grimaced at the choice of a Plymouth Argyle-themed mug, which bore the slogan 'Who Are We? Green Army!' He was a rugby man to his core.

Tedesco decided to open proceedings. "So, Jimmy. This must be important, giving up your Saturday morning."

"Okay, here's the big news. Hinton has closed the investigation on the tower case. The inquest is likely to deliver a verdict of misadventure, but I'm sure there's no way that Kerry would just leap off."

"What leads you to that conclusion?"

Bloomfield, while a bit irritated to be treated as if he was a new client of Tedesco's agency, inwardly conceded that the gentle interrogation was helping him to focus his thoughts.

"Firstly, everything we have heard about Kerry paints a picture of a positive, life-loving woman. She was independent – moving abroad, ditching the husband – and had everything to live for. Jools heard from her brother that she had been rescued from drowning as a kid and that had made her relish every second."

"Interesting. But you must have something else?"

"The holidaymaker who saw her fall and called the alarm. He described her as standing on one of the parapets as if she was about to topple over. Matt has interviewed the witness again – Mike Knowles – and he is still clear that Kerry was standing with her back to the drop. How many suicides plan to 'topple off', back first? And Knowles was definite about her mood. She was terrified and clearly didn't want to fall."

"It does seem strange. As you say, why would she clamber up there unless she wanted to jump – or someone had forced her to?"

"Exactly. And some of the people up there that day—"

"I'll butt in there, Jimmy. Nicky has already told me about Alan Meer and his obsession with her. I'm really grateful that you are taking it seriously. She may come over as the hardened reporter, but this has really got to her."

"My pleasure, Mr Registrar. And have you heard about Arabella Patrick?"

"Our prospective Member of Parliament? Yes, I have. Julie Stringer wasn't exactly subtle in trying to link her to the case on *Searchlight*, and I had an interesting discussion with the head tower guide."

"Old Barton? What did he have to say?"

"When he and Kerry were going through the list of the bank holiday tour group Kerry made a little joke: if Ms Patrick mentioned politics, she might be tempted to throw her off the tower, or words to that effect…"

*

105

Lynne Davey and Jools Tagg were joined by Jo, the dean's wife, as they made their way to the start of the weekly Parkrun, striding through the park like a middle-aged, middle-class Anglican iteration of *Charlies Angels*: more *Off to Evensong* than *Full Throttle*.

Sally Munks, the agency's redoubtable PA, was manning the registration desk but she was anything but her normal flamboyant self.

"Are you okay, Sally?" Jo politely enquired, prompting a stream of anger.

"It's that awful man. Barry Gulliver. Parkrun is special, it's for everyone. Look over there! He's turning it into a Trump rally!"

"Bit of an exaggeration, don't you think?" said Lynne.

Jools pointed to the other side of the King George Field from where what appeared to be a small motorcade was emerging.

Bazza had rigged up a truck festooned with posters advertising 'Gulliver's Travels! Next stop Westminster!'

A tinny sound system blared out 'I'm Your Man' as the candidate completed his circuit of the course, while the Rhyminster Majorettes had been inveigled into acting as somewhat pudgy cheerleaders, keeping up a steady chant of, "Give us a B, Give us an A, Give us an RRY!"

Gulliver signalled for them to stop, then proceeded to address the runners through an old school megaphone.

"Have a great run, people. I'm fully behind Parkrun and I guarantee that when I'm your next MP I will be joining you at the starting line. You try and stop me!"

And with that, the parade moved off in the direction of Woolford, to introduce the more rural of his prospective constituents to the Gulliver phenomenon.

*

Back in the quiet of St Budeaux Place, DCI Bloomfield listened intently as Tedesco took him through his case notes, immaculately inscribed as always, then he added his own findings.

"John, there's something else that bothers me. We've heard that Kerry was being hassled by a man she met on the cruise ships years ago. He's surfaced in Rhyminster."

"I know, Jools told Lynne about it on their flight back from Scotland. What are you thinking, Jimmy?"

"I may have mentioned Kerry's brother. Jools drove over to the outskirts of Bristol to see him yesterday, just as Hinton was pulling the plug. Graeme Franklin – the brother – recalled his sister describing the man as being loud, brash and northern."

"I don't suppose he was also an estate agent with an interest in politics?"

Bloomfield allowed himself a tight little smile. "How did you guess?"

"So," said Tedesco, "somehow, we have both the candidates embroiled in this mess. What was Arabella Patrick really doing on the tour? Had Bazza somehow known she was going to be there, and arranged for Kerry to be the guide? He must be seriously kicking himself. Let's not forget, it was down to Bazza's reckless greed that Arabella found her perfect home in the constituency. Talk about an own goal!"

"What are you thinking, then? Bazza persuaded Kerry to push Arabella over the edge in return for what – no more pestering? A cash reward?"

"Or was he frightened that Kerry would spill the beans about his inappropriate contact to Ms Patrick, thus ruling him out of the running, and so he arranged for Kerry's little accident?"

"I don't know, John. Perhaps there is a simpler explanation. But unless she did kill herself, I'm struggling to find one."

"I agree with you, Jimmy. But as you have often said, nothing is too far-fetched where that magnificent building is concerned."

They decided that Bloomfield and Jools would continue to operate in the shadows, the DCI convinced that the investigation would eventually reopen with adverse career consequences for Area Commander Hinton. Tedesco agreed that Lynne and Jools would liaise over the cruise aspect. Jools could call in favours and get hold of passenger lists, and Lynne could follow up.

"You don't fancy joining our agency, do you, Jimmy? There's no money but it's rewarding in other ways."

"How can I put this politely? You will see me in the Devonport End at Home Park wearing a replica Argyle kit before I go over to the dark side."

TWENTY-TWO

The post-Parkrun talk was all about Gulliver. The general view was that he had done himself no favours by disrupting the peaceful weekly workout.

"He hasn't even been nominated yet," Jo said, adding that she doubted if any of the local Tories involved in the final choice between Barry and Arabella would have been seen dead at a community event like Parkrun.

Lynne visibly blushed at this, and Jo looked at her aghast. "Lynne, I know we've never really discussed politics, but no! You can't be!"

Ex-DS Davey began to smile somewhat awkwardly. "It's okay, Jo, I'm not about to put myself forward as the next Priti Patel or Liz Truss, but I am attending the selection meeting."

"But you're not a party member, surely? You read the *Guardian*, for God's sake."

"I took some persuading. My esteemed colleague asked me if I was free next Friday then explained that his sister had arranged tickets for the candidate selection. You don't have to be a party member these days. The local Tories are trying to show how inclusive they are by inviting some members of the public to attend and vote. My initial reaction was to politely tell John to do one, but then it struck me that it would be a shame to miss out on Rhyme's version of the Rumble in the Jungle, and if I can cast a vote against the awful Gulliver, then happy days."

*

Once Bloomfield had left St Budeaux Place, heading for his next appointment at the golf course, Tedesco caught up with his copy of *The Times* until *Football Focus* began.

Dan Walker had been replaced as the presenter by Alex Scott and, whilst Tedesco welcomed any further move towards gender equality, especially in football, the change of personnel hadn't had any discernible impact on the programme's obsession with the big clubs. Yet again, no mention of today's real match of the day: Ipswich Town v Plymouth Argyle.

As the kindly detective finished his ritual weekend pasty, Barker, sensing possible movement, looked hopefully at his lead.

Tedesco got up, stretched, and gave his canine friend a gentle stroke.

"Great minds think alike, old friend. Where shall we go today? How about a walk down by the river?"

The well-trodden scenic walk began with a comparatively dull stretch of road, then you turned off for King George Field, home of Parkrun, a green expanse that led to the river, which boasted wonderful cathedral views.

As there was a surprising lack of other dogs Barker was unleashed and soon, somewhat knowingly, found a stick for his master to throw for him. It was as if the border terrier was indicating that he knew that this was the deal, tricking the humans into thinking they were in charge.

Tedesco let the dog have a splash in the shallows of the River Rhyme, and then put him back on his lead for the walk through the water meadows, as beautiful a stroll as you could imagine, culminating in a triumphant entry into the magnificence of the Cathedral Close.

About halfway along Barker started to sniff agitatedly around a bench sited near the old mill race by the Kingfisher, Rhyme's brave attempt at a fine dining gastropub.

"Well done, Barker! I agree. Time for a little rest. This is the very best view of the cathedral. Did you know that Turner painted it?"

Barker jumped up onto the seat and began to rub his head against the brass plaque at the top of it.

The border terrier had a history both of keeping the humans in the office relaxed but also of sniffing out clues.

Tedesco turned to the inscription and read it out loud. "Dedicated to the Eternal Memory of Angela Meer who drowned here whilst rescuing another."

There was no date, no further detail to embellish the starkness of the image that the words conveyed.

Tedesco turned to Barker. "I think we might need to interrupt Jimmy's game of golf, don't you?"

As he tried to reach Bloomfield – straight to voicemail – he had the presence of mind to take a photo of the inscription.

*

Area Commander Jacqueline Hinton and Felicity Gallant,

111

senior partner of her eponymous law firm, were enjoying a gentle hack along a bridleway in the folds of the Tamar Valley.

The conversation between them had been anything but gentle.

"Jackie, look, I really can't have your plods harassing my staff. If this gets out, then it isn't actually great for the bottom line. And it isn't just *Searchlight* and the *Herald* we have to worry about these days. All these leftie citizen journalists stirring up trouble."

"Don't worry! I've called off DCI Bloomfield. Unless he can come up with something new then the investigation is over. The poor woman fell off the tower, end of story."

"Good to hear, and I will of course hold you to that. But if any of my staff get bothered again there will be consequences."

*

Tedesco and Barker completed their walk in silence, interrupted only by occasional waves of recognition from various cathedral volunteers as they wandered home through the Close.

Tedesco had considered stopping off at the refectory, but it would be crammed with noisy and, frankly, bloody annoying tourists and he just wanted to curl up in his den and await the football results with his usual feeling of ninety per cent dread and ten per cent expectation.

Mug of Yorkshire Tea in hand he thought of trying Bloomfield again then decided to text Lynne before tuning in to *Final Score*.

"*Fancy an early evening drink at the Kingfisher? I have news...*"

Just as Mike West was getting to the result from Portman Road, Ipswich, his phone beeped.

"My dance card is free at the moment. How about 6.30?"

Then Mr West just had to go and lower the vibe. "Ipswich Town 2, Plymouth Argyle 1."

TWENTY-THREE

Barker tried his very best to look crestfallen at Argyle's result and seemed perfectly happy to stay in while his master retraced his steps to the Kingfisher.

As he was meeting Lynne, Tedesco decided to ditch his old barn jacket for his black pea coat and an old university scarf. He thought it made him look like a sixties icon, Alan Bates maybe, or at a pinch, Terence Stamp.

Making his way towards the river, shadows forming on the grassy banks, he consulted his internal play list. Nick Drake again: 'River Man'.

Not this time. Too obvious. The perfect track came to him as he looked up at the welcoming glow of the pub. James Taylor: 'Lighthouse'.

He saw Lynne's profile candlelit in the window, scrolling down a menu on her phone. Stooping to avoid the low ceiling as he entered the ancient inn, he saw that she was wearing a cashmere jersey under her 'Emma Peel' black leather jacket. As usual he felt conflicted. She was undeniably attractive, they got on well, but...

"Good evening, Mr Tedesco. I've already ordered a

couple of large glasses of Bordeaux in your honour."

"Before we settle down could you pop outside for a moment? I'll ask the barman to hold our table."

"Wow, you don't mess about! Couldn't you wait till we get back to your place?"

Tedesco make a useless attempt not to look embarrassed.

"It's work, Lynne."

"If you say so."

She followed him outside and they walked to the bench. He was glad that he had remembered a torch as that notoriously imprecise time called dusk had begun to descend on the little cathedral city.

"I think you told me that Kerry Franklin had been saved from drowning as a girl."

He shone his torch at the inscription. "What do you make of that?"

Lynne peered at the plaque. "I think we need that drink. And then another one…"

*

Rachel Bloomfield wasn't happy with her husband. He'd been late back from golf, and she had to delay supper. Before they settled down in front of *Strictly*, the first in the series to introduce the jeopardy of evictions after the previous week's series opener – Rachel felt that this was sufficient punishment – he went through his messages. Two missed calls: one from Tedesco, the other from Hinton.

The prospect of watching a bald actor from EastEnders who he'd never heard of dancing the American Smooth with a dead-eyed Russian woman was suddenly quite appealing.

*

Back in the Kingfisher the two detectives considered the new evidence.

Lynne, back in business mode, started out.

"Okay, so we are guessing that Kerry was the 'another' referred to on the inscription. So does it mean that she was rescued by Angela Meer?"

"And it is fair to assume that Angela is related to Kathleen and Alan Meer. It isn't exactly a common name."

"We can soon find out, and that could establish a link between Alan Meer and Kerry. But it's a big leap from there to suggesting that Alan killed her."

"Yes, though it's quite a coincidence, surely? By the way, how's the wine?"

"Not bad for this place. Listen, I agree it looks suspicious, to put it mildly, but why would Alan want to kill the person who was rescued by his relative?"

"I don't know. Perhaps he's been harbouring a grudge for all these years."

"What, that Angela should have lived, and Kerry should have been left to die?"

"That's putting it bluntly, but yes, it does make a kind of morbid sense, doesn't it?"

Lynne broke the developing silence between them. "Look, why don't we order another glass and some sandwiches to soak it up. Call it an early supper."

"Good idea, then we can order a taxi to drop me off at the Close and then take you back from there. And I'm putting this on expenses. This is work, after all."

TWENTY-FOUR

Just as Claudia and Tess were about to announce who was going home from *Strictly*, Bloomfield's phone vibrated with a palpable insistence.

It was Commander Hinton again. She wanted an urgent talk with him that evening.

He'd had more than enough crap TV for now and couldn't give a toss if it was the guy from *EastEnders*, some random influencer, whatever that was, or that blonde woman from BBC *Breakfast* who lost the public vote, so he was almost glad of an excuse to take himself up to his study and make some calls.

He called Hinton first.

"You took your time, DCI Bloomfield," she said briskly, not allowing for a response.

"It's about the tower, as you will have guessed. I had a very difficult conversation with Felicity Gallant today. I had to promise her that you won't be contacting any of her staff. Didn't I make myself clear?"

"Ma'am, no one has been in contact with Alan Meer since you told me that the investigation was a dead duck. But why should we be taking orders from a local solicitor?"

Bloomfield could almost feel the exasperation coming down the line.

"I will pretend that I didn't hear that, Jimmy. But what I will say is that Flick Gallant may work for a tiny firm in the back of beyond, but she has a formidable intellect and a client roster that is the envy of much larger outfits. She wouldn't hesitate in making life difficult for us if we strayed out of line. Just forget about the jumper on the tower. If the family want to look into it, they can always call Tedesco and Davey."

Yeah right, Bloomfield thought as he scrolled through his contacts section, *and isn't Ms Gallant a friend of Hinton's, and a leading light in the local Tory party? Wouldn't want to upset her, would we?*

He found Tedesco's number, realising at once that he could have saved time by simply returning the call.

The private detective yawned as he answered. "Keeping you awake, am I?" said Bloomfield.

"I had nodded off, but I'm glad you woke me in time for *Match of the Day*. Anyway, thanks for getting back. How was the golf?"

"My mind wasn't really on it. My first tee shot went into the trees, and it was downhill from there on in. At least it gave me an excuse to keep this wretched thing on mute."

"I can imagine. So, I was calling about Kerry Franklin. I, or to be fair, Barker, made an interesting discovery this afternoon. I think your investigation might be back on."

Bloomfield stifled a laugh.

"And I've just been politely warned by the area commander against any further contact with Meer or any of his colleagues."

Tedesco frowned. "Do I detect the cold hand of Felicity Gallant?"

"How did you guess? Anyway, my gut feeling remains that Kerry didn't just topple off that blasted tower by accident. Someone forced her up there, whether it was Meer, Arabella or her dickhead husband or maybe Bazza was somehow behind it all, pulling the strings. So, for now, we should continue to keep the lines open, but we will all have to tread more carefully. I'm going to bin this phone for starters and invest in a burner as well as a replacement."

"Have you finished? Don't you want to hear my stunning news?"

"Sorry John. Fire away."

"I took Barker for a walk through the water meadows today. About halfway home he seemed to be fixated on a bench. It's by the Turner view of the cathedral."

"Very bucolic I'm sure, but what's this got to do with the price of fish?"

"Patience, Jimmy. We stopped at the bench for a rest and Barker turned his attention to the memorial plaque, which I read. It was in honour of Angela Meer, who died while rescuing someone from drowning in the mill race."

"Hang on. Didn't Kerry's brother tell Jools that she nearly drowned when she was a kid?"

"He did. So can you see it now? Angela must have been a relative – Meer isn't exactly a common surname – and if it was Kerry who she rescued, then Alan may have borne a grudge."

"Let's think. How old is Alan? Late forties? I know he seems older."

"And how old would Angela have been when she drowned? Older than Kerry, presumably."

Tedesco sighed. "I'd stupidly assumed that Angela must have been Alan's sister, but the ages don't add up, do they?"

"How old was Kerry? Late fifies, early sixties? So, if Angela had been at least ten years older than Kerry she'd be well into her seventies now, wouldn't she?"

"About the same vintage as Kathleen. Are you starting to wonder…?"

"If Angela had been the first Mrs Meer."

"And Alan's real mother?"

They agreed that the agency would make some checks with the register office to confirm birth and death dates, then they would reconvene in secret, or use Lynne and Jools as conduits.

By now, Tedesco wasn't in the mood for Gary Lineker, and it was too late to call Lynne, so he opened a bottle of decent claret and went through his vinyl collection, settling on Gilbert O'Sullivan: 'Nothing Rhymed'.

Then he checked on Barker, who was sound asleep after all his efforts, locked up the house, turned out the lights and went to bed, his final conscious thought being of Sorcha in her bookshop in wonderful West Cork.

TWENTY-FIVE

The day started brightly at St Budeaux Place but there was more than a hint of autumn in the air as Tedesco and Barker made their familiar way over the bridge to the paper shop.

With his mind still buzzing from yesterday's revelations, the detective decided on a whim to go to the morning service of eucharist at the cathedral.

Despite his ongoing issues with the Almighty, he still found solace in the familiar words and rhythms of the Anglican church, the warp and weft of centuries of worship: it would also be useful to catch up on the gossip at the refreshments afterwards, even if it did mean forcing himself to drink Fairtrade coffee.

Barker silently intimated that he was quite happy to be left to his own devices at home, so Tedesco wandered down to the Close, noting the liberal sprinkling of leaves on the lawns, as if someone had just emptied an enormous box of cornflakes from a passing plane.

He was warmly greeted at the visitor entrance by two sidespeople, Chris Turner and Marion Budge. He'd acted for Marion's family when her husband had died.

"How lovely to see you, Mr Tedesco," she said. "Where would you like to sit today, quire or nave?"

It had always struck him that this was a bit like being offered white or red. The choice depended on the mood, the season and the time of day.

As the nights were drawing in, and the damsons had been harvested, he elected for the quire, the ecclesiastical equivalent of a velvety red.

Striding up through the Nave he remembered too late that there were two potential disadvantages to the quire. Firstly, there would inevitably be one of the miserabilist tendency of sidesmen guarding the entrance, often that gruesome toad Foster, and secondly that the choir mums had a habit of bagging the best stalls.

So he was more than relieved to find that the sidesman on duty today was none other than Jos Elsted, his favourite wine merchant.

"Jos! I didn't know that you had joined the Swiss Guard!"

A shy smile spread over Elsted's face. "The dean and his wife can be very persuasive – and they are very good at recommending my wine."

"A bit like influencers, then?"

"Very up to the minute, Mr Tedesco. Let me find you a good seat well away from the stage-door mommas."

As he settled into one of the exquisitely carved thirteenth-century stalls, he made a mental note to mention how good a sidesman Jos was next time he bumped into one of the cathedral canons, and he also remembered that Liz Gerrey – for a brief time employed as the dean's PA, and for a fleeting but bittersweet interval someone who might have meant rather a lot to him – used to sit directly opposite.

He was jerked back to the present by the appearance at the Tower Crossing of his friend Canon Wilf Drake, the precentor.

Wilf welcomed everyone, whether regulars or visitors, and reminded them that refreshments would be served in the cloisters today as a TV company was filming in the Chapter House.

That just about encapsulates life in today's cathedrals, he thought to himself as Wilf suggested a moment of stillness before worship began.

Izzie, the head verger, led an impressive procession through the building including both the boys' and the girls' choirs, the grimacing and gurning Master of Musick, who had recently and grudgingly ended his futile boycott of the girls' section, the lay vicars (the adult choristers), assorted servers and then the principal clergy with the dean bringing up the rear.

Tedesco wasn't the first person to note the similarities between this ritual and the quasi-religious atmosphere at sporting events.

Perhaps the procession should come out to a theme tune, and scarves be held aloft by the congregation? How about football-style chants? "There's only one Canon Wilfred," or "We love you Dean Dan, we do."

Or what about "Stand up, if you hate Dawkins?"

This pointless reverie was interrupted by the organ signalling the first musical number, the suitably rocking nautical anthem, Boys Brigade hymn and sure-fire cause of infantile sniggering, 'Will Your Anchor Hold in the Sea of Life', featuring the Master of Musick on lead vocals.

Things calmed down considerably after that, and Tedesco could enjoy some real mindfulness as the familiar liturgy began to exert its customary healing balm.

He noted that there was a visiting preacher, a long-winded retired suffragan bishop from Ilfracombe, who succeeded in bringing down the vibe, or cooling the scene, as Sorcha would have put it. Then the service ended as exuberantly as it began with a raucous rendition of 'He Who Would Valiant Be'.

Tedesco regarded this as the Plymouth Argyle hymn with its refrain of 'to be a pilgrim'.

Argyle are, of course, known as The Pilgrims, for the benefit of any readers from up country.

Once he had struggled his way out of the quire, squeezing past the screeching gaggle of choir mums, he was greeted warmly by a grinning dean.

"The precentor must have known that you were coming, John."

"To Be a Pilgrim, you mean? It was great to hear it again."

"I hope you we can persuade you to stay for coffee. I could use a minute of your time."

*

Tedesco soon realised that it could be quite a while before the dean would be free as most of the congregation seemed to want to speak to him on the way out, and then the poor man was assailed by Commander Foster just as he had reached the comparative safety of the cloisters.

"Who invited that preacher, Dean! Sent me to sleep. What we need is my old naval padre to stir things up. Muscular Christianity, that's the way forward!"

Not for the first time Tedesco realised that he could never have been a priest.

Apart from the flickering flame of his faith, which was all but extinguished when Sorcha died, he couldn't have stood and listened politely to muttonheads like Foster. He decided to wander into town and get a decent cup of takeaway coffee from Jenks, hoping that Dan might be free by the time he returned with something at least drinkable.

As he walked purposefully across the Green, he became aware of an oncoming commotion, as if the circus was about to arrive in town.

If only it had been. Instead he heard a familiar voice bellowing through a loud-hailer, "I'm Barry Gulliver and I'm gonna put Rhyminster on the map!"

Apart from the fact that his beloved city could do with being off the map for a while after the notoriety it had gained as a crime scene, the man had no right to bring politics into the Close.

As the 'Close constables', the cathedral's very own Keystone Cops, were a thing of the distant past, Tedesco decided to take matters into his own hands.

He ran towards the slow-moving truck from which Gulliver was operating and shouted at the driver to stop.

"Mr Tedesco! Glad to see that you want to join us!" said Barry.

"Mr Gulliver. You have no right to carry out a political demonstration here. Will you please go away and leave the Close. This is not a public space."

"I will do no such thing. Charlie Tantum gave me permission."

"Oh, he did, did he? Let's see what the dean has to say about this!"

To Tedesco's initial surprise Gulliver came down quietly

from the truck and followed him towards the cloisters, closely followed by his dodgy-looking driver, camera in hand. He was, presumably, Gulliver's campaign agent or whatever, and was no doubt looking for an angle such as 'Dean stands in the way of democracy as Gulliver silenced'.

Oh God, the detective suddenly thought. *Tantum is there. He will weigh in against the dean, as will Foster. And did I spot Julie 'It Makes Me Mad' Stringer in the congregation earlier?*

TWENTY-SIX

As he entered the cloisters Tedesco overheard Lady Derrington in conversation with Wilf Drake.

He had got to know her ladyship when she had instructed the agency in a delicate matter involving her son Rollo, who always seemed to be getting into scrapes. "Poor Rollo, it's not his fault, it's just dashed bad luck," was her constant refrain.

Married to the Lord Lieutenant, Lady Fiona bore a distinct resemblance to the late Celia Johnson, both physically and vocally.

Indeed, when Tedesco first introduced her to Lynne, his loyal colleague had nearly burst out laughing when she heard her ladyship's clipped tones, convinced that she must be putting it on.

Since then, Lynne and Lady Fiona had formed an unlikely friendship, based in no small part on their intolerance of stupid men.

"Sorry to interrupt you both," said Tedesco rather breezily, "but we have something of a developing situation. Fiona, Barry Gulliver is about to arrive, and so I was wondering if you could detain him for a while. I'm sure he will be only too happy to try and persuade you to vote for him on Friday."

The bird-like aristocrat looked startled, but soon got the plot.

"John, you want to talk to Wilfred and the dean, I expect. Good plan. Leave that dreadful little man to me."

Drake and Tedesco looked on in admiration as her ladyship made a beeline for Gulliver and his slimy-looking stooge.

"Mr Gulliver. Just the man I was hoping to see! Edward and I are having a real tussle about who to vote for. Perhaps you can persuade me?"

"That should keep him tied up for a few minutes," said Wilf, waving across at Dean Dan, who was being persistently harangued by Foster and looking increasingly desperate for an excuse to get away from the human battleship.

"I thought I would never escape!" exclaimed the dean as he reached safety.

"What was it this time?" Tedesco asked. "Time to abolish the girls' choir, end that dreadful left-wing handshake of peace?"

"How did you guess? Anyway, can you still spare me a moment?"

"I think so, I have no plans beyond a Nigel Slater lamb chop recipe, a glass of Jos' best and the Sunday papers. However, Dean, there is something, or someone, more pressing," he added, pointing towards Gulliver.

Canon Wilf spoke up. "Fiona is distracting Barry for now, but John spotted him campaigning in the Close and quite properly asked him to leave."

"That's right, and he told me in no uncertain terms that the Master of Musick had given him permission, so I reminded him that you should have been consulted."

The dean sighed and gazed up at the cloister roof.

"I shouldn't say this about a colleague, but bloody Charles! What does he think he is doing? Okay, I assume you indicated to Gulliver that he was trespassing. Let me go and join my mate Bazza and her ladyship and see if I can defuse things."

*

"I see, so you are positioning yourself as the local man. But aren't you from up North—"

Lady Derrington, noticing the dean hovering, allowed him to interrupt.

"Fiona, I'm so sorry to disrupt your obviously important conversation, but I need an urgent word with Barry."

"Oh aye? I suppose Tedesco has been telling tales out of school."

"John did explain that he saw you conducting a political rally in the Close, and that he asked you very politely to desist."

Gulliver shoved his head forwards with no little menace.

"What gives you the right to silence me? People like you, you've got no idea what life is really about. When have you had to graft? What do you actually do for the other six days of the week?"

Lady Derrington glared at the prospective candidate.

"Now look here. The dean works tirelessly for this cathedral and the city of Rhyminster. And if you think that we will support you on Friday you are sadly deluded."

Tedesco, spotting the photographer moving in, stood in front of him and blocked his view.

Realising that he was getting nowhere, Gulliver retreated with a truculent air, but not before turning around and pointing at the dean, shouting, "This is war! And if you think I'm going to sponsor your poncey concert you can think again!"

The dean smiled beatifically at the others. "Shall we all adjourn to the deanery for a pre-lunch drink?"

"What a super idea," said Lady Derrington.

"I think Barker can spare me for half an hour," said Tedesco. "And I have a funny feeling that my old firm might well be in the market to sponsor a prestigious event in the cathedral if Gulliver really does pull the plug."

Wilf Drake gave him a broad conspiratorial grin as they all set off across the Green.

*

Later that afternoon a grumpy detective was awoken from his post-prandial slumber.

"I know you hate the ring tone, Barker, but it needs to be loud in case I nod off."

"Tedesco? Lynne! I forgot to call you back, didn't I?

"And you sound half-asleep. What have you been up to?"

"Oh, just the usual, morning service at the cathedral, two or three glasses of sherry at the deanery…"

"And some claret with lunch, no doubt. You need to watch the units, you know."

"And deprive myself of one of my greatest pleasures? Thanks for the health warning. Anyway…"

"Anyway, indeed, you old soak. I was calling because I've been looking up old newspaper coverage about Angela

Meer's drowning. It never ceases to amaze me what you can find online. God bless Tim Berners Lee. And as I missed my lovely long cycle ride this morning due to my diligent research, I thought I might hop on my trusty steed and call round now."

Tedesco stifled a yawn. "Give me half an hour to clear my head. I need to tell you about my chat with Jimmy last night and the latest hapless stunt from Bazza."

TWENTY-SEVEN

By the time that Lynne Davey rested her impressive racing bike on the flint wall of St Budeaux Place the human occupant of number 17 had transformed himself.

Once he finished the washing up, he treated himself to the luxury of a long hot shower and now he felt like an old pencil that had been sharpened to a fine point.

Barker gave his usual effusive welcome. He liked Lynne, and in common with most of the inhabitants of the Close and its ancient liberty, gave the impression that he could see no just cause or impediment that should prevent the detectives from becoming more than business partners – or are we reading too much into canine intelligence?

Tedesco started to outline his revelation about the true identity of the late Angela Meer, but before he could get into his stride Lynne showed him her palm as if she was halting traffic.

"John, I think you need to hear this. The *Journal* and the *Western Morning News* both gave extensive coverage to the drowning. The girl who survived was Kerry. She was only six. Her rescuer, Angela, was described as a trainee nurse at Rhyminster General, aged twenty and married to one Kenneth Meer, a groundsman at Kelly College in Tavistock."

Tedesco stroked his non-existent beard. "So if Angela had survived…"

"She'd be pushing seventy. And I haven't finished yet. The *Western Morning News* said that she had a baby son."

"Alan, do we assume? He must be nearly fifty."

"I've checked and he is. I also checked out Kenneth Meer. He was remarried within a couple of years to the lovely Kathleen, who was quite a bit younger than him, and she brought Alan up as her own."

"No more children?"

"None that I can find. Kathleen is down as a laundrywoman on her marriage certificate."

"I wonder where she worked. Kelly College has boarders – I bet she met Ken there."

"Quite possibly. But where is this leading? Does this give Alan a reason for wanting to kill Kerry?"

"We have already discussed whether he was angry about Kerry surviving when Angela drowned, and now we know that she was his real mother…"

"But did *he* know that she was? Did Kenneth and Kathleen tell him?"

"Or did he find out for himself when he was an adult?"

"And what did you and Jimmy discuss yesterday?"

"The drowning. I'd been assuming that Angela might have been Alan's sister, but Jimmy soon realised that the dates didn't work and so we both wondered aloud if she might have been Alan's mum."

"So now it seems that she was. What do we do with this?"

"I take it you've brought me copies of the articles?"

Lynne removed an envelope from her smart leather messenger bag.

"I was going to attach copies to an email, but I know how brilliant you are at opening attachments."

"I will ignore that. I'm pretty good at IT these days."

His business partner rolled her eyes.

"Well, I think I am. Let me have a read through tonight then we'll talk again at the office tomorrow. Deal?"

"Good plan. I need to get another 10k under my belt before it gets dark, so I will love you and leave you. Hope to see you soon, Barker."

The border terrier followed her outside and stayed there until she was out of sight.

"Ah, there you are, old friend," said his master. "Time for a walk."

*

That evening he reviewed the cuttings. The press coverage of the drowning was written in the refreshingly non-sensationalist tone of the time. While out on his circuit of the Close with Barker he had wondered about witnesses. Would the local papers have mentioned any? Had there been an inquest?

Lynne had also printed out a brief article from the now defunct *South Devon Sentinel*. This might be something.

"Two potential witnesses came forward, Mr Reginald Landeryou and his wife Edith from Yelverton. They were leaving the Kingfisher Inn when they heard someone in obvious distress, but by the time they reached the scene it seemed that they were too late. A young girl was standing close to the riverbank, clearly in shock and so Mr Landeryou returned to the inn in order to telephone the authorities. However, Mrs Landeryou distinctly remembered seeing a young woman dressed in a dark cloak running away from the mill race, in the direction of the meadows."

"Landeryou. Now there's a weird name. Where have I heard that before?"

Tedesco's famed powers of recall produced a possible result. Didn't his brother-in-law employ a mechanic called Landeryou?

He texted his sister: "*Nicky – we must catch up soon. Do you remember Derek Landeryou? I might need to speak to him. Is he still working for Chag?*"

TWENTY-EIGHT

Barker, sensing his master's impatience to get to the little office on the other side of the Close that Monday morning, seemed to understand that there would be no time for fetch the stick or for sniffing the flowerbeds. They even managed to reach Minster Precincts before Sally.

Tedesco fumbled in his suit pocket, located the key and then struggled to recall the alarm code, before remembering just in time that it was the year that Argyle joined the football league. Autumn had set in, so he got the heating going. He wasn't a miserly employer.

However, any sense of enjoyment he felt at the unfamiliar sensation of being there as the workplace came back to life after the weekend was short-lived as, within minutes of his own arrival, he heard Lynne's familiar athletic steps bounding up the helter-skelter of a staircase. Clearly, he wasn't alone in wanting to crack on.

Lynne briskly indicated the meeting room and Tedesco meekly followed her in, Barker prudently deciding to remain close to his basket.

"We'll ask Sally to fix some coffee when she gets in, shall we? So, how did you get on with the old articles?"

"The standard of journalism was far superior back then, of course."

"I hate to agree with you, Mr Nostalgia for Ye Olden Days, but you are right – no lurid speculation, no heart-warming back story, just the facts."

"The *South Devon Sentinel* mentioned a couple from Yelverton who got to the mill race and found a shivering Kerry. They'd heard cries as they were leaving the Kingfisher."

"Yeah. I read it but was probably too fixated on the surprise news that Angela was almost certainly Alan's mother. Sorry John, do go on."

"Well. There are two interesting angles. Firstly, the wife very clearly recalls a young woman running from the scene. She wore a distinctive cloak. And secondly, the couple were called Landeryou."

"And why is the second point remotely interesting?"

"I am fairly sure that Nicky's husband had a mechanic called Landeryou. Anyway, I texted my famous sister and she called me just as I was on my way up to bed. Chag employed Derek Landeryou for twenty plus years. He's recently retired, and he still lives in the area. Ivybridge."

It was Lynne's turn to weigh things up.

"So, what are you thinking? The couple who saw the aftermath of the drowning must be long gone, I guess, so you think Derek must be a relative, the son maybe?"

"Landeryou isn't a common name round here, unlike Davey, for example."

"Ha bloody ha. And Ivybridge – that's where Kathleen and Alan live. Coincidence?"

"That's almost word for word how I put it in the casebook last night."

"So, do we go back to Jimmy? He must have enough to persuade the delightful Ms Hinton to reopen things, surely?"

"Well, he knows that we have established, at least on the balance of probabilities, that Alan is Angela's son. It would help to see the birth certificate to make absolutely sure but I reckon we have a plausible motive for him. Say that Alan only found out about Angela recently and then he sees Kerry return home full of energy: he may well have blamed her for ruining his life, condemning him to live with Kathleen all these years."

"But he still has an alibi. Don't forget that Betty Budden saw him emerging onto the roof as Kerry was falling."

"Good point, but I still think Jimmy should know the latest. Can you work with Jools?"

"She and I usually go to the gym on Monday evenings for a spin class. I'll have a word. By the way, you mentioned Nicky. Has she had any more trouble?"

"Not that she mentioned. But thanks for asking. I mustn't let my own reasons for wishing ill on Mr Meer cloud my judgment but I'm beginning to think that he's our man, despite his convenient alibi."

"What about Barry Gulliver?"

Tedesco reprised the story of the prospective candidate's rude interruption to the Sunday morning tranquillity of Cathedral Green.

"But that won't help his chances on Friday, surely. Rowing in public with our lovely dean, upsetting Fiona Derrington. I assume that she still has a big say in local politics."

"Without doubt. She told me something interesting over sherry in the deanery yesterday. I asked her why Arabella was conducting such a low-profile campaign. She told me that Ms Patrick is more than happy to leave Barry to make a prize fool of himself and that there has been a big increase in party membership recently."

"Which you would think might favour Arabella?"

"That was my first thought. I have heard that Felicity Gallant has been banging the drum for her. But then I wondered – Bazza is nothing if not a great self-publicist. Could the new members be of a rather different breed?"

"We will see on Friday. Will it be wall to wall hacking jackets, or men in shiny suits looking like footballers at an awards dinner?"

"I will choose to ignore your inverted snobbery, Mrs Davey. In the meantime, I might try and get in touch with Derek Landeryou. See if he knows anything. And why don't we both go on a tower tour?"

"Good idea, as long as there aren't any more psychopaths around. Shall I see if they have any space on Saturday afternoon?"

They were interrupted by an apologetic knock on the door.

"You can come in, Sally, we're finished in here," called Lynne.

The agency's loyal PA stumbled in with a pot of coffee and then sat down at the far end of the little table.

"Now that I've got you both together, I wondered if I could have a word about our carbon footprint."

TWENTY-NINE

Lynne Davey and her friend and former protégée, Julia Tagg, were the only customers in Crane's wine bar that dank Monday evening.

They didn't normally linger after their energetic workout, but this time Jools was more than happy to agree to a quick low-alcohol lager as she was curious to hear the latest on Kerry Franklin and the two friends hadn't seen much of each other since their Scottish break.

Despite the depressing lack of customers in the bar they had squirrelled themselves away in a booth, as they wanted to be out of earshot of the staff and any punters who might, against the odds, decide to rock up for a Monday night drink or two.

Jools quickly advised Lynne that Bloomfield had told her about his conversation with Tedesco, so she knew about the drowning at the mill race.

Lynne looked around the room then explained that her immediate research had confirmed that it was indeed Kerry who had been saved by Angela Meer, that Kenneth Meer had remarried, and his second wife had brought up Ken and Angela's child.

"Alan, I assume."

"The dates all work, I just need to check the birth certificate. And the local papers reported in some detail. There were two named witnesses to the immediate aftermath, and it looks like one of their living relatives may still live on the patch and get this, he used to work for Aspirational Cars."

"Chag Wills' outfit? Small world. I've always thought there were only about forty people in Rhyme, and a lot of mirrors."

"There's always a link to someone we know – funny how often it's Chag or Nicky. Anyway, John is going to see Derek Landeryou, the retired mechanic, see if he knows anything."

Jools chugged down some beer. "This isn't bad, but it seems to be lacking something."

"Alcohol, perhaps?"

"Probably. Anyway, what are you and John both thinking? Alan Meer, prime suspect?"

"John thinks so but there is the unfortunate question of his alibi."

"The nice American woman. She was very clear. How could Alan have forced Kerry onto that parapet when he wasn't on the roof?"

"Exactly. And that is why John and I are booked onto a tower tour on Saturday afternoon."

"Good call, but if you are thinking of a reconstruction please don't jump off. I've had a thought, bit left field…"

"Go on."

"There were no prints on Kerry's body when it reached the ground. That's always bothered me. Unless she really did commit suicide, and I don't think any of us are convinced, there would have been evidence of a struggle."

"Unless Alan, or whoever did it, had Hannibal Lecter-like powers of mind control."

"What, like 'You are going to climb up on to that parapet for me and then fall backwards.' Lynne, I'm trying to make a serious point here."

"Sorry Jools. Pray continue."

"It's probably nothing, but did we ask the tour group if any of them had been wearing gloves?"

*

A few hundred yards away, in the Georgian splendour of Stannary House, Arabella Patrick was preparing for her pitch to the party members.

Her friend Felicity Gallant had agreed to role play the part of the moderator, Vicki Thomas, and to come up with some audience questions to test the candidate's ability to respond under pressure.

"So, Arabella," ventured Felicity/Vicki, "what first attracted you to Rhyminster?"

"That's such an interesting question, Vicki. Crispin and I had been wondering for some time about moving out of London. Technology has given us all the freedom to work wherever we like—"

"Got to cut you off there. Not sure many of the members down here will feel that they are free to work anywhere they like. And a fair few of them are frightened of change, still refer to computers as 'new-fangled.'"

"Okay, point taken. How about, 'some of us are lucky enough to be able to take advantage of the freedom offered by the internet to work where we choose? And, while we are on the subject, Vicki, I will, as your MP, make improving broadband speed a priority."

"Much better. The business vote will lap that up, but you need to remember that our volunteers are often elderly retirees worried about things like cuts to bus routes and so on. Don't forget to offer them something."

"Golly, that's a good point. I rather assumed I'd just be addressing people like us."

"Right then," said Felicity, more than a touch briskly. "Back in character. It's time for some questions from the audience. So, random audience member, please could you say your name clearly and then ask your question."

Ms Gallant moved to another chair and, in a cringeworthy approximation of the local accent, announced herself as Carol Carrot Cruncher.

"Moi question is, woi should we vote for you? You isn't local. I've never seen you in Lidl's, not like that nice Mr Gulliver. He's one of us."

"Er, golly. Um, well, Crispin and I want to get you know you all and I've already joined the Woolford Hunt, for example, and met plenty of local people through that, of course."

The normally ice-cool solicitor put her head in her hands. "I think that needs a bit more work, don't you, Bella?"

THIRTY

"Chag has mentioned Derek Landeryou around the showroom. His wife died of a stroke shortly after he had put down his spanner for the last time. He spends most of his day in his allotment, this side of Ivybridge, so you should find him there."

"Thanks, Nicky," said her brother. "And thank Chag for me, will you? I look forward to seeing you on Friday."

"I can't wait. It promises to be a hoot, and a car crash for at least one of the candidates. Got to go. See ya."

"Sally."

The PA looked up from her desktop.

"Could you and Barker hold the fort? I'm going to Ivybridge. I'll make sure I'm back in good time for his walk."

"And your trip to the bakery. You should make your own lunch, Mr T! I can let you have some healthy options!"

Tedesco visibly gagged.

"Lynne will be popping out to collect a birth certificate from the register office, so the fate of the agency is in your hands."

As he made his familiar way downstairs then back through the Close to pick up the Lancia, he reflected on how rare it was to be driving somewhere on a Tuesday morning. What should he listen to on the way? It didn't seem right to play one of his favourite tracks. That was more of a weekend thing. Radio 4? Classic FM? Was Ken Bruce still on Radio 2?

His musings were interrupted by the sight of Arabella Patrick posing for photos for the *Journal* outside the West Front. He knew that it was for the local rag as soon as he saw Julie Stringer hovering, tape recorder in hand.

So, had the *Journal* ditched Barry? Didn't his estate agency, Mylors, pay for a huge ad in the property pages?

As he merged onto the ring road he was amazed at the volume of traffic. Who were these people? Why weren't any of them at work? No wonder the economy was tanking.

Once the traffic began to thin out he turned on Radio 2. Good old Ken. He was still there, as was his *Pop Master* quiz.

Today's questions were on 'Seventies Classics'. While he was surprised that he still recognised tracks by Donna Summer, Mud and Slade he was sufficiently irritated by the lack of questions about Carly Simon or Jackson Browne to switch over to Radio 4.

Woman's Hour was hosting a round-table discussion about the legal profession from a female viewpoint, and he nearly missed the turn-off to Ivybridge when he was both surprised and delighted to recognise the voice of his friend Gill Withers, who displayed her usual balanced, sane opinions. He'd message her later.

Parking was at a premium at the Paignton Road allotments, so he had to find a residential street about one hundred yards away. Despite the grotty weather the place was a hive of activity. He wandered up and approached a kind-faced, weatherbeaten old boy who was leaning on a fork, or maybe a spade. Tedesco had never been a gardener.

"Excuse me. I'm looking for Derek Landeryou."

"You've found him."

"Then I'm very pleased to me meet you. I'm John Tedesco, and—"

"I know you are. I worked for Chag for years. He told me to expect you. Let's get out of the drizzle."

In common with the other allotment holders, Landeryou had a shed. But unlike some of the others, which could have doubled as brick shithouses, his was immaculate.

"I'll put a kettle on. Builder's tea okay?"

It wasn't a question.

Once they had both settled down with their tea – Tedesco tried to ignore his new acquaintance's Torquay United mug – Landeryou became more expansive.

"So, Kerry Franklin. It was my mum and dad who raised the alarm. They were in the Kingfisher down in Rhyminster, just had a nice lunch and then they heard a commotion, went to see what it was."

"And they found a scared young girl."

"Correct. Mum was wearing a shawl and so she wrapped the poor kid up in it. Kerry had been on a picnic organised by the school and had got lost."

"And she'd fallen in the river?"

"Dad thought she must have been panicking and tripped over the ledge by the mill race. There may have been people coming the other way who forced her into the side. It's very narrow there even today. But you'd know that."

Tedesco nodded his head in agreement. "So, Derek, if I may, did your parents tell you anything else? Like if they saw anyone?"

"I was coming to that. Mother saw a woman running off back towards the town."

Landeryou looked around, as if he was frightened of being overheard by the Stasi.

"Anyway," he whispered, "this woman was wearing a navy-blue cloak. It was flapping in the wind as she ran off. Mum instantly recognised it as a nurse's cloak. Now Angela, she was a nurse. She must have ditched the cloak when she dived in."

"That makes sense. Did your mum or dad say anything else about the mystery woman?"

"They could never prove it, mind, but they both thought it was Kathy Hubbard."

"Kathy? Short for Kathleen?"

"Got it in one. She's Kathleen Meer now. Mum said that she was jealous of Angela, had her heart set on Ken. He was a good-looking bloke, apparently, and had a secure job over at the college. Very highly thought of, Dad said."

"Derek, you've been incredibly helpful. You are no doubt wondering what all this is about."

"I've got a pretty good idea. You are a private eye, after all. I guess you are investigating what happened to poor Kerry. I knew her a bit. She was really lovely, bubbly, you might say. I hope you get to the bottom of it. There's no way that this was an accident."

"I'm afraid that I have to agree with you there, Derek. Again, thanks for your time."

"Time's all I've got now…"

Tedesco checked his watch as he walked back to the car. Plenty of time to get to Jenks. And he did have a track to play. Clifford T Ward's take on Stevie Smith: 'Not Waving, Drowning'.

THIRTY-ONE

Having enjoyed a clear run home, he left the Lancia in its mooring at St Budeaux Place, then wandered around to Minster Precincts to collect Barker.

Lynne had picked up Alan's birth certificate. His parents were registered as Kenneth Redvers Meer, groundsman, and Angela Meer, pupil nurse.

Alan Redvers Meer weighed in at five pounds and twelve ounces.

"Not exactly a Devonshire dumpling then," said Tedesco, who had tipped the scales at over nine pounds.

"I can see that you guys are off for lunch," said Lynne, "but before I forget, there's something Jools mentioned last night."

"It's okay, Joan won't have run out of cheese straws just yet."

"DS Tagg wondered if any of the people on the tower tour had been wearing gloves."

Tedesco reached for his imaginary beard again and gave it three long strokes.

"Why didn't I think of it! Might explain the lack of fingerprints."

"She is going to have a sneaky look at the witness statements, but if they don't help, do you think we should contact the group?"

"Nothing to stop us, I suppose. Let me have a think about it after lunch."

Jenks Bakery was heaving by the time that Tedesco and Barker arrived, but Joan gestured to her favourite customers to slide in front, ahead of some ditherers.

"Tuesday," she said. "Let me guess. Tuna mayo?"

"Oh, go on then. A bit dashing for the middle of the week, but I need some brain food."

Having rejected Joan's kind offer of a two for one on lardy cake, he stopped outside the shop in order to bend down and consult his learned friend.

"Barker, I don't fancy the office yet, or the crossword either. Why don't we find a bench in the cloisters? What do you think?"

The benches were normally occupied by munching office workers, idling students or tourists, but the inclement weather ensured that for today they were the exclusive domain of the rugged and hardy.

As he knew, the cloisters were very well sheltered and, as it wasn't too cold, they made for a perfectly amenable lunch venue.

Then just as he was tucking into his second sandwich, Julie Stringer approached.

"Holey Moley! What is Mr Tedesco doing slumming it on a park bench? Hello Barker, how are you?"

The border terrier deigned to allow Julie to pet him for a minute or so. It was within his job description, after all.

"Why don't you have a seat, Julie? Did I see you interviewing our new MP earlier?"

"You're jumping the gun, aren't you? My spies tell me that it's going to be a very close-run thing."

"So, the *Journal* is backing the carpet-bagging Ms Patrick over the morally dubious Mr Gulliver, is it?"

"Not at all. We are remaining completely neutral. I'm interviewing Bazza at a boxing club later."

"I can't see you enjoying that for a minute, Julie. All those muscled young men."

The legendary reporter gave Tedesco a suggestive wink, which he found more than a little uncomfortable.

Recovering his poise, he asked her if Arabella Patrick had been wearing gloves for the interview.

"Yes! She always does. I asked her about it once. I thought she might have some hideous disfigurement that she was covering up, but not little Ms Perfect. The fact is, she is frightened about coming into physical contact with the voters."

"She didn't admit that, surely?"

"Not in so many words – she said she was worried about picking up an infection before the selection meeting – but I knew what she meant. Anyway, why did you ask about it?"

"That, Julie, is for me to know."

She reluctantly left Tedesco to finish his lunch and, as he still had twenty minutes of his notional break left, he decided to pop into the cathedral.

Ignoring the donations desk, he and Barker wandered up the nave, pausing at Tedesco's favourite side chapel dedicated to St Nonna.

Tourists tended to bypass the understated little chapel on their way to view the Rhyme Bible and so he was able to sit there quietly with Barker for a precious few minutes. Not praying, exactly, but something more than just thinking.

"John. I hope I'm not interrupting. Good to see you as well, Barker."

It was Wilfred Drake, the canon precentor.

"Not at all, Wilf. Bit quiet today?"

"It's the weather, and the main tourist season is pretty much over. It's good to have a break from the coach loads, even though we need them to pay the bills: even we clergy obsess about cash flow these days. Anyway, it will be Christmas before we know it, so a peaceful pause is a blessing. Unlike the public, we certainly don't 'Wish It Could Be Christmas Every Day'. How are you and Lynne managing?"

After taking a moment to get over his surprise at the precentor's unlikely reference to the festive hit, Tedesco replied to his friend.

"Lynne's branched out into executive background checks; we also have to watch the bottom line. And we are still looking into Kerry, as you are well aware."

"And we are truly grateful that you are. Dan and I are holding you both in our prayers."

With that, Drake glided off towards the vestry.

Barker stretched out as if to say, "Come on, back to work."

As they made their way to their little office, he felt that both he and his constant companion had a fresh spring in their step.

Wilf hadn't said anything profound, but his appearance in the chapel had somehow taken Tedesco's thoughts to a different place.

However, his spiritual musings were suddenly interrupted by the sound of his business partner, returning from her rather more active break from work.

"Come on you two, race you back!"

*

After remembering to send a message to Gill Withers, Tedesco spent the next half hour updating his casebook while Lynne was on a Zoom call to one of her HR director clients.

Looking flustered as she emerged from the meeting room, ex-DS Davey announced that she needed caffeine, before inviting her colleague to join her.

"For God's sake, John, I thought you lawyers had cornered the market in impenetrable jargon, but this lot! It's 'going forward' this, 'key stakeholder' that. Why can't they speak human anymore!"

Tedesco laughed. "You're getting like me! Anyway, why don't we turn to Kerry."

"Indeed, some real detective work. What did you discover in Ivybridge?"

Clearly intrigued as he explained about Derek Landeryou and his memory of his late parents' account of discovering Kerry, Lynne raised an eyebrow as he added the news of Julie's comment about Arabella's squeamishness around physical contact with mere civilians.

"So the gloves thing may be important? Where do you think we are on the big picture, John?"

He began to read from his latest entries in the casebook.

"Alan Meer – now our prime suspect despite alibi. Let's see if our trip up the tower casts any doubt on it.

Bazza – was he Kerry's stalker? Need to look deeper. Could he have bullied Kerry into getting rid of Arabella, but it all went wrong..."

Lynne cut across him. "I'll come to the stalking issue, but Arabella herself must be a suspect. The gloves!"

"Granted, but we need to check if any of the others were wearing them. And what motive could Arabella possibly have? If Barry Gulliver himself had been on the tour, then I can see that she might have spotted a chance to get rid of him, but a random tour guide who she had only just met – really?"

"Okay, I get it. But besides the possibility of Arabella being involved, what about the mystery woman who ran away when Angela drowned? If it was Kathleen Meer, could this have a bearing even decades later?"

"I've been wondering about that. Did she have a direct role in Angela's death, do you mean?"

"It sounds as if she was extremely jealous of her. And funny how she was in pole position to snap up the grieving widower, don't you think? Let's put it to one side for now."

"Or on the back burner," said Lynne, rolling her eyes.

"So," she went on, "Jools and I have been looking into Kerry's time on the cruise ships. The force works with all the main liners and so Jools was able to call in favours on the quiet."

"Good show, but I don't want her to risk her career over this. What did she find out?"

"It took a while, but she discovered that Gulliver was booked on a cruise to the Canaries at the same time that Kerry was in charge of entertainments for the Retro Line – they specialise in themed cruises. James Bond, Poirot, you know the sort of thing."

"Hmm. It sounds perfectly ghastly."

"I don't think you quite fit the key demographic, Mr Tedesco."

"You are getting good at the corporate speak. Anyway, does this mean that Bazza and Kerry were on the same cruise?"

"Almost certainly. And here's the thing; Mrs Bazza, the lovely Danielle, wasn't on the passenger list."

"Were they going through a difficult patch in their relationship?"

"Who knows? But Barry wasn't alone."

"What, he took a mistress?"

"How very Edwardian. No, he was on a corporate jolly. The directors of Mylors were treating themselves after a record-breaking year."

"And what goes on board stays on board?"

"That's how types like Bazza roll…"

"So what now?"

"I'm sifting through the passenger manifest to see if there was anyone from this area who might have recognised our future MP."

"Sounds good. Let me know how you get on. Anyway, what are you going to wear to the selection meeting? Twinset and pearls?"

"Hilarious. I think we both have work to do, don't you?"

THIRTY-TWO

The tiny cathedral city, or at least that part of it which took an interest in such things, was gripped by election fever.

Even the local bookies were offering odds, making Arabella Patrick the slight favourite but there had been a recent surge in backing for Bazza.

As they would form part of the electorate, Tedesco and Davey had been emailed candidate profiles and addresses followed by personal text messages from the rival camps, although Tedesco claimed not to have seen them.

The meeting was taking place in the Victorian Guildhall, a structure that Tedesco had always considered to look out of place in medieval Rhyme. It had a lowland Scots feel to it, as if it had been transplanted from one of the more prosperous Borders towns, Biggar, maybe.

As the meeting was due to commence at 7.30 Lynne had proposed a quick 'pre-theatre' supper at Buongiorno Italia, Rhyminster's go-to Italian, where they shared a seafood platter and a carafe of house white, which Tedesco rather too loudly described as a 'serviceable Soave', to Lynne's visible embarrassment.

On the sartorial front, Tedesco had done his best to look like a traditional Tory in his cavalry twill trousers, polished brogues and blue blazer.

Lynne had decided against her Emma Peel jacket and had opted instead for a relatively safe navy two piece but matched with designer heels.

"We look like that couple Margo and Jerry from *The Good Life*. Remember them?" said Tedesco, as he finished his coffee.

"Just about. Anyway, we'd better get the bill. Don't want to be late for the Big Fight, do we?"

They had a long wait to gain entry to the meeting while their invitations and ID were laboriously checked by party workers wearing hi-vis tabards.

Once inside they found themselves crushed into a foyer which resembled the bar scene in *Star Wars*.

"Who are all these weird creatures?" Lynne whispered. "I've never seen any of them before. Do they even live in Rhyme?"

"Over here," said Tedesco, guiding his colleague away from the melee and towards a quieter area where he had noticed some reassuringly familiar faces: Lady Derrington, and his sister, who were deep in conversation.

"John! And Lynne, of course," trilled Lady D. "How super to see you both."

"I've been having such a lovely chat with Nicola," she continued. "What a talented family!"

"We are honoured to be here," Tedesco said. "How are the candidates bearing up?"

"I haven't spoken to them yet, they are being held backstage. But have you seen Gulliver's supporters? These are our new members – employees of his horrid estate agency. He's trying to rig the election!"

Tedesco saw Nicky's ears prick up. She'd be looking to quote Lady D later if Bazza triumphed. She was a journalist, after all.

"Ladies and gentlemen," boomed a loud male voice over the PA. "Please take your seats in the hall, as the performance will begin in three minutes."

It was obviously a recorded announcement that the Guildhall used for concerts and the like, but 'performance' felt about right. Both candidates would be hamming it up, especially Barry, if the past week was any guide.

As they moved towards the auditorium, Tedesco was boringly unsurprised to find Commander Foster blocking the entrance, but his mood was lifted by the sight of his former partner in soliciting, Neil Sparkes.

Sparksy was rapidly draining a pint glass, before taking his seat with the other ticket-holding members of the public who had been segregated from the party members like away fans at a local derby.

Once HMS Foster had safely dropped anchor, Tedesco and Davey took their seats in the row behind Neil.

As the lights dimmed and the hubbub gradually subsided a tall, elegant figure walked out onto the stage.

It was Vicki Thomas, *Searchlight*'s respected lead presenter. She had let her hair go grey in recent years, which, taken with her aquiline features, gave her an air of considerable gravitas. She was smartly dressed in a dark-green trouser suit, a look that Tedesco described to himself as subdued glamour, just right for the occasion.

"Good evening," began Vicki, confidently. "I am very

pleased to be here tonight to moderate this evening's meeting. Like several of you, I am not attending here in a partisan capacity, and I confirm that I have no political affiliation.

"My role is to introduce the candidates by way of a brief interview and then each candidate will have the chance to make a short presentation before you have the chance to ask questions.

"The candidates tossed a coin a moment ago and I can tell you that Barry Gulliver called correctly but asked Arabella Patrick to go first."

"Typical Yorkshireman," whispered Tedesco. "Putting the opposition in to bat on a sticky wicket."

THIRTY-THREE

The atmosphere in what passed for the green room had been frosty.

Arabella had the more impressive entourage, comprising Crispin, her father Sir Maxwell Patrick MP, as well as Felicity Gallant and her husband.

Sir Maxwell's train from Paddington was delayed, which had put him in a foul mood.

Barry Gulliver was backed by his agent, the knavish character who had been seen driving him around the constituency, and his wife.

Before setting off for the Guildhall he and Danielle had enjoyed the mother of all rows, her last-minute agreement to attend secured only by the promise of a weekend in a luxury spa for her and three girlfriends.

"Dashed unsporting of Gulliver to put you in first, Bella," was the verdict of the MP for Somerset Central.

Arabella remained calm, unlike her husband, who was pacing around, eyes glued to his smartphone.

Back on stage, Vicki Thomas concluded her opening remarks and asked Arabella to step forward.

The candidate appeared to a brief flurry of camera clicks and flashes and to loud applause.

Lynne noted that she had opted for a modern twist on Mrs Thatcher, silk ski pants with a pink blouse featuring the Iron Lady's signature pussy bow.

Vicki led Arabella to a breakfast-TV-style sofa for the interview and lobbed her some fairly gentle questions about her background and experience, for which she had been well prepared by Felicity.

"So, Arabella, you moved to Rhyminster earlier this year. How are you settling in?"

"Very well. Crispin and I both love our home, and the people are so welcoming."

"Good to hear. We are a friendly bunch down here. And have you had much chance to meet your potential constituents?"

"Oh yes. Cris and I always look forward to our shopping trips to Trago Mills and Lidl. Such good value."

Tedesco noticed Felicity Gallant smiling and giving a thumbs-up to that answer.

However, things got more difficult for the candidate during the Q and A session.

Commander Foster pointedly asked her why she hadn't waited for her father's seat to become vacant, which she handled well, but then Lynne put her hand up to ask a question.

As she awaited the roving mike her colleague hissed in her ear, "What the hell are you doing?"

"Lynne Davey, member of the public. My question is this. You have told us how at home you feel in Rhyminster, one of the locals even. Perhaps you could direct me from the Cathedral Close to the general hospital."

Felicity Gallant turned a shade of puce as she watched Arabella squirm.

"Er, well, you leave the Close by the main gate, of course, and then you take Broad Street, and then, er…"

"Let me help you," said Vicki. "You are in the one-way system now so you need to drive back around the ring road."

Arabella tried to make light of it. "You know what, Vicki. I'm the same as everyone else these days. I rely on sat nav."

Barry Gulliver had been hermetically sealed off from the proceedings and was only released onto the stage when his opponent had departed.

He had organised a claque of noisy supporters to greet him, some of them blowing hunting horns, and Vicki had to call the meeting to order.

Once he was safely ensconced on the sofa, the *Searchlight* stalwart posed her first question, taking her cue from Lynne's question to Ms Patrick.

"Barry, you have been very keen to emphasise your local credentials. Now, suppose I am a lost tourist. How would I get to the bus station from here?"

The ebullient estate agent avoided the elephant trap with ease but was less than comfortable with the first question from the floor.

It was from Fiona Derrington.

"Do you believe in family values, Mr Gulliver? I understand that you have several families of your own."

"I have been married more than once, but that's the way of things these days."

"Not down here, it isn't," yelled an anonymous heckler.

After the allotted number of questions had been dealt with, and the candidates had delivered their closing pitches for support, Vicki explained that everyone should remain seated while ballot papers were distributed. Once they had made their choice, delegates should then proceed to the exits where stewards would be in place with collection baskets.

"The counting process will take a while and so you may want to retire to the bar until we have a result."

"I've never spoilt a ballot before," whispered Tedesco, "but I'm sorely tempted this time."

Lynne glared at him and then he made a reluctant show of marking his cross.

The bar was packed with nut jobs and oddballs again, so Tedesco suggested that they went outside. He had Neil Sparkes on his contacts list so he could keep in touch with the count.

"Good call, John. I need to escape from the asylum. Some of those questions! How about Cranes?"

Unlike the previous Monday, when Lynne and Jools had been the only customers, the place was rocking.

They eventually managed to find a relatively quiet space in the upstairs function room and Lynne went back to the bar while Tedesco texted Neil.

"No sign of any white smoke yet!" was the instant response.

After what seemed an age Lynne appeared with two large glasses of red wine.

"It's their house Shiraz. See what you think."

He sniffed and swirled, and then pronounced that it was actually not bad, before updating his partner on the news from the Guildhall.

"So, John. Full disclosure. Who did you vote for?"

"I am assuming that we both voted for Arabella, despite your attempt to sabotage her."

"It felt really odd. I've never voted for a Tory before, but when it came to it the choice was between an amoral wide boy and the first woman to have a serious chance of representing us, so it was a no-brainer. Why did you vote for her?"

"Although she isn't my cup of tea, at least she is demonstrably intelligent and, as we discussed earlier, while they are both actors in the Kerry drama, she is less likely to have been implicated in any murder plot."

"Not exactly a ringing endorsement, is it?"

Tedesco's phone vibrated. It was Neil. *"It's all kicking off here. There's going to be a recount. Too close to call, apparently."*

He showed the text to Lynne.

"Shall we finish these and wobble back? We don't want to miss the fun."

She finished her wine, then responded, "If it's that close, then you know what this means? We might have swung the vote."

THIRTY-FOUR

The scene that greeted Tedesco and Davey as they approached the Guildhall was barely distinguishable from the noisy, lairy vibe of the nearby Wetherspoons. There was even a small police presence on the steps to greet them.

Voices were raised and allegations of fraud and malpractice were being thrown from both sides.

Tedesco suddenly felt a familiar nudge in the rubs.

"Nicky! This must be your lucky night."

"Neither of the candidates is available for comment until we have a result, but I've interviewed their supporters."

"Any idea who called for the recount?" asked Lynne.

"Each side is blaming the other. Lady Derrington is suggesting that Bazza has infiltrated the party by inviting a 'bunch of ruffians' to join, while Commander Foster is muttering darkly about Central Office rigging the result for Arabella."

"Lady Fiona may have a point, Nicky," said Lynne. "There do appear to be a lot of thick necks and tattoos on display."

"That's the inclusive new party, Lynne," Tedesco said. "And your question to Arabella might have just won Bazza the vote."

"Bit harsh, bro, but I would give the Patricks a wide berth if I were you."

"Ladies and gentlemen." Vicki Thomas had commandeered the PA system, and her BBC-trained voice immediately stilled the mob.

"Please would you return to your seats as we can now announce the result. Thank you for being so patient."

Once the delegates were seated, Vicki reappeared, this time accompanied by the retiring member, Sir Vere Alston.

"We are going to miss him," said Tedesco. "He's got more class than Bazza and Bella put together," Neil called over.

"Thank you all once again for your patience. It's been a long night. We are not going to announce how many votes were cast for each candidate, but we do have a result which has been verified by our friends from the Electoral Reform Society. Sir Vere, would you please announce your successor as prospective parliamentary candidate."

The distinguished knight of the shires, immaculately tailored as always, stepped forward.

"I am delighted to announce that Arabella Patrick will be the candidate for the party at the next election. Please give her your support, as I will. She is bound to face a serious challenge and so we are starting our fighting fund tonight!

"Please be generous and give what you can on your way out. Let's get her in!"

The newly elected candidate appeared in the wings and was ushered onto the stage by Sir Vere.

Tedesco realised that Vicki had quietly left the stage, as matters were now decidedly partisan. She would already be heading back over the Tamar to her riverside home near Fowey.

Arabella gave her very best, 'Gee shucks, I never expected this' smile and then took to the microphone.

"First of all, this is the greatest honour of my life. I am not taking the voters for granted but I cannot wait to be your next MP."

After the usual Hollywood-style tributes to her family and her supporters she dragged a frazzled-looking Crispin onto the stage, describing him as her absolute rock – *more of a wet pebble*, thought Tedesco – before Lord Derrington, the president of the association, drew proceedings to a close.

"So that's it, then," said Lynne, as they made their way past the party stewards, ignoring their loud appeals for donations.

"Or maybe it isn't," said her partner, pointing across the Square, where Bazza was standing on a plastic crate addressing his supporters with the megaphone he had deployed earlier in the week.

"I will be seeking urgent legal advice from my solicitors. This is very much not the end. This election has been stolen! The fight goes on!"

"Lynne, why don't we share a taxi? I think that's more than enough excitement for one night."

His colleague readily agreed and very soon a cab drew up and the familiar features of Mickey Hunn appeared at the driver's window.

"Usual routine, is it? Water Lane and then St Budeaux Place?"

*

Once Mickey had dropped him off outside number 17, Tedesco apologised to Barker for leaving him on his own for longer than expected, then turned on the TV. The late edition of the local news would be on in a few minutes, so he muted the sound and retreated to his den with a mug of coffee before riffling through his vinyl collection in search of the '*chanson juste*'.

"Got it. How about some peerless song writing?"

He tenderly removed the record from its sleeve, then carefully placed the stylus over the grooves before unlocking another gem from his collection: 'Song for the Asking', from the *Bridge Over Troubled Water* album.

As the track faded, he put the arm back in its dock and, once the record had slowed to a stop, gently put it back in its place.

Remembering that the local news report was about to start, he switched the sound back on just as Nicky appeared on the screen.

"The eagerly anticipated selection of the prospective parliamentary candidate for the Rhyminster constituency took place tonight amidst a frenetic atmosphere. Police were called after one of the candidates, Barry Gulliver, was backed by a threatening group of supporters as he angrily demanded a recount.

However, it was Arabella Patrick, the daughter of Somerset Central MP Sir Maxwell Patrick, who finally emerged triumphant on a night of high drama.

Despite this, Mr Gulliver is still threatening to challenge the result through the courts if necessary. This is Nicola Tedesco, for BBC *Searchlight*."

Seeing Barker make for his basket, he opted for an early night.

"Good plan, old friend. Why don't we go for a decent walk in the morning?"

He could do with some down time with the terrier: he would need his wits about him when he went up the tower later.

THIRTY-FIVE

The sun was breaking through the clouds as Tedesco and Barker made their familiar way across the little bridge that led to the newsagents.

Copy of *The Times* duly secured, and canine ablutions successfully completed, they sat out in the garden while Tedesco skimmed the headlines and plotted that morning's walk.

"We haven't been out to Langdon Lakes for a while, have we?" he said aloud.

Barker responded with a quizzical look, as if to say, "How the fuck do you expect me to remember? I'm a dog."

"Well, that's settled. If we leave now, we should get a parking space."

As Barker hopped into the back of the Lancia, his master chose some classic Dusty Springfield – 'Little by Little' – as a suitably breezy Saturday morning opener, before switching to the Reverend Richard Coles on Radio 4.

Langdon Lakes was a series of man-made ponds that had been transformed into a nature reserve, which boasted an excellent café: Tedesco had already decided to treat himself to some of their excellent lemon drizzle once they had completed their circuit.

Barker remained on his lead as they maintained a good pace along the well-marked route, slowing down as they approached the hides, well-patronised by the local twitcher community. Tedesco wondered if any of them had been at the vote last night but decided that twitchers probably voted Green.

A swan set off on a well-rehearsed majestic glide towards them and then somewhat pointedly glided back when it realised that there was no food on offer.

Having done whimsy for now, the detective pulled his thoughts back to the events of the previous evening.

Barry Gulliver had not just looked angry: he was furious. He had clearly expected to win. And had Arabella shown just a tiny glimpse of surprise at the result?

"Come on, Barker, stop sniffing down there, the café is just around the next corner."

As the weather was unseasonably warm there were seats outside and Tedesco, having ordered a coffee with his lemon drizzle, headed towards a table right on the water's edge before securing Barker's lead to his chair.

The waitress, probably one of the sixth-formers at the grammar school, had taken a predictable shine to the border terrier who was happily drinking from a branded dog bowl.

"Hello Barker! What are you doing here?"

It was Lynne.

"If he could talk, Barker would be asking you the same question," Tedesco noted. "No Parkrun today?"

"I'm training for the Torbay Triathlon, so I've just cycled out here. And I've got the Rhyme Tough Mudder a fortnight after that, so I'm having to up the pace."

"Not sure I could manage a Tough Mudder. A 'Tough Malbec Tasting' might be more my scene. I'll suggest it to Jos Elsted. I don't suppose I can interest you in joining us for coffee?"

"Hardly. I've just had an energy drink. Look, I need to get back and I'll see you in the cathedral for the tower tour. Listen, I was up at five this morning, couldn't get back to sleep so I had a look at those passenger lists."

"Anything come up?"

"Possibly. A couple from Woolford were on the same cruise. Ross and Valerie Saxton."

Tedesco looked out across the lake where some ducklings had formed a peloton and were now paddling away in urgent pursuit of their mother.

"Saxton? The electricians?"

"That's right. We used them when we rejigged the office."

"Everyone uses them. Doesn't the son run it now?"

"Aaron? That's right. His dad has practically retired from the business."

"More time for cruises then," said Tedesco, barely concealing a sneer as he could envisage nothing worse than being stuck on a liner for weeks on end in the company of uncultured retirees.

"Look, must dash and all that but I know Aaron a bit – he's a serious triathlete – and he's arranged a meeting for me with Ross and Valerie. I'm going to see them on Monday."

"Good. I'm so pleased to see that all this exercise is benefitting the agency."

She shot him a look. "Do you know how many calories there are in that cake?"

He shrugged. "I'll do my best to delay the coronary until we've been up the tower."

As Lynne cycled off at what he felt was a terrifying speed, Tedesco reflected that his usual Saturday pasty might not be a wise addition to the delicious lemon drizzle. On the other hand, he needed all the sustenance he could get before climbing up all those steps...

*

While Tedesco and Barker had been enjoying the gentle idyll of Langdon Lakes, Barry Gulliver and his campaign team were meeting in emergency session in the kitchen of his riverside apartment.

The apartment was part of the exclusive Leatside development, which Barry's firm had marketed, and within which he had somehow managed to secure the pick of the units on offer.

Also present were Commander Foster, Danielle Gulliver, Nicola Tedesco's husband Jeremy 'Chag' Wills, and the sinister agent who had driven Bazza's battle truck, now revealed as Jake Seabury, who owned what passed as Rhyminster's only night club. With his slicked-back hair and obsequious manner, there was something of the courtier about him as well as the knave.

If Satan employed a PR man he'd look just like Seabury.

"How the fuck did this shit show happen? How?" said Bazza.

"Calm down, Barry," said Wills. "There were only a couple of votes in it. Get some legal advice. Was it even constitutional to allow those non-party members a vote, for example?"

"I thought they were just going to observe," added Danielle.

"Chag's got a point," Foster said. "Look at the types who came. Assorted local Lib Dems, the odious Tedesco and his pretty sidekick, none of them natural Barry voters."

Gulliver stood up, bristling with aggression, as if he was in search of the nearest bar fight to join. "How in the name of Christ does this help? Get legal advice, Chag says. Who from?

"Sir Maxwell? Who's his daughter, eh? And if some do-gooding commission looks at it, won't they notice the sudden rise in party members from my firm?"

He glared at Wills. "And your missus didn't help, or that bitch, Vicki. We all know that the BBC hates Conservatives, especially ones like me."

"Nicola has no idea that I'm involved in the campaign. And it would put her job at risk if it came out that she did."

"And don't you just love being Mr Nicky Tedesco, you little—"

The previously reticent Jake Seabury spoke up.

"Ladies, please. Look, there may be another way. Barry, why don't you run against Arabella as an Independent candidate?"

"What, split the vote and let the Liberals in? Or those tree-hugging Greens? Great idea, Jake. Do you want to destroy my business?"

Danielle looked up. "Calm down, dear. Look at Sir Maxwell. He's standing down because that independent woman in his area looks like winning next time."

"Your wife makes an excellent point," said Foster. "And we have plenty of ordnance to use up against Arabella Patrick. She has no local following, except for the Derringtons and nonentities like Flick Gallant."

"Yes," Dani Gulliver added, "and what was Ms Patrick really doing on the cathedral tower when that guide was killed? Bit of a coincidence, don't you think?"

"Well said, Dani," Seabury said. "I reckon it's time to play dirty, don't you?"

THIRTY-SIX

Having suffered death by slow-moving traffic on his return journey from the nature reserve, Tedesco indulged in his regular bout of irritability as he tried to drive into the Cathedral Close.

"How many times! This is a road!" he shouted at the groups of drippy tourists blocking his way.

"Woof," said Barker, with a distinct lack of menace.

Late for his regular date with *Football Focus*, Tedesco decided to give it a miss for once, but he very deliberately indulged in his other Saturday lunchtime ritual, scoffing his Jenks pasty as he read the paper.

Barker wasn't allowed on the tower tour but seemed remarkably relaxed over missing out on the opportunity to climb up 300 steep steps.

Leaving his friend to a contented afternoon of snoozing, Tedesco headed over to the cathedral, to find that Lynne was already lying in wait with the other tourists by the pull-down blind marked 'Tower Tours. Please Wait Here'. She had changed out of her Lycra cycling gear into jeans and a thick jumper. It could be very cold up there.

The head tower guide greeted them warmly then asked the group to follow him for the safety briefing, to which they must all pay close attention.

Lynne had deliberately arrived a little early so that she could chat with the other members of the group.

There was Toni and Bianca, a charming young Italian couple from Perugia, a retired Australian couple called Vic and Lesley who were doing a tour of English cathedrals, and a gaggle of curious locals who had always meant to do the tower but had somehow never quite got around to it.

Although she was slightly disappointed that none of the suspects had decided to return to the scene of the crime, as they would have done in a Poirot novel, Lynne reflected that at least there should be no clear and present danger from this group.

Tedesco listened attentively to the briefing, watching carefully as the members of the group emptied their pockets prior to placing their belongings in the lockers.

Although Jock Barton was observing them closely, it would still just about be possible to smuggle something small onto the tour if you were determined to avoid detection.

But if Alan Meer had been intent on taking a weapon on the tour, why did he make such a fuss over handing over his Morrison's bag? Perhaps he had been playing double bluff; he wanted to draw attention to himself.

Betty Budden and Mike and Sue Knowles had all commented on his rudeness to Kerry.

Barton, as befitted such an experienced guide, took plenty of opportunities to give his charges a breather, but the Aussies still weren't impressed.

"Jesus, Lesley. This is worse than, where was it?"

"Lincoln. I thought that was bloody hard work."

"We are almost at the first viewing platform, folks. Just a few more steps."

The view from beneath the west window was stunning. Tedesco hadn't been up there for several years and envied the first-timers taking in the view of the nave, interrupted only by the large stone screen dividing the public part of the building from the quire and the high altar.

Toni pronounced the view to be 'fantastica', whilst Lesley thought it was 'beaut'.

Lynne was by far the most confident climber, and when they reached the little door leading to the outside of the tower she squeezed through with no hesitation or difficulty.

As others needed encouragement and assistance from their guide, she had a few uninterrupted minutes in which to survey the scene.

The door onto the roof opened out on to the east. Kerry had fallen from the opposite side.

If Meer had persuaded Kerry to jump, would he have been able to get back to the opening before she fell? How would he have remained undetected, and how did he manage to get up there in the first place?

She set the stopwatch on her phone, then ran from the western parapet to the door. Even allowing for the fact that she was almost certainly fitter than Meer it should only have taken him a few seconds.

But how would he have avoided detection? He could have been lucky – the tourists may have all grouped together in the same area – but how long would Kerry have been dangling from the wall? Her scream was heard as Meer appeared, or possibly reappeared, on the roof.

Her deliberations were disturbed by the tower guide.

"I should be reprimanding you, Lynne, you know. I am supposed to keep all my charges in my sight at all times."

Before she could respond Barton added that Tedesco had outlined the reason behind their visit. "But try and stay where I can see you."

She gazed down at the view over the little city, looking beyond the river towards Rhyminster Down. She silently agreed with the Aussies. It sure was 'beaut'.

Once the group had reassembled, and Barton had invited them to take in the views and to enjoy any 'Kodak moments' – God, that showed his age – she sidled up to Tedesco, quietly suggesting that they each move to opposite sides of the roof and see if the other tourists followed.

The random group turned out to be sheep rather than cats. They followed in Tedesco's footsteps, slightly to Lynne's chagrin, and stood on the south side of the tower overlooking the Cathedral School and towards the Kingfisher.

If Kerry's group had behaved like this lot, and it was a big if, then Meer could have been home and dry.

Tedesco busied himself by using his local knowledge to suggest the best views for photos.

He even managed to drag up his limited Italian for the occasion.

"*Allora, Toni e Bianca. Guardate! La vista – Bellissima!*"

On the way down the two detectives paid particular attention to any nooks and crannies where evidence could have been secreted and then, once they had regained the safety of the viewing platform, Barton asked if anyone had any more questions.

Vic asked where he could get a beer after all that climbing

and one of the locals, a noted pedant, asked a technical point that even Barton struggled with.

Tedesco, remembering that there was an annual safety inspection, asked when it was scheduled to take place.

"I can't be too precise, John, so I will get back to you if that's all right. Are you volunteering to be winched down?"

The group laughed politely before they were gently led down the final set of steps where Barton opened the lockers and gave each member of the tour a badge to 'wear with pride'.

The badge had a drawing of the tower with the wording 'I Made it to the Top, and I didn't Stop!' underneath it. Another triumph for the marketing department in the light of recent events.

Tedesco had several of these at home so declined the offer of another badge. Then he reflected sadly on how Kerry had set off to climb the tower that August day, never for a moment thinking that it would be for the last time.

Having said their fond farewells, the tourists headed out, some to the refectory and Vic and Lesley to the pub, having been directed to the Rhyminster Arms by Barton.

"You old misery," said Lynne. "Where's your badge?"

"If you come back to my place I'll show you…"

THIRTY-SEVEN

"So, here's my collection of tower tour badges," said Tedesco, revealing a tin of rusting discs that he produced from his cutlery drawer.

"Makes a change from 'Come up and see my etchings,'" his colleague responded.

"Anyway, shouldn't you be checking the football results about now?" she went on.

"Nice try. Argyle don't have a match today. They are playing tomorrow. 5.30pm kick-off."

Lynne detected the disdain in his voice. Messing about with kick-off times was one of Tedesco's long litany of complaints about the modern game, along with shirt sponsorship, the disappearance of the terraces, corporate hospitality and the sad decline in Bovril drinking at half time.

He made a pot of tea, and then they retreated to his den. He drank from his Argyle mug and she used one embossed with the Devon flag and the slogan 'Cream first, Jam on top'.

Since she had teamed up with him there had been moments when she felt herself becoming seriously attached to this kind, gentle man of principle, but they were balanced by times like this when she realised that it would never work. No woman was ever going to change him. The only one who might have stood a chance, Sorcha, had gone.

But could even his Irish muse have got rid of his dreadful mugs or persuaded him that the sun would still come up if he missed the football results? Or that plenty of decent songs had been written in the twenty-first century?

"So, DS Davey, what have we learned from our little outing?"

"Okay. Meer could have done it; he would need to have got up on the roof undetected then hidden behind the back of the roof opening. Then he'd have had to pick a moment when Kerry was on her own and the tourists were looking the other way."

"And we saw, didn't we, that today's group gathered in one place so it wouldn't have been impossible."

"Indeed. Then he would have had to have persuaded Kerry out onto the roof, run back to the opening, climbed back inside and waited for someone, Betty Budden in this case, to give him an alibi."

"What are the flaws here? Would Meer really have been able to get onto the roof without anyone noticing?"

"Jools said that Matt Lovell told her that Meer was the most insignificant, colourless guy he could remember meeting."

"A real 'Mr Cellophane man', then. But even if the rest of the scenario panned out as you suggested, why wasn't there any evidence of fingerprints on Kerry's body? The only person wearing gloves that afternoon, as far as we know, was Arabella Patrick."

"Fair point, but if Bloomfield is able to reopen the case,

he could reinterview Betty and the others. One of them must have seen Meer get out onto the roof."

"And he should ask about the gloves."

"But what is it going to take for Hinton to allow a reopening, especially when she's subject to political pressure?"

"I really don't know. But Meer has motive, assuming he found out that Angela was his real mother. We know he is obsessive – just ask Nicky – and he did behave oddly over leaving his stuff in the locker. Has anyone actually seen his inhaler?"

"What we need right now," said Lynne, "is something a little stronger than your builder's tea. And a breakthrough."

"I can't magic up the second of your wishes, but I think I can help with the first. Why don't we take Barker for a stroll over to the Kingfisher? I haven't had an early evening pint there for ages."

THIRTY-EIGHT

He blamed his disturbed night on his second pint of Deacon's Delight. It must have come from the bottom of the barrel.

Whatever the reason, he needed to get up and go outside, so a slightly puzzled Barker found himself accompanying his master to the 8am communion service at the cathedral.

Tedesco loved this service and he thought that it should be branded as 'suitable for persuadable agnostics'.

The liturgy was spoken, no hymns or choir to disturb the peace, and there was minimal input from the congregation.

The unique combination of the simplicity of the service and the magical stillness of the Lady Chapel at that hour of the morning created a space that allowed his thoughts to run clearly like a mountain stream rather than the usual muddied waters.

He couldn't entirely switch off his internal playlist though. Van Morrison: 'It's So Quiet in Here'.

Barker had soon drifted off into a gentle sleep so there were evident mental health benefits for dogs as well.

It disappointed him that so many groups dismissed this quiet mystical aspect of the Church: these ranged from some of the volunteers, who seemed more interested in discussing flower rotas or gossiping about each other than in spirituality, to noisily earnest happy-clappy clergy, who were, thankfully, somewhat thin on the ground in Rhyminster.

He sensed a gentle tap on his shoulder. It was Bishop Bob. He sometimes slid into the back of the chapel for this service. Then Izzie McCalliog, the head verger, made an unobtrusive entrance as she led a tiny procession consisting of a volunteer server, who Tedesco recognised but couldn't quite place, and Dean Dan.

The New Testament lesson was taken from John, the one about the Lord's house having many mansions.

Tedesco had always liked this reading, imagining that there would be a place reserved for him in the Kingdom which looked suspiciously like 17, St Budeaux Place. He also rather hoped that border terriers would be welcome in the afterlife, as well as a large collection of vinyl albums and old football programmes and an eternal supply of heavenly claret.

Dan gave a brief sermon: the full version of this would be delivered at the choral eucharist later that morning.

The Dean's interpretation of the gospel reading differed somewhat from that of his favourite private investigator, his more conventional take being that Jesus has procured the right for every sinner to enter heaven.

When the small but respectable number of worshippers started to go up for communion, Tedesco sat it out. He didn't have a fixed policy on this: he sometimes went up at Christmas and Easter as it seemed as much a cultural as a religious statement then.

His internal soundtrack kicked in once again. Ralph McTell: 'Sometimes I Wish I Could Pray'.

As the service rather prettily came to its end, he resolved to seek out Izzie. She had been a key actor when the tour group had been rescued in August and he felt sure that she wouldn't mind having her brain picked.

Just as he was making his way towards the vestry, the bishop appeared and asked how he was. Both Bob and his lovely wife Hilary, a ward sister at the general, had been part of his informal support group when Sorcha had lost her battle with cancer.

"I'm getting there, I think. I comfort myself by thinking how lucky I was to have known her, if that makes any sense."

"It certainly does, John. Anyway, I'm back to work now, off to preach at Kingsbridge. Be good to yourself."

"Take care, Bob."

With that he headed to the vestry. The previous head verger, Roy Baird, had turned his office into a veritable hobbit's den, a candlelit lair dominated by the pungent smell of his pipe tobacco.

Izzie had transformed the space into a light, bright, welcoming little enclave within the vastness of the cathedral.

She greeted Tedesco a touch warily, but any hesitation soon melted away when she saw Barker, as her parents owned a beloved border terrier called Otto and she was a huge fan of the breed.

Once she and Barker had become reacquainted, she offered Tedesco the seat opposite her desk.

"Izzie," he began, "I can quite understand that you may be a little surprised when a private investigator turns up after early communion, but I was wondering if you could assist me."

"I guess it's about poor Kerry. I'd do anything to help. Canon Wilf told me that you were still looking into it – in the strictest confidence."

Tedesco cleared his throat. "This will seem a bit odd, but bear with me. If you could cast your mind back to the August bank holiday: when the group got down from the tower did you notice if any of them was wearing gloves?"

Izzie turned to Barker and stroked him, before replying.

"That is a bit random. It was a hot August day, so why would anyone be wearing gloves?"

"Think, Izzie, this could be important. What about Arabella Patrick, for instance? Can you remember what she was wearing?"

"Let's think. Something summery? Hang on, she *was* wearing gloves – a glove, to be precise."

Tedesco looked at her expectantly. "Carry on, Izzie. What exactly do you remember?"

"That's it. She had a single glove on when she got down. I remember thinking how odd it was and wondering if it was a fashion thing. She's very London, isn't she?"

He smiled. "Yes, she is. I don't know how she will find us lot down here when she becomes our MP. Can you remember anything else? What the colour was, perhaps?"

"She took it off when she got down the ladder. The fire brigade were called, as I'm sure you know. She looked a bit surprised, as if she had only just realised that the other one was missing."

"Was it a long glove, like women in costume dramas wear?"

"No, I don't think so. It was white, I think, but short. It

looked like leather. I wonder what happened to the other one?"

"So do I. Izzie, you have made my day."

*

Tedesco and Barker walked back through the Close, greeting various friends and acquaintances on their way.

A puzzled Barker was led past number 17 and over the little bridge. The usual routine may have been disturbed, but a Sunday paper was non-negotiable.

They were both hungry, so Barker tucked into some Waitrose essential dog biscuits while his master enjoyed some toast and marmite and an hour with the main section of the paper.

Remembering that Lynne had told him that she was going onto the moors for a Mudder Boot Camp, he sent her an old-fashioned email, headed "Breakthrough?"

He divided the rest of his morning between clearing some leaves off his back garden, chopping vegetables to go with his Sunday lunch of baked potato and sausages and thinking about Arabella's glove.

Reaching for his casebook he inscribed some thoughts.

"If the missing glove was lost on the tower, then why didn't the scene of crime people find it? Could it still be up there? Is it worth checking the vestry for lost property?

And what about the one she was wearing? Has she still got it?"

He had a late lunch, which included two glasses of claret, so had fallen asleep with the Review section by the time that Lynne called him.

She listened carefully as he gave more details of his discussion with the head verger.

"So, it's like Cinderella, is it? Instead of a glass slipper it's a white glove, and whoever it fits becomes our number one suspect."

"You may jest, Mrs Davey, but yes, it is a bit like Cinderella. And Arabella may have just knocked Alan Meer off the number one spot."

"But why on earth would she want to harm Kerry?"

As the question hung in the air Tedesco asked after the Boot Camp.

"It was very tough. And extremely muddy."

THIRTY-NINE

Ross and Valerie Saxton lived in Woolford. The village was effectively split in two and they lived in the lower part, which was mainly Victorian cottages, spatchcocked with occasional modern infill.

Tedesco's sister lived on the upper side, just over the River Rhyme, where barn conversions and 4x4s dominated.

Lynne discovered that Lower Woolford contained too many cars for the space available and she soon became tired of trying to find somewhere to park on the road. Even Bishop Bob's motorist's prayer hadn't worked: "Dear Lord, by your grace, find me a bloody parking space," so she was forced into using the public car park.

After the obligatory wrestle with the machine, it eventually agreed to spew out a ticket, leaving her two stressful minutes to dash down the hill to her meeting.

She detested lateness in others and was highly self-critical on the rare occasion when she was other than bang on time.

The Saxtons lived in what appeared to be a small Victorian or Edwardian terrace, but on entry Lynne sensed a

Tardis-like quality – the place was far more spacious than the exterior had suggested.

She was greeted by Ross, a sprightly senior wearing a baggy sweatshirt which proudly proclaimed that 'Old Guys Rule'.

I can just see Mr Tedesco in one of those, she thought to herself with a considerable dose of irony as she was ushered into a knowingly tasteful garden room extension.

"So, Lynne – can I call you Lynne? I'm Ross, but you probably guessed that, and this is Val."

Mrs Saxton was short, blonde and immaculately made up, as if she was just about to appear as a guest on daytime TV.

A cafetière of coffee was already in position on the glass-topped table, as well as some Danish pastries.

Lynne made to refuse the offer, as she was on a strict training diet, but gave in to a combination of politeness and temptation.

Ross started to chat about his career in the electrical trade, how Val had done the books, kept him on the straight and narrow with all the paperwork, adding that Aaron was keeping up the family name. "He's got lots of new ideas—"

Val, who Lynne had quickly assessed as someone not to be messed with, broke in. "Lynne hasn't come all the way out here to talk about Aaron's expansion plans, has she?"

Establishing laser-like eye contact with her guest, she continued, "I gather from my son that you are a fellow keep-fit fanatic?"

Before Lynne could respond Val went on, "Anyway, he spoke very highly of you and your colleague, so how can we help?"

"That's very kind of him. My agency has always enjoyed excellent service from Saxtons. Mrs Saxton – Val, I'm not sure how much Aaron explained to you, but I am looking into the death of Kerry Franklin."

Ross rejoined the conversation.

"I thought that she had jumped off the cathedral?"

"Well, that's the official view, but we believe that there is some room for doubt. I can't give too much away but no one who knew Kerry thinks that she would have taken her own life."

"But it could have been an accident," said Val.

"Yes, it could, but the building is surveyed on a regular basis and the tower guides are very well trained in health and safety."

"That's a fair point," Ross noted. "But how can we assist you?"

"Okay. For some years Kerry worked on the cruise ships. I've been going through the relevant passenger lists, and I found that you had been on a cruise to the Canaries with Retro Cruises."

"That's right," said Val. "It was a theme. We all had to dress up as characters from the *Titanic*."

"I was one of the orchestra and Val went as Kate Winslet."

"We were quite a bit younger then."

Lynne paused, then continued, "Kerry Franklin was on that cruise."

"I don't remember her – do you, Val?"

"She was working behind the scenes, so I didn't expect you to remember seeing her," Lynne said. "But do either of you remember this man?"

She handed Val a photo of Barry Gulliver, taken from one of his election leaflets.

The Saxtons stared at it intently.

"It's him, isn't it, Ross?"

"No mistake. He was a right pain in the arse, pardon my French."

"In what way?" Lynne asked.

"He was a real loudmouth. They all were. He was with a group of other blokes, all of them behaving like they were on a rugby tour."

"And they hadn't made any effort to get into character – they just wore cheap-looking tuxedos."

Lynne showed them the photo again. "Do you know who he is?"

"No," said Ross. "I think he called himself 'Gazza', maybe?"

"The person in the photo is Barry Gulliver. He lives locally and he has been seeking selection as our next MP."

Val tutted. "We wouldn't know, Lynne. We take no interest in politics. They are all crooks these days."

"Hang on," said Ross, scratching his head. "There might be something. These blokes, Gazza and his mates. Weren't they chucked off the ship in Lanzarote?"

"I think it was Tenerife. That's right, love, I remember it well. There had been a lot of complaints from passengers about this mob. They were ruining the cruise for everyone. And they were so arrogant the way they spoke to the crew."

"And," said Ross, "wasn't there a rumour that one of them tried it on with one of the female staff?"

"I think it was rather more than trying it on, from what I heard," Val replied.

Then she took a sip of coffee and fixed Lynne with another gimlet-eyed stare.

"Lynne – are you suggesting that Kerry might have been the victim of these brutes?"

The former CID officer carefully considered her response.

"Not in so many words, Val. But Kerry made a formal complaint about the behaviour of one of the guests when she got home, so this may be relevant."

Having secured the couple's agreement not to discuss matters with anyone else, she got back to her car and checked her phone. The interview had been successfully recorded.

She would get hold of Jools, hoping that the force still had links with their colleagues in Spain, Brexit notwithstanding.

*

Over at the office in Minster Precincts, Tedesco was being harangued by the agency's PA.

"Sally, I know we need to do more about reducing our carbon footprint, but we would need to talk to our landlords for permission to install solar panels. And this is a listed building, don't forget."

His phone gave out the irritatingly jolly 'you have a message' jingle but, for once, he was glad of the interruption.

The message was from Jock Barton. The head tower guide was as good as his word. He confirmed that the next safety check on the tower was due in a couple of weeks' time.

"Let me know if you and Lynne want to observe. We allow a few trusted spectators, and the local media will be there."

Reliving the fun he always had in teasing Nicky about *Searchlight*'s over-excited annual coverage, he reached for his diary and sent Lynne an email.

If nothing else, it would be good to see another strange Rhyminster tradition acted out.

What he would really like to see would be Charles Tantum, the corpulent Master of Musick, being winched down from the tower, but Barton had added that this year's brave volunteer was Andrea Hutchins, the manager of the cathedral shop.

This made sense. Unlike with Tantum, there was no danger of the petite Ms Hutchins getting stuck in the roof space.

FORTY

Any lingering air of celebration in the Vote Arabella Patrick camp had evaporated by the time that the candidate and her key people had gathered in the little boardroom of Gallants solicitors to plot her path from selection to election.

Instead, there was a palpable sense of anxiety melded with relief at the result.

"A win is a win," said Felicity Gallant.

"Of course, it is. Well done! Now let's forget about Friday and concentrate on holding the seat."

"It's easy for you to say that, Lady Fiona," said Arabella, adding that they would have to take Gulliver's threats seriously.

"Oh, I wouldn't worry about him. He's just a bad loser. Awful little man. Why can't he join the Labour Party?"

"Listen, Bella," said Felicity, "he hasn't got a hope in hell of overturning the result, and, crucially, his pockets aren't deep enough."

"But he has completely divided the local association, and he can cause me real damage if he doesn't shut the fuck up," retorted the newly selected candidate.

Lady Fiona Derrington looked as if someone had just urinated on her carpet.

"My dear Arabella. I trust that you won't be bringing the language of the stable yard into your campaign!"

"I'm sorry, but this is serious. Gulliver is threatening to stand as an Independent. You know the trouble that Daddy is having with that deranged woman in his constituency. Gulliver could easily split the vote and let the lefties in, or he could even take the seat if he can convince enough of the knuckle-dragging locals to vote for him."

"Maybe better to refer to them as 'wonderful and friendly', like you did on Friday," was the calm advice of the glacial solicitor, who continued by suggesting that Arabella should make a public attempt to invite Bazza to support her campaign.

"What a splendid idea," said Lady Fiona, who proved that there was a political schemer concealed behind her natural bonhomie by making the point that such a move would disarm Gulliver.

Flick Gallant weighed in behind the avian-like aristocrat.

"Fiona makes a good point. Bella, I suggest that you draft a statement congratulating Gulliver on running a brilliant campaign which pushed you all the way and suggest to him that you could make good use of his formidable public relations skills. I know it would stick in your craw, but how could he refuse without looking petty and spiteful?"

"An appeal for party unity always goes down well with the members," said Lady Fiona.

The candidate appeared to be less than convinced. "Patrick and Gulliver, the dream team. Really?"

Her husband Crispin was busy working on his latest legal case from home. She would get his input before thrusting any olive branch in the direction of that vile man.

*

Lynne Davey soon got a response to her message to DS Julia Tagg.

"How about tonight, after yoga?"

Lynne had been in two minds about going to the little studio next to the deanery that evening. She was planning some serious gym work as part of her intensive training. But this settled it; the two friends could go to Cranes after their session. And it would be good to see Jo, the dean's wife, again.

FORTY-ONE

The yoga group was a little depleted that evening. Autumn colds were starting to kick in, mainly amongst the Cathedral School mums.

"Probably picked up a bug from their darling little Henry and Henriettas," whispered Lynne as they began.

The elder members of the class were made of sterner stuff. Myrtle from the Holy Dusters, the indefatigable team of volunteers who cleaned the cathedral's woodwork and polished its treasures, proudly announced that she had never missed a single session, before adding that she was seventy-five, you know.

Once the session had ended, the two friends and former CID colleagues walked the short distance out of the Close and into Broad Street, Lynne wondering aloud if they should have invited their instructor to join them for a drink.

"I'd wondered that too – she looked tired, not her normal bouncy self. But as I guess we are going to be discussing matters of interest to DCI Bloomfield…"

"You are right. That's what I thought. But let's invite her next time, yeah?"

"And maybe Myrtle as well?"

*

On the opposite side of the Close from the deanery, within the Georgian splendour of Stannary House, the atmosphere was rather less convivial.

Arabella and Crispin were sitting at opposite ends of their antique dining table situated in the centre of the library.

The previous owner had been a retired property developer, and during his tenure the shelves contained fat volumes of ghosted autobiographies from the likes of Harry Redknapp, Jeremy Clarkson and Richard Branson.

Crispin and Arabella had replaced these with volumes of old law reports, political diaries, and collections of *Wisden* and *Who's Who* going back over several decades.

The irony of how the couple had acquired one of the most desirable residences in England, let alone within the Close, was not lost on Tedesco.

Sir Maxwell Patrick had instructed Barry Gulliver to act as his property search agent with a brief to find him the perfect home in the Close, failing to disclose that it was intended for his daughter.

Sir Maxwell had been introduced to Bazza by the Master of Musick at the cathedral, Charles Tantum.

Bazza and Tantum might seem to be unlikely confreres, but Gulliver's daughter Scarlet was a pupil at the Cathedral School where Ginny Tantum worked as a housemistress, and so the master networker ruthlessly exploited the connection.

The estate agent soon ingratiated himself with Tantum, then he managed to persuade the directors of his firm to sponsor a prestigious cathedral concert by the Tuneful Company of Minstrels, on the basis this would open up a new world of networking opportunities.

Tedesco – and DCI Bloomfield – had taken an interest in the suspicious circumstances by which Gulliver had secured the property for his client. It was as if he had a premonition that David Helford, the then owner, was about to die. Barry was placing an offer for Stannary House on behalf of his client before rigor mortis had set in.

However, as no evidence of anything untoward could be established, Sir Maxwell secured his dream house and Bazza greedily snaffled his fat fee.

The huge irony was that Gulliver had failed to check out his client. A simple Google search would have shown him that Ms Patrick was seeking a safe seat, and so perhaps it should have led him to at least question what Sir Maxwell's motive had been in employing him.

He might have secured a six-figure finder's fee, but Barry had also installed his rival for the nomination into one of the best addresses in the constituency.

"So, what would you do about Gulliver?" Arabella asked her husband.

"Other than shove him off the tower, you mean?"

"Not even slightly funny. Listen, if I screw up then this hits you as well."

Crispin rose from his Regency chair and paced the room.

"I agree with Flick – be the magnanimous victor. Even if Bazza takes the bait you don't actually have to work with him. You just need to keep Gulliver and his cretinous crew on side until you are safely sitting on those green benches with your stonking majority."

"And if he doesn't bite?"

"Then he will look like a sore loser. It's a win-win."

"Okay, I thought you would say that. I'll message Flick to get things moving.

"But what about our other little problem? How the hell did you manage to lose the bloody glove?"

"I'm always losing things, as well you know. I might have taken it off when we were descending the stairs, get a better grip on the rope, I really don't remember. Just shut up about it, okay!"

*

Cranes wine bar was quiet again. Lynne wondered whether they should restrict opening to weekends when it was permanently rammed, but she was glad they didn't. Where else would they go after their workout?

As it was a school night, and Lynne had already broken her strict diet, they stuck to non-alcoholic cocktails. These all had Rhyminster-themed names.

Jools went for a 'Chapel Juice', while Lynne chose the distinctly dodgy-sounding 'Bishop's Banger'.

"So, how was your meeting with the Saxtons?"

"She was harder work than he was. A real little shrew. But they did positively ID Bazza from his election leaflet."

"So they saw him on their nostalgia cruise, or whatever it was?"

"It was a *Titanic* theme, can you imagine? Anyway, Bazza and his mates were celebrating a record year, behaving as if they were on a stag do—"

"Hardly surprising, Lynne," interrupted Jools. "A group

of bonus-wielding estate agents are hardly going to behave like choirboys, are they?"

"Granted, but if you let me finish, their behaviour must have gone beyond a bit of high spirits, as they were taken off the ship when it docked in Tenerife."

"Go on."

"And Val Saxton said that there were rumours circulating that one of them had misbehaved with a female member of staff. 'It was more than trying it on', she said. I've recorded it."

"And when you interviewed Kerry all those years ago her description fitted Gulliver to a tee."

"It did. But I'm wondering why Kerry didn't mention about the group from Mylors being chucked off the ship."

"So do I but, the more we look at this, Kerry's previous history with Bazza must be linked to the tower, however tangentially?"

"So, what are you about to ask me to do?"

"You old cynic. Is there any way that you could see if the Spanish authorities have kept any record of the men being taken off the cruise? I assume they were arrested?"

"I'll see what I can do. Jimmy still has contacts in what he hilariously refers to as 'InterPlod'. You know what, this whole situation makes me mad."

"You are in real danger of sounding like Julie Stringer, you know."

Jools laughed, then said, "Seriously though. How can Hinton still refuse to investigate. As you say, the links between Kerry and Bazza are more than a little whiffy especially with the election in the background."

"When you hear what I'm about to tell you about Arabella Patrick you will see that things are even murkier.

But before I do that, I got some inspiration from my visit to the Saxtons – the perfect Christmas present for Mr T."

"Go on, surprise me."

"An 'Old Guys Rule' sweatshirt."

FORTY-TWO

DCI Bloomfield's customary dapper appearance – think Philip Schofield with a dash of David Dickinson – was replaced by a slightly ruffled look as he entered Rhyminster police station.

He'd been in Truro for a meeting about future funding and then he got stuck in the roadworks near Liskeard.

"Anything going down?" he said to Adie Maher, a cheerful Scouser who had washed up in Rhyminster as desk sergeant via a spell in the merchant navy.

"Something's just come in. A domestic in Ivybridge. I was about to send a couple of uniforms over there. Neighbours very agitated, they think it's going to kick off."

"Where exactly is it?"

"Let's have a look. The old council estate. Oates Close."

"Leave it to me, Adie."

Bloomfield knew who lived in Oates Close – the Meers. And although it was his job to direct investigations rather to respond to call-outs, this was too good an opportunity to miss.

Spotting Matt Lovell heading to the car park he asked him if he fancied another little outing to Ivybridge.

*

"So you let me believe for all this time that Angela had been my older sister and all along – all along – you knew that she was my real mother!"

"She wasn't fit to be a mother. Me and your father would have been together if it wasn't for that little tart. You were mine by rights! Anyway, who told you? Come on, cat got your tongue?"

"So, you don't deny it? You are an awful, dried-up old hag. You have completely screwed up my life. And why didn't Dad tell me? Because he was just like you, stupid, thick as shit and terrified of the truth."

Kathleen Meer stood up and walked towards her son, then she slapped him across the face with a sudden ferocity that appeared to shake the paper-thin walls, and which drew blood.

"What have you got to say for yourself now, you little failure? And if anyone's life was ruined it was mine!"

Alan Meer got up slowly.

"Are you crying, you little pansy? We always thought you were queer. No girlfriend, never getting into scraps in the playground like normal boys."

"So, the truth is out. Just because I wasn't a violent moron like good old Ken, you thought I was gay."

"You are – as a bunch of flowers. And who told you about Angela?"

"One of my clients."

"Really? Which one?"

"I don't suppose you know what client confidentiality means, do you, Mother? Too many syllables for you."

Kathleen grabbed a large glass paperweight from the mantelpiece. It had been given to her husband when he retired from his job as head groundsman.

As she moved to bring the item down on her son's head he moved aside and she fell face down on the threadbare carpet, then turned and snarled at Alan.

"I know who it must have been. Derek Landeryou. His parents were there."

Alan bent over her and whispered in her ear, "Tell me everything. Or else I'll suffocate you with one of your moth-eaten cushions."

He let her stand up and, as she moved towards the sofa, he turned to face her.

"All right," she said. "It was a holiday and I'd taken the train into Rhyminster with some girls from the laundry. As we were walking by the river, I heard shouts and screams and ran over. Angela was there. She left her cloak by the riverbank and dived in as soon as she saw Kerry. It must have been freezing. Then she swam out to the girl. She managed to rescue her and got her close to the path by the pub, but then I could see that she, Angela that is, was getting dragged under down by the mill race. There's a dangerous current there."

"So you did nothing!"

"I'll tell you what I did. I got her cloak and wore it myself and ran back to town. I dumped the cloak in a litter bin by the station before I caught the train back with the others."

"You evil old woman. You could have rescued her."

Kathleen Meer shrugged. "But I didn't. And I got Ken, and God help me, you."

Decades of resentment suddenly transformed her son into an avenging angel.

He grabbed a 'Keep Calm and Carry On'-inscribed cushion and advanced on his mother.

*

Lovell tried to hide the fact that he was a little cross about missing his five a side football again: work came first.

Bloomfield let him in the car and explained on the way about the reports of a disturbance in Oates Close, adding that the house number matched that of the Meers.

Having reached Ivybridge in record time, they stopped outside the property, blocking the road. Bloomfield remained with the vehicle while Lovell ran to the door and pressed urgently on the bell.

"Police!" he bellowed through the letter box, shouting over the sounds of struggle coming from behind the front door.

"Shall I charge it, boss?"

Bloomfield calmly exited the car and tried the front door: it was unlocked, and once inside they were greeted by the heart-warming scene of a son in the course of asphyxiating his mother.

Lovell pulled Alan off Kathleen with ease and dragged him to his feet as Bloomfield administered the caution.

"Alan Meer, I am arresting you for the attempted murder of Kathleen Meer. You do not have to say anything. But it may harm your defence if you do not mention when questioned something which you later rely on in court. Anything you do say may be given in evidence."

Lovell called for an ambulance for Kathleen. Was that a self-satisfied smirk he detected as her son was led away?

FORTY-THREE

Alan Meer showed negligible emotion as he was driven from Ivybridge to the Bristol Road station.

On arrival, he was led into an interview room where his right to consult a solicitor was explained to him.

"I could call Felicity Gallant, but she doesn't do criminal work and I don't know her private number."

"We can call the duty solicitor."

"No point. You saw me suffocating my so-called mother, so I waive my rights."

Bloomfield asked Alan if he wanted a drink and called the duty desk to get one sent up before pausing the tape, after remembering to confirm that the interview was suspended.

He stepped outside with Lovell. "Okay, this is what we do. We keep him here till the morning, then we decide whether to charge him."

"You want to see what his lovely mum does first?"

"You've got it in one. And I wonder whether we should use our twenty-four hours to ask him about the tower?"

"How does that relate to what we saw tonight?"

"After a good night's sleep he may decide that he wants to help us with our enquiries."

Lovell called the general hospital. Kathleen was surprisingly well, considering the attempt on her life. They would be keeping her in overnight as a precaution.

*

The tower looks at its floodlit best on a dry, brackish autumn evening, Tedesco thought to himself as he took Barker for a walk around the Close.

His reverie was disturbed by the sound of a pushbike slowing down beside him.

It was Hilary, wife of Bishop Robert.

"John, Barker. It's getting cold, isn't it? Why don't you come back to the canonry and warm up by the fire? I'm sure Bob would be thrilled to see you. And Jos delivered some samples yesterday."

She led them through the main door of the North Canonry, which had become the bishop's residence when the former palace was converted into a school for the choristers.

She and Bishop Bob occupied a flat on the first floor, where they found his grace warming himself by the blazing fire after getting back from General Synod in London.

"Ah, splendid!" he said, as he rose to greet Tedesco. "Some blessed relief from three days stuck in a stuffy hall with my fellow Anglicans. And Barker's here as well!" he added, bending down to give the terrier an informal blessing.

"I hope Hilary tempted you over with the promise of a wine tasting. While I was away Jos Elsted dropped off some interesting Italians to sample. How does a glass of Barolo sound to mark the turning of the seasons?"

While his grace went to the kitchen in search of a corkscrew, Hilary asked Tedesco how he was.

"Really? I wouldn't admit this to many people, but I still miss her. It was," he started, hesitating as he realised that he was speaking of Sorcha in the past tense, "a unique relationship, one that others couldn't understand, the way we needed each other without having to be together."

Hilary took his hand. "Your trouble, Mr Tedesco, is that you over-analyse everything. And worry far too much about what others think. Of course, you will never completely get over her, but you still have such a lot of love to give. And Barker, you agree with me, don't you?"

Before the terrier could express an opinion, the bishop returned with an opened bottle and three glasses.

"John, you are the expert," he said, pouring a sample for him to taste.

Tedesco obliged with an exaggerated display of sniffing and swirling.

The first sip of the wine felt like a late autumn morning in a Piedmont forest; the mist about to burn off to reveal some precious sunlight.

"Is the wine to your liking, sir?" said the bishop, smirking.

"Of course it is! It's from Jos, isn't it!"

Barker and his master left the canonry only once the bottle had been finished and, as a deep darkness began to descend as they walked back through the Close, Tedesco suddenly realised that his hosts had deliberately omitted to talk about the Kerry Franklin mystery. Nor had they spoken about themselves. They had concentrated solely on their guest, giving him the space to open up about his grief.

"Rhyminster is a blessed place, Barker. One of God's little miracles, perhaps."

Even after all that had happened in the last year, the detective remained a persuadable agnostic with the softest of soft spots for the Church of England.

What had he once heard Ian Hislop say? Something about the initials which summed up the best about this country – BBC, C of E, NHS. He'd vote for a party who stood for that.

Barker tugged impatiently on his lead. "Autumn nights are all very well, but my paws are getting bleeding cold," was the implicit message.

"Fair enough, old friend. Let's snuggle up in the den and have some supper."

FORTY-FOUR

After decades of sleeping under the same roof, Kathleen and Alan Meer found themselves waking up in different places.

"Did they let him out?" Kathleen enquired of PC Clare Evans from family liaison, who had appeared as if by magic at her hospital bed, before answering her own question.

"I thought not. He will never survive on his own."

Before Evans could speak the old woman added, with more than a hint of menace, "Now, young lady, should I press charges?"

*

Over at the brutalist Bristol Road police station, DCI Bloomfield was asking the custody officer, Jim Furnell, how their guest was this morning.

"Our Alan? Do you remember Scooby-Doo, sir?"

"I'm just about old enough. Why?"

"Alan puts me in mind of Shaggy. He's terrified of his own shadow."

"Thanks for that glowing insight, Jim. Is DS Tagg in?"

"She's just coming now."

Once they were behind the security door Jools said that she had hoped to catch Bloomfield as she had a favour to ask.

"Is it about the tower? Look, it will have to wait. We arrested Alan Meer last night. He tried to smother his own mother."

"Hell's teeth! You don't think this is linked to Kerry, do you?"

"That's why I want you in the interview with me." He led her to his office.

"Okay, let me take you through last night's events, then we'll see what he has to say."

*

It was a rather gentler start to the day in the offices of Tedesco and Davey.

Sally was burbling on about her book club, "Some of them hadn't even read it! I do wonder if all they come for is to drink wine and gossip," while Barker was contentedly sprawled under Tedesco's desk as his master updated his casebook.

Their momentary peace was soon disturbed by the sound of Lynne powering her way up the rickety stairs.

"Have you seen this?"

She thrust her phone at Tedesco, who displayed his usual annoying discomfort around technology.

"What am I supposed to be looking at?"

"Oh, give it here! Arabella Patrick has written an open letter to Barry Gulliver inviting him to join her election campaign. The crafty cow!"

"A very clever move, certainly. An arsenic-tipped olive branch. It's going to be hard for Bazza to stand against her when she's been so magnanimous."

"And my other news – I saw Jools last night and told her about my visit to the Saxtons."

"What did she think? Any chance of them reopening the investigation?"

"No, there's still nothing to directly link Bazza to the tower."

"Granted, but they must understand that placing Barry on the cruise when she was attacked supports the idea that Gulliver would want to buy Kerry's silence?"

"Maybe. Anyway, Jools is going to talk to Jimmy. He still has contacts in Spain. There must be something on file."

"You'd think so. It isn't every day that a bunch of pissed-up-west-country estate agents gets hauled off a *Titanic* cruise in the middle of the Atlantic, is it?"

*

DC Matt Lovell interrupted his colleagues. "Sorry to butt in. Alan has asked to make a call."

"His mother?"

"No, Felicity Gallant. He was anxious to let her know that he would be late in for work."

"That's all we fucking need. Fragrant Flick will be straight on to Hinton. Does he want a solicitor?"

"He says not, but once he's got through to his boss, who knows."

"I agree. Okay, Jools, we'd better get on with it while we can."

A startled-looking Alan was produced from custody and, after Jools had switched on the tape and introduced the cast of this little play, Bloomfield reminded the suspect that he remained under caution.

Meer again waived his right to a solicitor but wanted to know when he could talk to his employer.

"One of the officers will let us know when she is free. She was probably on her way in to work when you called."

"So, Alan. Tell us what happened last night."

Meer spoke with a surprising frankness, as if he had wanted to get things off his chest.

"I had a huge argument with my so-called mother. I had just found out that my real mother drowned when she rescued Kerry Franklin."

"That must have been a terrible shock, Alan," said Jools, going on to ask him how he had found out about this.

"As you know, I work for a firm of solicitors. My work is in the area of wills – elderly people stuff. One of my clients had been to see me about a Power of Attorney."

"Can you tell us more?"

"He had recently lost his wife to dementia and was worried about going senile himself, so he wanted to make his affairs easier for his family to deal with. A Lasting Power of Attorney allows named individuals to act on your behalf, to stand in your shoes, as it were."

"I know about LPAs," said Bloomfield. "My parents have done them. Sensible. Now how did this mundane meeting lead you to find out about your mother?"

"I was coming to that. My client—"

DS Tagg interrupted. "Does your client have a name, Alan?"

"Oh, I can't tell you that. I'm bound by client confidentiality."

"Not in here you're not," growled Bloomfield, provoking an exasperated sideways glance from his colleague.

"Alan, your professionalism is a credit to you," Tagg said, "but DCI Bloomfield is right. We can easily find out the identity of your client."

Meer, looking distinctly uncomfortable, volunteered that his client was called Mr Landeryou.

"Would that be Derek Landeryou?" Jools asked.

Meer's temporary display of confidence visibly drained away as he reverted to Shaggy mode.

"Er, how do you know about Derek? Have you had me followed?"

"I thought that was your department, Alan," Bloomfield muttered, before adding, "we know all about your fixation with a certain *Searchlight* presenter."

Jools tried not to let her fury show: Bloomfield was on course to blow the entire interview. The defence would have a field day when they heard this: bullying the suspect, duress...

She stepped in. Time to play nice cop.

"Alan, let's go back to your client, shall we? What did he tell you?"

Meer glared at Bloomfield then he spoke, addressing his answer to Jools.

"My client – it was Derek Landeryou – signed the legal paperwork then, as we were finishing up, he asked if I was related to Angela Meer. I told him that she was my late sister, who died before I was born."

"Go on," said DS Tagg, trying her best to sound empathetic.

"Derek looked puzzled and said that Angela couldn't have been my sister. Then he told me that his parents had been in Rhyminster when Angela drowned and that they had found Kerry Franklin in a state of distress, so they looked after her."

"Do you need some water?" asked Jools.

The suspect shook his head and carried on with the story.

"Anyway, Derek's mother spotted a woman running away from the scene. She was wearing a cloak, like nurses wore back then. And this is the awful thing: she recognised this woman. She thought she was Kathleen Hubbard."

Bloomfield, sensing that it was safe for him to rejoin the interview, asked Meer if his mother's maiden name was Hubbard.

"No! The woman who I lived with all my life was born Kathleen Hubbard. She is NOT my mother!"

Jools intervened again. "Alan, this must be so difficult for you. Do want a break? You only have to ask."

Meer shook his head. "No, I want to finish the story. Maybe you will understand when you've heard it."

I very much doubt it, thought Bloomfield.

Jools glanced towards the door. "For the purposes of the tape, DC Matthew Lovell has entered the room."

Lovell leaned over and whispered in Bloomfield's ear, causing the DCI to announce that the interview would be paused.

There was a call for Mr Meer. Felicity Gallant was on the line.

FORTY-FIVE

Commander Foster had captured and roped off the section of the refectory reserved for the use of the cathedral guides and had successfully managed to repel all boarders while he awaited Barry Gulliver and his erstwhile election agent, Jake Seabury.

Just as Foster was about to abandon ship, the Dastardly and Muttley of local politics crashed into the room, noisily pushing through the gaggle of tourists queuing for their Minster Blend cream teas.

"That miserable bastard in the hut who controls the parking. Can't you get rid of him? He knows bloody well who I am. Tried to tell me that I couldn't park in the Close. I wasn't having it."

"Calm down, Barry. Have some tea."

Seabury tried, with limited success, to supress a snigger.

The commander took charge. "I've been looking at the legality of this so-called contest. I can't find anything in the association rules that allows non-members to vote."

"Yes, but wouldn't they have thought of that and amended the rules?" Seabury suggested.

"Can't see our Felicity allowing them to cock it up, can you?"

"Not likely. But as members, we see minutes of meetings. I've been through them with a fine toothcomb. Nothing about the rulebook. And I've checked – they would have had to call an extraordinary meeting of the membership to change the constitution."

"Commander, you're a legend! But how do we persuade them to rerun the vote?" said Barry.

"And," noted Seabury, "there's no guarantee of a different outcome, is there?"

Foster produced a letter from a document folder. It was addressed to the president of the Association, Lord Derrington.

"I've got copies for you both. If you are happy, then I recommend that we all sign it and then we send it today by registered mail. Think of it as a warning shot across the bows."

Seabury scanned through the draft. "It's brilliant. They can't ignore the rules, surely? What if someone was to leak the contents of the letter to, for the sake of argument, someone like Julie Stringer?"

"Aye," said Barry. "Good call. Could cause no end of trouble if it got out."

*

While Meer was taken out of the interview to speak to his employer, Bloomfield and Tagg took the opportunity to regroup.

"Felicity will tell him to insist on a solicitor. She may even come down here herself."

"Don't be daft, Jools. Felicity Gallant in a police station? There's more chance of seeing her at the dog track. Or shopping in Lidl's."

"But you know who she will be calling next?"

"Area Commander Hinton? That's what I'm really worried about."

"But Hinton can't object to us questioning him, surely? He's a murder suspect, for God's sake."

Their musings were interrupted by Matt Lovell, who had returned with the suspect.

"Mr Meer wishes to continue with the interview."

Bloomfield rubbed his hands together, a little too gleefully for his colleagues' liking.

"Okay, so let's get the show back on the road, shall we? Interview recommenced at 10.25am."

But before Bloomfield could resume, Meer announced that he wanted to say something. He had been advised by his solicitor to await representation, but he had decided to ignore her advice. "I want to conclude where we left off."

"Thank you, Alan. DS Tagg, would you remind us of where we got to?"

She referred to her notes. "Alan, you had just confirmed that Kathleen Meer was born Kathleen Hubbard, is that right?"

"Yes, that's right. And Derek – Mr Landeryou – told me that she was jealous of Angela and that's when the penny dropped. Angela was my real mother.

"And when I heard that Kathleen just ran off and let her drown..."

He started to sob.

"Shall I pause the interview again?"

"No, please. I must finish this. I confronted Mother – Kathleen – about it last night. She hinted that she and Dad had been seeing each other before Angela came along and that she was happy that Angela drowned. She invented the story about her being my sister."

"I see," said Jools. "So, she was covering her tracks, in case anyone mentioned her name to you as you were growing up."

Bloomfield decided that it was time for 'not really very nice cop' to make a comeback.

"But none of this detracts from the fact that DC Lovell and I saw you attempting to kill Kathleen, does it? Had you planned it?"

"Of course not! If you had arrived a few minutes earlier, you would have seen her hitting me. She drew blood! And then she threatened me with a heavy object. I had to stop her!"

"You were suffocating her."

"But I wasn't going to kill her!"

Seeing Jools make the 'throat cutting' sign, Bloomfield let her continue with the interview.

*

Over at Derriford, the large regional hospital in Plymouth, Kathleen Meer was waiting to be discharged.

She had decided. She wasn't going to press charges against Alan. She knew that he lacked the balls to go through with killing her and she didn't want awkward questions to be asked about her role in the death of Angela. She had seen enough of those cold case TV programmes to know that the past could still be dragged up. She couldn't face that.

FORTY-SIX

Tedesco and Davey spent the rest of their morning engaged in the agency's bread and butter work.

Lynne had received two more enquiries from local companies seeking her help with scrutinising job applicants and Tedesco had a conference call on his latest missing beneficiary case.

As the cathedral clock struck one, he was to be seen heading out of the office towards Jenks bakery, Barker trotting along behind him. "Good to stick to our routine, don't you agree?"

Emerging from the shop with a workaday BLT for his lunch he was assailed by a familiar voice.

"Mr Tedesco! And Barker! How are our infamous sleuths today?"

"And how is our veteran columnist?"

"Less of the veteran, cheeky," said Julie Stringer. "Anyway, glad I bumped into you. Have you read today's *Journal* yet?"

"It may surprise you to learn that I've been working all morning."

"We are Mr Grumpy today! At least Barker seems pleased to see me. You should read my column – it's an exclusive on the candidate selection. There goes my phone. Must dash. By-eee!"

*

DS Tagg was at her most emollient as she resumed the interview with Alan Meer.

"I realise that this must be stressful for you, Alan."

She paused, ostensibly to give the interviewee time to compose himself, then continued, "Why did you visit Rhyminster Cathedral on the August bank holiday, Alan? Did you know that Kerry would be leading the tour?"

DCI Bloomfield scowled at his colleague. Had Alan elected to have a solicitor present these questions would have been stamped on.

"What has this got to do with last night?" said Meer, who wasn't as naïve as Jools had assumed.

She considered carefully before responding.

"You attacked Kathleen because she allowed your real mother to drown when she saved Kerry. It might seem like a bit of a coincidence that you booked a tower tour led by Kerry, which ended with her tragic death."

"I didn't know that Angela was my real mother when I went on the tour. Kathleen had always told me that Angela was my sister, and if she hadn't saved that girl, she would still be alive today."

"So, what are you telling us, Alan? That you murdered Kerry?"

"Bloody woman. What do you think, Barker? Shall I buy the *Journal* instead of *The Times*?"

Deciding to buy both papers on the basis that he could attempt the crossword at home just as well as at the office he hurried back to Minster Precincts, a confused Barker struggling to keep up.

As soon they had climbed the stairs Tedesco fixed lunch for his friend – Waitrose essential dog biscuits and a bowl of water – then opened up the local paper.

Skipping through the local news section, a quick glance at which might convince a casual reader that the Rhyminster crime wave rivalled that of Naples or Palermo, and ignoring the increasingly shouty letters page, he located Julie's column artfully sandwiched between 'Forgotten Rhyme' and 'Musings From Our Member of Parliament'.

The 'It Makes Me Mad!' feature was accompanied by a picture of its author tearing up what appeared to be a sheaf of utility bills while looking extremely angry, verging on the psychotic.

This week's offering was subtitled 'One Rule for Them?'

La Stringer had seen a copy of a letter addressed to the president of the Rhyminster and Woolford Conservative Association, in which representatives of the defeated candidate, Barry Gulliver, had accused the Association of breaching its own rules by allowing a vote in the candidate selection process to a group of non-members.

Reading on while trying to ignore Julie's increasingly excitable tone, Tedesco gleaned that the local Tories should have amended their constitution in order to allow for the public element of the vote, the implication being that failure to do so put the result in doubt.

"No one from Arabella Patrick's office was available for comment today, but a spokesman for Mr Gulliver indicated that unless a suitable explanation could be offered the defeated candidate would be seeking a rerun."

The kindly detective glanced out of the skylight, from which he could see a section of the tower. Perhaps he should go over to the cathedral and pop into the Chapel of St Nonna. The editor of the *Journal* would need all the prayers he could get once Felicity Gallant and Sir Maxwell got hold of him.

FORTY-SEVEN

Just as Alan Meer was about to answer the question from DS Tagg, DC Matt Lovell stepped into the room and slid a slip of paper across the table.

"Kathleen Meer has decided not to press charges," it read.

Bloomfield ignored it.

"So, Alan, did you murder Kerry Franklin? You are still under caution."

Meer glared at the smooth DCI.

"NO! I did not!" he shouted, before adding almost in a whisper, "But I was going to…"

"Take your time," said Tagg, "this is important. What happened? Did you lose your nerve?"

"No, nothing like that. Look, let me explain. I did book the tour because Kerry was the leader or whatever. I'd seen a feature on *Searchlight* and Kerry had been interviewed. I checked with the cathedral, and they told me that she was going to be on duty that day, so I booked the tour."

"We can check that, Alan," noted Tagg.

"But do go on," said her colleague, with more than a hint of impatience.

"I'd been brought up – or as I now realise, brainwashed – by my so-called mother into believing that my sister would have lived if it wasn't for Kerry. So when her name popped up on the screen when she was interviewed, I knew that I had to take revenge for my parents. Why should they have lost Angela, and why should I have lost my sister, when this silly woman lived a full life?"

"What were you going to do, Alan?"

"I was going to get her on her own and then threaten her. I thought I could scare her into jumping off the tower, you see."

"You didn't think this through, did you?" said Bloomfield. "And how would you have threatened Kerry – by waving your inhaler at her?"

It was Jools' turn to glare at her colleague but, before she could smooth things over, Alan decided to plough on.

"Of course not. I don't have an inhaler. I'm not asthmatic. I made that up. I had managed to take my Swiss army knife up with me. It was already in my pocket when Kerry told us to leave our belongings in the lockers. I deliberately made a show of not wanting to leave my bag."

"Very clever. But how were you going to get Kerry on her own?"

"I had planned it. The cathedral website has a lot of videos on its YouTube channel, including one that shows part of the tower tour. I saw that the visitors tend to group together when they reach the top."

"So you decided to bide your time and wait until Kerry was on her own."

"It wasn't difficult. She stood with her back to one of the parapets so she could keep an eye on the group. I had deliberately been the last of the group onto the roof and my plan was to threaten Kerry into jumping, then scurry back to the opening, wait for someone to come close and then climb out onto the roof as if I had only just made it up there."

Jools joined in, "So you would get your alibi. And Betty Budden very kindly obliged."

"But it didn't matter in the end. Someone beat me to it. I heard Kerry scream before I could get close to her so went straight back to the roof door."

"Did you hear any other voices, Alan? Perhaps someone else had decided to threaten her?"

"No, I don't think so. It's very windy up there, so voices don't carry. But I heard that scream. I will never forget it. And I feel terrible about Kerry now."

"I'm sure you do, Alan," said Bloomfield.

"Now, as we have you here, do you want to tell us about your fixation with Nicola Tedesco?"

"I see what you're up to. You are trying to suggest that I stalked her. Absolutely not. I just think she is the most wonderful woman that ever lived. I wouldn't do anything to harm her. The only stalker I know is Kathleen. She followed Angela, she would do anything to split her and Dad up."

With that, Tagg and Bloomfield went into a little huddle before the DCI spoke.

"We are going to leave it there for now, Alan."

"So are you going to charge me?"

"As I said, we are going to have a break. DS Tagg and I need to discuss this and so DC Lovell will escort you back to your cell for now."

"I really do know my rights, you know. I'm a lawyer!" Meer said as he was led away.

DS Tagg turned to her boss.

"He's right, we can only hold him for twenty-four hours. What can we charge him with? Mrs Meer isn't pressing charges, we aren't even supposed to be investigating Kerry's death, and as for asking about Nicky!"

Bloomfield took off the granny glasses that made him look a bit like John Lennon, removed his silk pocket square and polished the lens.

"On the first point, it's up to the Crown prosecutors to decide whether to press charges and I was there when he attacked her, don't forget."

"Fair enough, but if the old bat doesn't want to go ahead then why involve the CPS? And how do we justify raising the tower with him?"

"I thought about that while we were interviewing him. Meer brought up the subject of Angela – the role Kathleen played in her death – so I decided that this was a game changer as far as the tower was concerned. Meer had effectively admitted a motive and so it was reasonable to ask him about this in the course of our questions about the attempted murder."

"Not sure that's how Hinton will see it. Or Flick Gallant. So what do we do? Let him go?"

"I think so. If he's got to spend the rest of his life with Kathleen, then he will suffer enough."

"And at least we can eliminate him from Kerry's murder."

"Which we aren't investigating. Time for an informal pow-wow with Tedesco and Davey, do you think?"

FORTY-EIGHT

Frank Uglow knew that he was a dinosaur, unable, or at least unwilling, to adapt to the world of social media, influencers, bloggers and vloggers.

His position at the *Rhyminster Journal* had been the pinnacle of a career spent in local news but deep down he feared that he would be the last editor, at least of the print version.

Local news mattered. Getting to know the patch, reporting from parish councils and magistrates' courts. This was how all the great journalists started, not by pimping out beauty products online.

Julie Stringer was cut from the same cloth. He knew that he would get in trouble for publishing her column, but it was a genuine public interest story, and it might even generate some much-needed sales.

So it was absolutely no surprise to him when Felicity Gallant sent him a brief email warning him of an injunction – a bit late for that now – quickly followed by a call from Arabella Patrick threatening not to speak to the paper, which struck him as particularly stupid. She would be desperate to get her voice heard if there had to be another election.

Lynne was happy to drop her book club in favour of a meeting with Jimmy and Jools.

"I haven't actually read it – some worthy coming of age novel – and I'm not drinking so, all in all, it's a no-brainer."

"I was going to suggest a takeaway back at mine, but if you're in training for your mud fest…"

"Even Rhyme 'n' Rice does veggie curries these days. I assume that's what you were planning?"

Rhyme 'n' Rice was a local institution, positioned conveniently next to the Rhyminster Arms. Generations of Rhymesiders had followed the Friday night tradition of ordering a curry then popping next door for a pint or two while it was cooking.

Tedesco kept a copy of the takeaway menu attached to his fridge with an Andy Warhol magnet – double Elvis – and Lynne arrived to find her three colleagues studying the list of culinary delights with a deep intensity, as if it was a crime scene.

Bloomfield, normally the type to order English food from an Indian restaurant, was persuaded by the fluency of Tedesco's advocacy skills to join him in a Sally Lamb, a house speciality which was claimed to be based on an ancient Persian wedding dish.

Lynne and Jools had been studying the limited vegetarian offering and eventually settled upon a lentil dhansak as the nearest thing to a healthy option.

Tedesco phoned the order in, adding two portions of lemon rice and some poppadoms, then he went to the fridge and produced a choice of alcohol-free lager or chilled IPA.

At the same time as the investigators were expecting their takeaway a darker scene was playing out in Ivybridge, where Alan Meer was removing his meagre belongings from the house in Oates Close.

Felicity Gallant had offered him the use of the small caretaker's flat at the top of the office. It hadn't been used as such since the seventies, when old Colville had finally decided to retire after decades of glowering at anyone who crossed his path. Felicity's father had kept him on, tolerating his alarming ways as he was a fellow ex-Navy man.

Since then, the flat had been used as an overflow to the deeds room and, so rumour had it, as somewhere for the younger employees to retire to for a crafty snog or a punch-up after the boozy Christmas lunches of the eighties and early nineties.

There was still a rusty old shower in there and a gas ring, so Meer could survive until he found somewhere more permanent.

Only a few hours earlier it had looked as though his choice would be between a prison cell and a return to Kathleen, so the legal executive was only too happy to accept his new accommodation.

*

While they were waiting for their food Tedesco produced his case file, updated to the previous day, and Lynne powered up her tablet.

Jools and Bloomfield took them through the events of the past twenty-four hours, which Tedesco meticulously recorded in copperplate, like a monk working on a medieval document, Lynne simply using the notebook function on her device.

If he had been a sweary man then he would have let out a choice series of expletives at the latest revelations, but as he was endlessly courteous, Tedesco just raised an eyebrow, and said, "Good grief!"

"Let me take a moment to process this," said Lynne. "You get called out to an incident in Ivybridge, you arrive to see Alan Meer about to murder his mother, you arrest him, he refuses a solicitor, then he confesses to attacking her with a cushion, provides a plausible reason for hating Kathleen because she lied to him about his real mother, and now he blames her for letting Angela drown. Just a normal day at the office, I suppose."

Before Bloomfield could respond there was a knock on the door, which sent Barker into guard dog mode, albeit the least fierce guard dog imaginable.

The border terrier could sniff the curry and probably thought it was for him.

Tedesco recognised the lad on the delivery round: it was Costel, who had pitched up in Rhyme from the streets of Bucharest a few years ago. After a spell as a *Big Issue* seller, he had become the go-to guy for any odd jobs, from garden clearance to takeaway delivery. He also coached a junior football team on Saturday mornings.

"Good to see you, Cos. How much do I owe you?"

Tedesco gave him a generous tip. The locals hadn't all been welcoming when the trickle of East Europeans started to arrive at the turn of the century, but Costel had been determined to win them over.

After a pause while Tedesco shared out the food, Bloomfield continued. He outlined how they had been able to introduce the subject of the fall from the tower into their questioning of the suspect and ended with the news that Kathleen had decided not to take matters further.

Tedesco finished chewing a chunk of the lamb dish. "Mmm, not bad, good to see standards haven't slipped. Look, Jimmy, it's a lot to take in, as Lynne said."

He popped the top off another bottle of IPA, took a sip and went on, "To summarise, in the course of a single interview you got a confession, some possible mitigation, if you believe that Kathleen assaulted Alan first, confirmation that Angela was indeed Meer's real mother and then Kathleen drops the charges, but not before you get Alan to own up to going armed for his tower tour."

"And," Lynne added, "it looks as though Betty Budden really did give him an alibi for Kerry's death. So, do we scratch him from the list of suspects? And did he tell you anything that might get the case reopened?"

Before Bloomfield or Tagg could respond, the loud ring tone from Tedesco's phone blurted out, setting Barker off.

"I'd better take this. Nicky? What's happened?"

FORTY-NINE

He always worried when his sister called. This went right back to their childhood when he had been the protective brother, guarding his little sister against their alcoholic father, and had continued into their adult life. He remained anxious about the state of her marriage and had even suggested a meeting with one of his divorce lawyer contacts when it seemed as if the point of no return was imminent.

Things were much better between Nicky and Chag at the moment but now Tedesco had his local TV star sister's stalker to worry about.

"Don't sound so worried," said Nicky. "I've been talking to Julie."

"And what is she mad about this time? Sorry, I can never resist it."

"Listen, I'm trying to help you here. Have you seen her latest column?"

"Yes. I bumped into her outside Jenks and she all but frogmarched me to the newsagents."

"You will have read that Barry Gulliver has effectively told Arabella where to stick her olive branch."

"So it would seem. Sorry to be rude, dear sister, but I do have company."

"Not a woman, is it? Lynne? Please say it is."

"She is here, but so are Jimmy and Jools."

"Okay, understood. But here's the thing. Frank Uglow has been threatened by both Arabella and that hard-faced Flick woman. It looks like all-out civil war."

"They're frightened that Bazza isn't going to go quietly. Look, perhaps we can catch up later in the week. All I can say is that the plates are spinning."

*

A matter of yards away, within the confines of the Close, Crispin was doing his best to act as referee between his wife and Felicity Gallant.

"Flick, I thought I could rely on you. The others on the executive are what I now know to be NFR – Normal for Rhyme – but you were like us."

"What, AME – Arrogant Metropolitan Elite – do you mean?"

"Ladies, this is getting us nowhere."

"Shut up, Crispin," they replied in unison.

"Look, Flick, I take that back. I'm stressed to bits if I'm honest. I shouldn't be taking it out on you."

"No, you are right. I should never have allowed that pompous wanker Commander Foster to take charge of the selection process. But we are where we are."

"What are you going to do?" Crispin asked. "I hate to say it, but Gulliver has a point. If the rules didn't provide for a public element in the vote, then the result is void *ab initio.*"

237

Arabella took a sip of her negroni. "Okay, so why don't we remove the public votes and only count the genuine members?"

Flick, on her second vodka martini, was glad that she had brought a change of clothing. She would have to stay the night now she was over the limit.

"It sounds like a plan, and Gulliver could hardly complain, as it meets his key objection."

"Do I detect a 'but'?" said the candidate.

"You do. How confident are you that you would have won without the public vote?"

Crispin spoke up. "Felicity does have a point, darling. Look at those oiks who turned up. They were bona fide party members, recruited by the ghastly Gulliver."

"And look at the public who applied for tickets. People like John Tedesco, Neil Sparkes. Just the kind of people who would have voted for Sir Vere, despite being uncomfortable with some of our harsher rhetoric. They'd have voted for you."

"So that idea doesn't work. What the fuck do we do now?"

"Wait and see might not be a bad tactic," advised Flick.

"But if Gulliver pushes this we could end up in judicial review."

"Okay. There's only one way to deal with this," announced Felicity. "We need Lord Derrington to convene an emergency meeting of the membership."

"At least it will buy us some time," Crispin added, looking anxiously across at his wife and wondering for the umpteenth time why they had moved their lives to the back of beyond if there wasn't going to be a seat in Parliament as compensation.

*

"That was my sister," said Tedesco. "Frank Uglow has been threatened with court action by Felicity and Arabella for publishing Julie's column."

"I heard about that," Jools said. "Irregularities with the vote, wasn't it?"

"Jimmy, did you get anywhere with your contacts in Spain?" asked Lynne, changing the subject.

"They're still digging through their files, though they did confirm that a group of Brits were taken off the boat in Tenerife. There were no charges, but it sounds as if this may have been down to pressure from above."

Tedesco stroked his imaginary beard. "Wasn't Sir Maxwell Patrick a Foreign Office minister back then?"

"Okay," said Lynne, somewhat impatiently, "so if Meer is out of the frame, and we still agree that this was no accident, then where are we? Barry must be the main suspect now, but do we have anything concrete to go on?"

Bloomfield looked up from his Sally Lamb curry, pronouncing it a bit hot for his liking, and gave his verdict.

"That's it in a nutshell. It's all circumstantial with Bazza. From what Kerry's brother said, Gulliver was probably the bloke who had been bothering her after she settled back in Rhyme. The Saxtons put Bazza on the Retro cruise with her, and we now know that his group were ejected from the ship."

Tedesco butted in. "But we have nothing to join up the dots. No one actually saw Gulliver with Kerry."

"We have her statement, don't forget, the one she gave me before I left the CID."

"Yes Lynne. But she didn't name any names, did she?"

DS Tagg, who had been listening carefully, was now ready to offer her sixpenny-worth.

"Let's look at this another way. Instead of trying to fit the suspect to the crime, perhaps we should look at the surrounding circumstances. What was behind Kerry's death?"

"It's all about the election of our new MP, isn't it? Would this tragedy have even happened if that hadn't been going on in the background?"

"I don't think so, Jimmy," said Tedesco. "Think about it. If Kerry had been trying to blackmail Gulliver, and he wasn't standing for election, would he have been that bothered?"

"And," Lynne added, "why would she blackmail him in the first place if he was just another provincial estate agent? The prospect of losing his only realistic chance of becoming an MP would have been enough to persuade Gulliver to take decisive steps. It was a game changer. And Arabella was only on the tour because she wanted to show off to the voters."

"Are we back to one of the earlier theories, then? That Barry paid Kerry to get rid of Arabella and to keep quiet about the incident on board?"

"It's still possible, Jools, but we haven't got anything to justify calling Barry in for questioning, have we?"

"It's one step forward and two steps back, I'm afraid," was Bloomfield's dismal conclusion.

"I agree," said his fellow officer. "We need a miracle."

Tedesco leaned back in his chair and smiled.

"Cheer up, everyone. This is Rhyminster. We've had centuries of miracles, and I'm sure we are due another one soon."

FIFTY

It was definitely a morning to throw those curtains wide. As he glanced at the TV while he scoffed his breakfast, Tedesco didn't need Carol Kirkwood's upbeat forecast to corroborate the evidence from his own kitchen window, nor her daily greeting to Bono and the Edge: "And good morning to U2!"

It was a sparkling, crisp autumn day, perfect weather for heading out to the coast for a walk on the beach or for wandering over to the cathedral to view the annual safety inspection.

As he led Barker on their familiar route across Cathedral Green, the terrier seemed surprised when they stopped outside the West Front rather than continuing towards Minster Precincts.

The local media was already setting out its stall and, as well as Julie Stringer, Tedesco thought that he recognised a reporter from the *Western Morning News*.

Duncan Chivers had been sent to cover the story by *Searchlight* and was sharing a joke with Lynne, who had already racked up 10k on her exercise bike before he'd even started breakfast, while various cathedral bigwigs were gathering by the great west door, including the dean, Wilf Drake and Lady Derrington.

Just as Darrell Harris (the clerk of the works) was about to welcome everyone Julie suddenly materialised at Tedesco's elbow.

"You'd think that our new MP would be here, wouldn't you? She only had to walk across the road for God's sake."

Harris, bronzed in appearance and sporting a long beard worthy of a member of ZZ Top, moved uncertainly towards the mike stand.

"Good morning, guys. Can you all hear me okay? Yeah? Great stuff."

Having warned the little crowd to stand well back, he proceeded to explain that there was a very serious purpose to the exercise.

"Have you ever thought about what would happen if someone had injured themselves up on the tower or had fallen down the steps? I think most of you guys have been up there, so you know all too well that there isn't much room for a stretcher or any specialised equipment."

"I wouldn't mind being winched down by him," whispered Julie, rather too loudly.

Harris continued, "This means that the best way of rescuing someone in that scenario would be to reach them from the outside of the tower. Our good friends from fire and rescue are here today and they are going to test our procedure."

Then, to a ripple of polite laughter, he explained that each year a victim – "or perhaps I should say volunteer" – from the cathedral staff is given the dubious honour of acting as an injured tourist in need of rescue.

"This year, it is our legendary gift shop manager, Andrea Hutchins!"

Andrea stepped forward from the crowd and curtsied.

"Andrea is going to climb up the steps to the tower, as if she was on a regular tour. She will then be strapped into a safety harness and put on a stretcher. Once she's ready to rock and roll I'll tell you what happens next."

The diminutive but plucky volunteer walked over to the visitor entrance to a burst of applause, accompanied by head tower guide, Jock Barton, who was going up with her in accordance with the health and safety protocol.

"She's frightfully brave," said Lady Derrington, who also noted Arabella's absence.

Mark Tubbs from the refectory had produced some warming drinks to keep the spectators occupied until the show was about to begin, which provoked some light-hearted teasing.

"Don't fancy it this year, Tubbsy?" asked Lynne, well aware of the fact that the catering manager had been in real danger of becoming permanently wedged in the small exit room at the top of the tower when he had been the guinea pig.

"I think that's why they went for the smallest person on the staff this year. Why don't you do it next time, Lynne?"

"Seconded!" said Tedesco.

Before Ms Davey had the chance to accept or reject the challenge there were audible gasps at the apparent signs of movement from on high.

"If I can have your attention, guys!" Harris shouted. "The descent is about to commence! So, stand well back!"

The *Searchlight* cameraman trained his sights on the tiny

yellow blob that had appeared hundreds of feet up the tower, which gradually became clearer as it was slowly winched to earth.

But where was Barker? Tedesco had taken him off his lead and he was surprised to see his normally obedient canine companion hurtling across the Green.

As he looked up, Tedesco became aware of something falling from the sky.

Was it a leaf – no, too big – or a bag of some type?

The answer came as soon as Barker ran up to him and deposited a white leather glove at his master's feet.

*

The injured tourist reached the ground, was carefully detached from the winch and then the stretcher was expertly carried to a waiting SUV which was playing the role of an ambulance.

Meanwhile, Tedesco had carefully placed the glove in a poo bag, which was the nearest thing to an evidence bag that he could find.

Andrea was checked over by a paramedic and was subsequently released to a rousing three cheers led by Dean Dan, then the poor woman was led away to be interviewed for *Searchlight* while Julie Stringer hovered impatiently in the background, keen to speak to the heroine of the hour.

"Shall we leave them to it, Lynne?" Tedesco asked. "I think the show is over."

"And don't think that I didn't see you put that glove in one of Barker's bags. Time to get back to work, I reckon."

*

Arabella Patrick hadn't been at home that morning. She'd been hacking through Woolford Forest with Felicity Gallant.

FIFTY-ONE

"Sally, could you look after Barker this morning, please? Lynne and I are going to be engaged. No calls, please."

"That sounds exciting. Can I ask—"

"NO!" said her bosses, in stereo.

"Okay Tedesco. Spill," said Lynne.

"I noticed something falling from the sky just as Andrea was being winched down, and before I knew it Barker was off in hot pursuit."

"And I assume that the something was a glove. Are you thinking what I'm thinking?"

"That it belongs to Arabella? Of course. And why wasn't she there today? Did she know something?"

Tedesco took a slow walk around the little meeting room, as if to order his thoughts.

"I said we needed a miracle. And there is a circularity to this. The mystery started with a fall from the tower..."

"And you think it could end with another one? Very poetic, but let's look at the reality. A glove falls out of the sky, presumably from the tower. Why did this happen, today of all days?"

"Was it dislodged when the firemen were getting Andrea down?"

"Hmm. Arabella lost the glove when she was on the tower tour, so I suppose it could have dropped down the escape hatch and stayed there until today."

"And if that is what happened there is a chance that there might be some trace DNA left on it."

"I wouldn't bet on it if the glove had become wedged somewhere on the outside of the tower. DNA degrades if exposed to weather, as I assume you know. And if Arabella set out to kill Kerry, then wouldn't she have taken pains to avoid touching the outside of the glove?"

"Look, two points: do we really think that she set out with the intent to kill someone when she went on the tour? And how do you put a glove on without touching the outside?"

"Fair point, I suppose, but it's still a long shot."

"Okay, dear colleague, so what do we do with it? See if Jools can call in a favour with the lab and run some tests?"

"Fine, I'll talk to her. They will have Kerry's DNA on file so they can soon see if there is a match."

"Assuming there's still something on the glove, of course."

"Right then. Back to work, I reckon."

"Lynne, there was something else. You seemed to be getting on very well with Duncan Chivers."

Just the faintest hint of red began to reveal itself on the Dutch-doll complexion of Tedesco's fellow detective.

*

At this point the bridleway was wide enough to allow for the horses to ride two abreast.

"I've been thinking through what you suggested last night," Arabella said. "We need to call a meeting, but do we really have to involve the entire membership at this stage?"

"What are you saying, we just get the executive together? I can see why this might be less risky but don't forget that Gulliver has his supporters on the exec as well – Foster, for one."

As they trotted on Arabella's mind was turning to the safety inspection. *Perhaps I should have gone after all*, she thought. *What if that bloody glove is found up there?*

*

"Sally, I may be back late from lunch," said Lynne.

"That's not like you. Are you meeting someone?"

"As I said, I may be a bit late, that's all."

It had all happened so casually. Duncan Chivers had mentioned to her that he would have wrapped up the filming by lunchtime and had asked Lynne if she could recommend anywhere for a quick bite before he headed back to the studio.

She suggested Cranes, and then it seemed only natural for him to ask her to join him and for her to accept.

So, while Tedesco was queuing for his ritual sandwich at Jenks, Lynne found herself sitting opposite the self-proclaimed Alan Partridge of the south-west, weighing up whether to choose from the specials board.

They both opted for the catch of the day, which prompted a knowingly lame riff on *Match of the Day* from the veteran sports reporter: "We've got some tasty encounters coming up on tonight's 'Catch of the Day', starting with Turbot Town against Sea Bass City. So let's join your commentators at the Emirates Aquarium, Clive Whiting and Roy Bream."

Lynne found herself giggling. She had a surprising weakness for silly humour, and for men who didn't take themselves seriously.

It was half past two by the time they left the little wine bar.

"Can I call you if I'm in Rhyme again? When another murder takes place, perhaps?"

"Oh, I hope it might be sooner than that," she replied, hardly believing what she was hearing herself say.

She was still laughing to herself when she got back to Minster Precincts.

"Good run, was it?" asked Tedesco.

"Mind your own business, trunk," came out as, "I was networking with one of my HR clients."

Tedesco, feigning a lack of interest, changed the subject.

"Nicky just shared something with me. She wasn't due in to work until this afternoon as she's doing the late news summary. She thought we might like to know that she saw Arabella and Flick on horseback in the village earlier."

"So that's why the notoriously publicity-shy Ms Patrick was absent this morning. Perhaps they are having second thoughts about rejecting Bazza's sticky advances?"

"Oh, and Jimmy called in on the off chance. His contacts in the Canaries have confirmed that Bazza *was* held overnight while the others were released."

"So, he must have got up to serious mischief on that cruise?"

"Looks like it. But the Tenerife equivalent of Jackie Hinton told the local guys to back off. However, one good thing, I gave Jimmy the glove and he was going to call in at the lab on his way to a gender awareness session in Totnes."

"Which I am sure he was looking forward to."

"Like a kid on Christmas Eve."

FIFTY-TWO

While they awaited news of the DNA results Lynne started to involve a truculent Tedesco in her executive recruitment work, which had become rather more than a side-line.

Lynne's reputation had spread well beyond the local area, and she didn't want to turn away new business so, despite his frequent complaints about the corporate jargon deployed by their new clients, Tedesco grudgingly began to enjoy the forensic aspect of the work.

However, they only had a couple of days to wait before Jools called with the news that there was a clear match for Kerry's DNA on the glove.

"If we can get a sample from Arabella and this matches what we have on the inside of the glove…"

"Then we have the connection," said Lynne.

"But how do we get a sample?" said Tedesco. "Break into Stannary House and look for her hairbrush?"

"Jools and Bloomfield want another get together. I said we could meet here after Sally goes."

"Okay. I'll clear it with Barker."

Brad Budden had been helpfulness personified when Jools tracked him down in Massachusetts to ask if he could forward copies of any pictures he had taken on the tower.

He'd not got round to deleting the thousands of images he had saved from their European adventure, so the pictures of Arabella and Crispin posing on the tower with Stannary House in the background were still there. Ms Patrick was clearly wearing gloves, and it would be easy to expand the pictures to see if they were of the same make as the one that Barker had rescued.

Also, Jools remembered, Izzie the head verger had told Tedesco that she had seen the gloves, so that could be useful if Arabella claimed not to recognise them.

*

Sally Munks was normally out of the office door like a greyhound out of the traps as soon as the cathedral clock struck five but, to her employers' exasperation, this was the one day when she seemed determined to hang around.

"Haven't you got a book club tonight?" asked Lynne.

"Or a vegan tofu knitting evening," Tedesco muttered under his breath as Lynne eventually manage to shoo the PA down the stairs and safely off the premises before Bloomfield and Tagg arrived in the courtyard.

"Lynne, tell me, have you ever considered a career as a shepherd?"

"Why? Are you thinking of joining the diplomatic service?"

Moments later, a knackered DCI Bloomfield arrived hot-foot from his training session.

"I'm getting too old for this. Perhaps I should just jack it in and join you two? I bet you don't have to waste your time on the latest woke crap."

"No, we don't, but there's no pension scheme and the pay is lousy."

"And," Lynne added, "we may not go to gender awareness seminars, but we do practise it."

One of the myriad reasons for her joining Tedesco in setting up the agency had been the continuing prevalence of a toxic masculine culture in the CID. And she had always felt that Bloomfield was amongst the more enlightened!

"Shall we make a start, or shall we wait for Jools?"

*

DS Tagg had managed to squeeze into the last available space in the tiny car park at the far end of the Close.

Like her friend Lynne, she hated being late, so she jogged through the Close at some speed. However, she slowed to a walk as she went past the magnificent residences on the far side, increasingly convinced that she could hear frighteningly loud voices being raised.

As she got closer, she could sense that they were coming from Stannary House, so she stopped to listen. She distinctly heard Arabella Patrick shouting at her husband, something about him being bloody useless; he shouting something indistinct back at her which might have been, "You didn't burn them!"

She should have called in a uniformed officer but, as Bloomfield was around the corner, she rang him.

"Sorry folks, it was Jools," he said, taking his leave of Tedesco and Davey.

"Will you be back?" Lynne asked.

"Oh yes. Jools just called from outside Stannary House."

"In that case we await your return with bated breath."

*

Bloomfield was on the scene within a minute, just as the shouting turned to screaming. DS Tagg approached the huge oak door and yanked at the bell pull several times before banging on the window, while DCI Bloomfield tried the back door, which he was less than surprised to see still bore a notice marked 'Tradesmen's Entrance'.

Good to see that our next MP is down with the levelling up agenda, he thought to himself, just as he became aware of a light coming on, the bulb exhibiting a certain reluctance to shine.

An agitated Crispin Atherton appeared at the door, looking for all the world as if his game of billiards had just been rudely interrupted.

"How dare you make all this racket!"

"And good evening to you, sir."

As the identity of his visitor began to dawn on the up-and-coming barrister, he resorted to charm.

"Ah, DCI Bloomfield! So sorry. I thought it was one of those young thugs who lurk about the Close bothering the residents. It's about time that the dean and chapter reinstated the Close constables."

"If the residents are experiencing problems of that sort, our doors are always open, Mr Atherton."

Overhearing the conversation, Jools joined her boss at the tradesmen's entrance.

"Good evening, sir. I am DS Tagg. I overheard what appeared to be sounds of distress emanating from your property."

"We would just like to make sure that you and your family are safe. Do you mind if we come in?" asked Bloomfield.

"Look, officers, my wife and I were just discussing a few things and the conversation became a little heated. I'm sure you both have better things to do with your time."

"As DCI Bloomfield said, we just want to make sure that all is well—"

Before Jools could finish an almighty scream came from within.

*

While they awaited developments from Stannary House, Tedesco and Davey caught up with other news.

"Neil called while you were still out at lunch," said Tedesco, somewhat pointedly.

"You aren't going to let me forget that, are you? Anyway, what did Sparksy want?"

As we have seen, Neil Sparkes had been a partner in Tedesco's old legal practice, which had recently been merged with a large regional firm.

Neil had taken to the merger like a frog to boiling water, and during the early months he had started meeting Tedesco in the pub after work to off-load his frustrations with life under the new regime, frequently expressing the wish that he had bailed out when Tedesco left.

The kindly detective soon wearied of these sessions and had spoken to Neil's strong wife, Mary, a legal executive with the local authority, sharing his concerns about his old friend's drinking, and so he took the lack of recent contact from Neil as a positive sign.

Tedesco responded to Lynne by explaining that Neil had divulged that he had offered Alan Meer a job with Easlick Creber (the merged firm) as his assistant. Sparkes was the partner in charge of wills and probate, which was also Meer's line of business.

"Sounds like a match made in heaven. Isn't Neil a bit of a geek too?"

"Hmm. He does go to *Star Wars* conventions, and he likes Pink Floyd and Genesis. Probably harmless. Anyway, he wants to meet for a drink after work tomorrow."

"I hope you turned him down."

"I would have done, but he insisted that he had something important to share about the tower. Something Meer told him."

FIFTY-THREE

Ignoring Crispin's lame protests, Tagg and Bloomfield entered Stannary House as if they owned the place, wandering through a boot room and a huge utility area before arriving in what the property porn mags refer to as a 'farmhouse kitchen'. It boasted a huge, suspiciously pristine Aga, the oven equivalent of a massive SUV. It just needed a personalised number plate.

Arabella Patrick had her head down on the table and, as she was sobbing uncontrollably, Tagg instinctively went to comfort her. She was completely taken aback when the normally thermostatically controlled Ms Patrick responded by literally crying on her shoulder.

Crispin was soon by her side. "Look, officers, can't you see that Bella is distressed? She's been under huge pressure with the selection meeting and now that odious runt Gulliver is refusing to accept defeat, like he's Donald fucking Trump, not a jumped-up oik. I don't know, perhaps the people down here deserve him."

"I am aware that feelings are running high locally, but DS Tagg wouldn't have called this in if there hadn't been signs of distress. And what I heard sounded like rather more than a routine domestic."

Jools turned to the putative MP, who was rapidly composing herself.

"What happened, Arabella, if I may? Would it help if we spoke alone?"

"No, not at all. It's as Cris says. I'm fed up to my back teeth with Gulliver, the dim-witted, clumsily conspiratorial peasantry and that bloody woman who writes for the local rag. I took it out on Cris, which was unfair. He's got a stressful enough career without coping with my shit."

Tagg and Bloomfield glanced at each other knowingly, then Bloomfield said that they would leave things for now, but they would send someone round in a few days' time to make sure that everything was all right.

As Crispin showed them back out through the tradesmen's entrance, he whispered to Bloomfield, "Look, all that stuff we said about the locals. We didn't mean it, you know. Just letting off steam. Now, you will be a good chap and never mention what you just heard to a living soul, won't you?"

"A very good evening to you, sir – oh, and for future reference, I don't take kindly to being asked to be a good chap, if that's all right with you, Mr Atherton."

*

"We were wondering if we should call for back-up," quipped Tedesco as Tagg and Bloomfield returned to Minster Precincts.

Jools ignored the knowingly flippant comment.

"John – strange request alert – but have you got something you could put my coat in? It needs to go to the lab."

"Er, what?" said Lynne.

"Arabella the Ice Queen literally melted on my shoulder. I've got traces of her all over my coat."

While Lynne rootled around in the cleaners' cupboard, Bloomfield summarised the scene at Stannary House.

"Okay, so where are we now?" asked Tedesco, rhetorically.

"It looks like we've got plenty of Arabella's DNA on Jools' coat, so if it matches with what the lab found on the inside of the glove…"

"Then we know that the missing glove probably belongs to her," said Lynne, returning with a plastic drawstring bin insert that could approximate to an evidence bag.

"Fine," Jools added, "but don't forget that we have Kerry's DNA on that glove as well, so if Arabella comes up trumps we have clear evidence of a coming together."

"Although any half-competent defence lawyer will question the admissibility of what you got hold of tonight."

Bloomfield groaned. "Once the lawyer, John. Look, I was there when Arabella cried on Jools' shoulder. She moved towards her. There's no way that we came by the evidence illegally."

"Isn't this for another day?" said DS Tagg. "What are our next moves?"

"You get that coat to the lab, obviously," ventured Lynne, "but then what? Have you got grounds to call her in for questioning?"

"Hinton will put the kybosh on that, I fear. We need a bit more. We've got the glove and we know what Arabella was wearing, so it will be interesting to see if she still has the clothes."

"You think she could have got rid of them? Interesting, Jimmy. You are of course right. We do need something else. I've got a meeting tomorrow evening, and I have a feeling that this might move things along."

"Care to tell us more, Hercule?" asked Bloomfield.

Tedesco grinned. "Oh no, I need to keep my informant's identity secret for now. So if you don't mind," he added, "I need to check up on Barker and get some supper."

FIFTY-FOUR

The border terrier appeared less than gruntled as he waited for what seemed like several dog years for his master to finish whatever was keeping him from going home on time.

Didn't he understand that a professional, highly skilled pet needs routine?

As soon as Tedesco had unlocked the front door to 17 St Budeaux Place, Barker ran expectantly to his empty bowl.

"I'm so sorry, old pal," said Tedesco, opening a new packet of dog biscuits. "You must be starving."

"I don't suppose I can interest you in a glass of claret? No? I'll have one on my own then."

He spotted a half bottle of a decent Chateau Lamothe that needed finishing, so he poured himself a glass before heating up some spag blob – an old family joke – from the freezer.

Once he had eaten, he planned to retire to the study with his casebook and the remnants of the bottle, but in the meantime, he was in urgent need of some music. He hadn't listened to Carole King for a while, so he placed *Tapestry* on his turntable, carefully lowering the needle to gently line up the opening bars of 'So Far Away'.

Sorcha was always there in the background, and his coping mechanism was in listening to songs like these.

*

"Do you have a death wish or something?"

"How was I to know that the CID were patrolling the Close just as you were being a total fucking beast?"

Crispin fell silent for a couple of heartbeats. "That's it! What exactly were they doing outside our house? Are we under surveillance? I think a call to the chief constable is in order, don't you?"

"And I know just who should make it – Daddy. Bloomfield and his little helper won't bother us again once Sir Maxwell sets the hounds on them."

*

The prospect of an early retirement and helping out at Tedesco and Davey seemed even more appealing once Bloomfield had put the phone down on AC Hinton.

"I've already had the chief on my case. What the shitting hell were you and Tagg doing in the Close last night? It isn't even on your way home. If I find out that you are helping Tedesco on the sly, then I don't have to spell out the consequences."

He *almost* felt sorry for Hinton. As well as the chief constable she'd have had Felicity Gallant pecking her head off, not to mention Arabella's pompous twat of a father.

Despite the pressure, Bloomfield remained resolute. He still believed in old-fashioned things like justice and fair play and in the old dictum that what goes around comes around. He had also become surprisingly, even reluctantly, persuadable by Tedesco and his innate feel for a case. John wouldn't have dangled the prospect of something coming out of his mystery meeting without good reason.

*

"This is a bit different from last time," Tedesco observed as he joined Neil Sparkes in the Broad Street branch of Caffè Nero.

At their previous meeting the venue had been the dingiest pub in town, where Neil had already finished his first pint by the time that Tedesco joined him.

"I'm a new man now. Mary got me to see what I was becoming, and I gather that I have you to thank as well."

"I did have a word with her, yes. But you haven't taken the pledge. I saw you downing a pint at the selection meeting."

"That was a Friday night. I've cut it out during the week, but still need a beer or two to celebrate the weekend."

"I think that's great Neil. You are certainly looking well on it."

Sparkes had clearly lost weight, and the sweaty countenance had all but disappeared.

"I've discovered walking football – one of the few benefits of the merger is that we have enough people to take part – and I have suddenly acquired an assistant to share the load."

"So, things are looking up. I couldn't be happier for you.

Now, tell me about Alan Meer. It sounds as if he has turned his life around as well."

Sparkes explained in rather too much detail how he had the brainwave of approaching Alan, recognising someone else who could use a fresh start. It would be impossible for Alan to stay at Gallants with his mother living around the corner.

"I was pushing at an open door, really. Alan had been living with Kathleen all those years and he hardly spent anything, no dependants, no car, no holidays. He had stashed away the best part of thirty years' salary in the Dartmouth Building Society, so he can afford his own place. Not that Gallants had paid him much. He's more than doubled what Flick gave him by joining us, and that's no more than the going rate."

Meer had just taken a short lease on a flat just off Fancourt Terrace, one of Rhyme's ritzier addresses, and was actively looking to buy a house.

Fascinating as it was to ponder on Alan Meer's *Great Expectations*, Tedesco was becoming impatient to learn the real reason why his old mate Neil had summoned him for a swift flat white or two.

"So, Sparksy. You wanted to tell me what Alan said about the tower."

"Er, yes, of course." He looked around in the manner of a pantomime villain, checking that no one was eavesdropping on their conversation, then he went on again, lowering his voice.

"As you know, John, poor Alan was on the tower tour when Kerry Franklin died, and the police seemed to blame him. You'd have more insight, but I think they picked him out because he's a bit, you know, different—"

"I don't think that was the only reason, Neil, but pray continue."

Sparkes leaned in, whispering now.

"Alan was terrified when the police interviewed him. That heartless monster Felicity had told him not to say anything and that the firm's reputation was on the line. She also reminded Alan that Arabella and her husband were not just important clients, but her personal friends."

"I'm afraid that doesn't surprise me one bit," Tedesco said, trying his hardest not to sound irritable.

"So, what didn't Alan tell the police?"

"He saw a struggle. Between Kerry and Arabella. Then they moved outside his field of vision for a brief moment, and the next thing he remembers is hearing one of the other tourists shouting for help."

"Wow, okay. This could be the missing piece in the jigsaw, Neil. Do think he would speak to the police now? Or at least to me?"

FIFTY-FIVE

Arabella Patrick. Is she the new chief suspect? But why would she want to get rid of Kerry? Gulliver remains the one who had animus against her, surely? If he had been the one who assaulted her on the ship and who had tracked her down in Rhyme, then he would want her silenced.

But if it was Arabella then are we witnessing a cover-up? Flick Gallant suppressing evidence, Hinton, and possibly the chief constable, warning Bloomfield off the case. And Sir Maxwell Patrick is involved somewhere, no doubt about that.

And what was really behind the terrifying argument which Jimmy and Jools interrupted the other evening?

Tedesco's immaculate writing up of his latest thoughts was disturbed, as it often was, by the insistent ringing of his phone.

"Nicky, to what do I owe the pleasure?"

"Just wanted to pick your brains, bro."

"Pick away."

"Have you heard anything about the bishop?"

"And have you and Chag been on the scrumpy again? What on earth are you driving at?"

"So, you haven't heard, then?"

"Heard what, Nicola?"

"Never mind, have a good night. Love to Barker."

He worried about his sister sometimes. But why on earth would Bishop Bob be visible on her radar?

*

As he made his way to work the following morning, he felt completely uninspired. The weather didn't help, and nor did his internal playlist.

There were plenty of good candidates to match his empty mood, from 'Monday Monday' by the Mamas and Papas, to the Carpenters' 'Rainy Days and Mondays' and, perhaps not quite his thing, 'I Don't Like Mondays' by the Boomtown Rats.

But this was a Thursday, dammit. Why weren't there any songs about miserable weather on a Thursday?

The conclusion of his deep philosophical musings would have to await another day.

He really needed to sit down with Lynne and see what she thought about Neil's revelations, but before he could do so he and Barker were assailed by Sally. Again! Wretched woman!

"Look, Mr T! You've got an official invitation. I bumped into Barbara as she was cycling through the Close this morning and she gave me this!"

Sally handed her bemused employer an impressive-looking envelope containing what Charles Tantum, the Master of Musick, would leeringly refer to as a 'stiffy'.

"Ooh, go on, what is it? Barbara wouldn't give anything away."

Barbara Battershill, who had served as secretary to three bishops of Rhyminster, was renowned for her discretion and her formidable diplomatic skills.

Tedesco slit open the envelope, deploying his uncle's old letter knife with a certain ceremonial panache, carefully removed the card and then read aloud, "Bishop Robert and Hilary would like to invite their friends John Tedesco, Lynne Davey and Barker to the North Canonry to mark their retirement from the Diocese…"

So that is what Nicky had been driving at! He checked his old-school paper diary – in Plymouth Argyle green, of course – and marked the date.

"And guess what? I've been asked to help out with the food. The bishop's wife has roped me in to produce some vegan options, so I will be there as well!" burbled the loyal but exhaustingly up-beat PA.

In all the excitement, Tedesco had failed to hear Lynne's familiar gallop up the stairs.

"Sorry I'm late, folks. Jools caught me just as I was about to leave the house. We need to talk."

"We do – Sally, hold any calls, please."

"I really don't know what's happening, Barker," Sally said to the dog after Tedesco and Davey had shut the meeting room door behind them. "That's the second time this week that they've gone off in a huddle. I don't like it. Not one bit."

*

"Come on, put me out of my misery. How was the meeting with your informant?"

"It was Neil Sparkes."

"And how many flagons of ale did you have to pour down his throat?"

Tedesco gave his imaginary designer stubble another stroke before he responded.

"He's a cheap date these days. Neil has become a weekday teetotaller. Anyway, do you want to know what he told me?"

"Oh, if you must, but then can I get down from the table and play on my X Box?"

"This is serious, Lynne. As you know, Neil has taken on Alan Meer as his assistant and, as I am sure you will be glad to hear, the new boy is doing very well."

"Yeah, thrilled to hear that your sister's stalker and our former number one murder suspect has turned his life round."

"Can I finish? Good. Anyway, Alan had a heart to heart with Neil and told him that Felicity Gallant had ordered him to keep schtum when interviewed about Kerry and the tower tour, effectively warning him that his job was on the line."

"Okay, so far so predictable."

"May I continue?"

Lynne, mischievously enjoying her colleague's discomfort, gave a sly grin.

"Of course you may. So, what did the delightful Mr Meer say that was so important?"

"When he was on the tower, he witnessed a struggle between Kerry and Arabella."

"What did the little pervert do next? Jerk himself off?"

"What has gone into you today? There's no need for your police canteen vulgarity! He only saw them for a split second, then they disappeared out of sight. The next thing he remembers is hearing cries for help."

269

"So what are we supposed to think? That Kerry attacked Arabella, presumably at Barry Gulliver's instigation, but Ms Patrick managed to hold her off and push her over the edge?"

"Maybe, but remember what Mike Knowles said in his statement. *She was about to topple over.*"

Lynne ignored the prompting of her phone, warning her of an incoming message.

"I get it, but could Arabella really have lifted Kerry onto the parapet and blithely wandered off, assuming that Kerry would just jump back to safety?"

"Seems a bit far-fetched, I grant you, but Arabella was by some way the younger of the two and presumably the fitter. She could have lifted Kerry up, I suppose, or swung her round, like you do in a barn dance. Not that I dance in barns," he swiftly added.

Lynne's phone beeped again.

"Hadn't you better take that?"

"Sure… It's from Jools. The results from the lab test on her coat are in already. As we knew it would be, Arabella's DNA is all over it. And it matches what they found on the inside of the glove."

FIFTY-SIX

As Bloomfield had the house to himself – Rachel had just driven off to join her prosecco-guzzling, shopaholic girlfriends on yet another long weekend in a spa hotel recommended by *Good Housekeeping* – he invited Tagg, Tedesco and Davey round for an early working supper.

The DCI lived in Derrington, an anonymous suburb of Rhyminster made up of aspirational four- and five-bedroomed detached houses, with a few older bungalows strung somewhat apologetically along its main road.

Tedesco had picked Lynne up from Water Lane and, as he took the fourth exit off the Trago Mills roundabout towards Derrington, he began to moan about their destination.

"Do you know what I think of when I hear the name Derrington – 'Pleasant Valley Sunday'."

"I have absolutely zero idea what you are getting it. Let me guess, another easy listening masterpiece from the early seventies? James Taylor? Carly Simon? Neil Sedaka?"

"I cannot believe your shocking ignorance sometimes. It was late sixties. Carole King. But the Monkees had the hit with it."

"Oh really. If my mum was still alive then I'm sure she'd remember them."

Any further pointless discussion was cut short by their arrival outside Bloomfield's perfectly pleasant four-bedroom detached house, snuggled away down a quiet cul-de-sac.

Their host greeted them at the door, a vision in Gant.

"Could you take your shoes off? Rachel's orders. The boss will kill me if she finds any evidence of footprints. She'll have the SOCOs crawling all over the carpets."

Lynne's intended reply – *"Oi, chauvinist! Have you even noticed that it's the twenty-first century?"* – somehow came out of her mouth as "No problem, Jimmy."

The DCI's idea of a working supper was some slices of supermarket pizza and a tantalising choice of Heineken alcohol-free beer or elderflower.

They all opted for elderflower, aside from their host, who opened the meeting by swearing the participants to secrecy.

"Look," said Lynne, "I understand as well as you do that the powers that be want to distance themselves from the events of last August."

"But," Tedesco added, "you must know that something stinks here, Jimmy, and that we have the makings of a case. Or am I missing something?"

Bloomfield put his hands together and then opened them out to form a church steeple, a gesture that Tedesco had always found somewhat prissy.

"Why don't we look at what we know. Jools?"

DS Tagg set out the case against Arabella Patrick with clarity, as if she was speaking in bullet points.

"Number one, forensics have examined the glove that fell down from the tower during the safety inspection. They

272

found traces of DNA that matched the samples found on Kerry Franklin's clothes. Number two, an examination of my coat revealed samples of Arabella's DNA which were identical to those found on the inside of the aforementioned glove."

"And continuing with DS Tagg's numbering system," Tedesco interrupted in his most annoying lawyerly manner, "point three, the head verger recognised the glove as the one that Arabella was wearing and point four, Brad Budden has supplied photographic evidence of the clothes that she was wearing on the day, including the gloves."

"So what we have so far," said Bloomfield, "is evidence that the suspect was wearing a particular pair of gloves, and that she touched the deceased with them. Hardly a slam dunk, is it? Arabella could have brushed against her when they were climbing the steps. I've done that tour myself and it gets pretty narrow in there."

Tedesco, sensing that it was his turn to speak, announced that it was time to reveal point five.

"And before I do so, I need Jimmy and Jools to respect confidentiality. What I am going to tell you involves another suspect."

Bloomfield tugged on his beer, then smiled. "I hope it was Gulliver. What have you found?"

"Sorry to pour cold water," interjected Lynne, "but we are talking about Alan Meer."

"We've interviewed him. What are you saying, he withheld evidence?" Jools asked.

"Did he tell you about the struggle he witnessed?"

"No Lynne, he didn't. He just said that he overheard raised voices, which put him off trying to attack Kerry himself."

Tedesco waited till he had finished chewing his undercooked pizza before rejoining the discussion.

"Don't lose sight of the pressure Meer was under from his employer and her links to the establishment. Poor old Frank Uglow has also been threatened from on high as well, don't forget."

"Okay then John, time for the big reveal."

"Meer is now working for my old firm, as Neil Sparkes' assistant."

"What is he assisting him with, I wonder? A yard of ale competition?"

Tedesco rushed to the aid of his former colleague. "Neil's changed. We met for coffee this time. He looks much better as well. Anyway, let me get back to Alan. He told Neil that he had seen a brief struggle between Kerry and Arabella just before he heard the screaming."

"And is he prepared to confirm this?"

Lynne re-entered the fray.

"He is understandably anxious about another interview under caution."

She reached down to her elegant leather document folder.

"However, what I have here are copies of an affidavit he swore at Neil's office."

She saw Tedesco look across at her and cross his fingers as the two CID officers read the statement.

After what seemed like an age, Bloomfield sighed.

"Okay, so what does point five really add?"

"Does it point to the DNA being transferred during the struggle?" said Jools.

"Come on Sherlock, what do you think?" Bloomfield asked Tedesco.

Ignoring the tedious jibe – the Europhile former ecclesiastical law specialist would have preferred to have been compared to Maigret – he paused for effect before pronouncing, "Lynne and I have been through the evidence, and this is our theory. Gulliver is really behind this, but we have nothing concrete on him. My guess is that he found out that Kerry had moved to Rhyme, realised that she could spill the beans about the cruise and thus thwart his political ambitions."

"What are you suggesting? That he tried to buy her silence?"

"Not just that, Jools. Bazza could easily have found out that Arabella was going on a tower tour on the day that Kerry was leading it. He's best mates with Commander Foster, who in turn lurks around the cloisters with Jock Barton."

"Barton is the head tower guide," Lynne explained, "and he and Foster are both ex-Navy."

"Thanks Lynne. So, Barry could have offered Kerry a sizeable amount both for her silence and for arranging for a little accident."

"But then Meer decides to pitch up with evil intent."

"Yes Jools, before Alan could execute his plan, and from what I know of him, I doubt if he ever would have, Kerry waits until she can isolate Arabella from the rest of the group, attacks her, but is overcome by the younger, stronger woman."

"Hang on, John. What are you asking us to believe? That Arabella calmly threw Kerry off the tower and just carried on as if nothing had happened?"

Tedesco tried to conceal his irritation.

"You have read the interviews, Jimmy. If you need to refresh your memory, then look at what Mike Knowles said."

Jools butted in. "I remember. He saw Kerry toppling on a parapet. Arabella didn't throw her off. She left her to dangle."

FIFTY-SEVEN

"I've cleared it with enough of the executive members. Lady Fiona is about to send out notice of an extraordinary meeting. She's quite the operator – she thinks that if Foster takes the blame for bypassing the constitution, then we can apply pressure on him to shut Gulliver up."

"And what are we going to propose?" asked Arabella.

"Oh? Didn't I say? After we've duffed up Foster, we retrospectively decide to allow non-members to vote."

"Flick, don't look now, but I think we need to leave."

*

"Will they do anything about it now?" asked Lynne as they walked to the Lancia.

He let her in via the passenger door. "Why don't we stop off at the Kingfisher on the way back? I think I'm allowed a small glass of house red after all that awful cordial."

"Why not, it's kind of on our way home."

Tedesco lucked in, as there was only one space in the awkward car park and, after ignoring Lynne's offer to reverse the car in for him, he eventually managed to squeeze into the space without causing any damage to his paintwork or to that of the adjacent Range Rover.

"Something tells me that you haven't been on the police driving training course," she said, laughing.

"You can pay for the drinks for that!"

As they ducked under the perilous beams at the entrance, they noticed two expensively dressed women getting ready to leave.

"It's either Felicity and Arabella, or the pub is hosting a Cruella de Vil evening."

"Can you whisper a bit louder? I don't think they heard you in Cornwall."

"What do you think? Do they know about Alan's statement?"

"Why don't I get the drinks? Your usual, madame?"

While Tedesco went to the bar to order a glass of house red and a white wine spritzer, Lynne surreptitiously reached over to the adjoining table, which had been vacated by the two women. There was a piece of paper next to their discarded bar bill.

"What's that?" her colleague asked her when he returned with the drinks.

"Not sure. It looks like an agenda of some sort, but there's some handwriting on it. It's not as neat as yours, of course, but I think I can just about make it out."

She handed the page to Tedesco, who peered intently as if he was examining an old title deed, just like the solicitor he used to be.

"Yes, it looks like a draft agenda to me. Must be the local Tories. And the writing – looks like 'Blame Foster'."

"Oh dear," Lynne said. "What if Julie Stringer got hold of this?"

*

"Look, sir," said Jools, "if this was a run-of-the-mill suspect we'd at least question them now, surely?"

Bloomfield looked distinctly queasy.

"But what have we really got? Granted, the DNA evidence shows that there was contact between the two of them and then there's Meer's rather convenient statement."

"Let's look at this another way. We approach Arabella and tell her that we are looking to eliminate her from our investigations. And, during questioning, we ask her what she has done with the other glove and whether she still has the clothes she was wearing that day."

"You think she might have got rid of them?"

"It did cross my mind, yes. I was wondering whether that might have been what she was arguing about with her husband. As I said before, I thought I heard him shout something along the lines of 'You didn't burn them!'"

"But all this presupposes that Tedesco's little theory adds up. I know he's often been right in the past – he always suspected that Swain was behind the murder in the Chantry – but I can't see Hinton letting us reopen the case on this flimsy evidence, can you?"

"She might if she thought that interviewing Arabella and clearing her would end any media speculation. You've been around the cathedral long enough to know how it works. The Close is powered by intrigue and rumour."

"Mmm, maybe. And Ms Patrick would insist on a

lawyer, probably that smooth operator that her father used to represent Charles Tantum."

"Raj Purbani? I thought he was pretty fit, as it goes. But I get it, Arabella is so arrogant, she'd assume that her lawyer would eat us for breakfast."

"I will sleep on it, DS Tagg. Lots to mull over before I ask to see Hinton."

*

Once she was safely behind her front door in Water Lane, Lynne scrolled down her contacts, found what she was looking for and sent a direct message.

"Haven't eaten yet. Fancy meeting up in Cranes for a late supper."

It took a nanosecond for the response to flash up.

"Sounds good. See you in twenty minutes."

FIFTY-EIGHT

As Lynne slyly slid the single sheet of A4 towards her, Julie Stringer rummaged in her bag for her glasses.

"Just for reading, in case you were wondering. Let's have a look…"

"It's clearly an agenda for a meeting and, as Flick and Arabella left it behind at the Kingfisher, it must relate to the local party."

Julie handled the paper carefully, as if she was the curator of an ancient artefact.

"Yeah, I agree. And what's this handwritten note about blaming Foster?"

They had decided to share a baked camembert with a side order of nachos, so Lynne gingerly speared a piece of molten cheese before responding.

"Commander Foster? You must have come across him. Built like a battleship. Key ally of Barry Gulliver."

"Isn't he a sidesman at the cathedral? I know him, always pretends he doesn't recognise me when I go there."

"That's the jolly old commander. John gets the same treatment. He had a reserved seat in the quire at the candlelit advent service last year, and Foster tried to bar him on the basis that he wasn't on his list."

"I bet Mr T didn't take that lying down."

"Oh, he didn't need to. Hilary, the bishop's wife, rescued him, and he sat next to her. She asked John if he knew under which rock the cathedral found pompous pricks like Foster."

Julie threw her head back and laughed. "I'll quote that in my next column."

"And if you do, I'll never speak to you again."

"Ooh, touchy! It was only a joke. Anyway, back to that cryptic note on the agenda. What are the Ugly Sisters blaming Foster for, do you think?"

"Come on Julie, isn't it obvious? What was your last column about?"

"You mean my exclusive on the constitutional cock-up? Of course! Duh, wake up Stringer! They are going to use the meeting of the executive to blame the pompous prick himself for not checking the rule book!"

"You missed your calling, Julie. You should have joined the CID."

"Hilarious. Listen, I don't suppose…"

"That the sheet of paper could go missing again? The very thought. But if you decide to use this, won't you need to run it past Frank?"

"Mr Uglow has his own issues with Flick Gallant. Don't forget that she threatened to serve him with an injunction and then Bella pitched in, refusing to be interviewed by the *Journal*. He's remarkably relaxed about it – retirement is on the horizon, one last scandal to expose. He's already talking to *Private Eye*."

"Good on him. One more for the road?"

"Not this time, I need to get this into the online edition as soon as I can. And I might just send a cheeky text to Luke."

"Luke Barnard? The police media guy?"

"It would only be polite. Nighty night!"

As the indomitable Julie disappeared in a puff of smoke, Lynne realised too late that her calorific supper was hardly conducive to taking part in the Torbay Triathlon, let alone the Rhyminster Tough Mudder.

*

Over the county border the day began early at police HQ. Area Commander Hinton, who had never understood how the cursed, faraway cathedral city had snuck into the edge of her bailiwick, was doorstepped by an anxious-looking Luke Barnard the minute she entered the building.

"Luke. This had better be important."

"One word: Rhyminster."

"Christ almighty! Okay, my office!"

*

Meanwhile at 4A Minster Precincts, Sally Munks was gearing up for one of the highlights of her year, the annual BBC *Children in Need* appeal.

For this year's event she was leading a group of 'brigands' made up of members of her Monday book club, the Thursday group deemed too stuck-up to take part, as well as assorted friends from her pilates and beginners Spanish classes.

The piratical theme would be acted out around the city and the cathedral precincts, and Sally was very proud of the snappy slogan she had devised to elicit donations.

"Give us your doubloons, you paltry poltroons!"

She asked Lynne if she could spare any time to dress up as a pirate. Ex-DS Davey said she would certainly think about it but warned the PA against trying to involve Tedesco.

"I'm sure he will give a generous donation, but I think he would rather saw off one of his limbs without anaesthetic than pretend to be an old sea dog. I know – why don't you ask Commander Foster?"

Tedesco and Barker arrived slightly late as they'd been to morning prayers in the cathedral, the private detective feeling in need of some quiet space, and also wondering if he might pick up some news on what his sister had been hinting at about Bishop Bob.

He managed a quick word with his friend Canon Wilf Drake at the end of the service, but the precentor was giving nothing away about the episcopal retirement.

As Tedesco got to the office and reached his desk he looked up and saw his colleague staring into space.

"Lynne – you are looking uncharacteristically vague this morning."

"Rude! Actually, I am a little on edge. I've lit the blue touch paper…"

*

"Well, Luke. This had better be important."

"It is, ma'am. I've had a tip-off from a local journalist up there that they've got hold of a confidential document which could be used to suggest that the local party is trying to cover up the irregularities in the selection of Arabella Patrick as the candidate. And they are running it in the paper this week, with an online teaser from today."

Hinton lasered in on Barnard.

"So I should expect calls from Flick, Arabella and probably the chief? It's one thing for the chief to get involved when a member of the public claims harassment, as Crispin Atherton did, but what am I supposed to do about a leak to the press, unless we can show that the document was stolen?"

"It's a 'no comment' if I get asked, then?"

*

It didn't take long for the sparks to fly. The allegations of a fixed election followed by a cover-up were given further credence by Julie's piece: 'Bella Gate latest: cathedral volunteer thrown under the bus'.

While Frank Uglow waited for the inevitable storm to break over the *Journal*'s Dickensian office in Parchment Street, word of Julie's piece had reached DCI Bloomfield and DS Tagg.

Bloomfield took out his pocket square and gave his granny glasses a thorough polish, which Jools correctly recognised as the prelude to a pronouncement.

"I've slept on what we discussed yesterday. I think this latest development might be what we need to get Hinton to back me up."

"And why would that be, sir? How does mad woman Julie Stringer's latest bit of tittle-tattle add to the evidence?"

"It doesn't. But think about this from Hinton's side, and Arabella's if you like. The stench from the selection meeting is getting stronger by the minute and it's only a matter of time before Julie, or someone on the nationals, starts to link the botched election with what happened on the tower."

"I think I follow. And if a cover-up is revealed, and the proverbial hits the fan, Hinton could be brought down if she was shown to have colluded with Flick and Arabella."

"And if they start asking questions about her halting our investigation…"

"What are you saying? We demand a meeting with her and set out what we have got? It still isn't a slam dunk, as you said yesterday."

"No, but we've got the glove, we can ask about the clothes, and we've got the statement from Meer. The CPS have prosecuted on less."

"And if we persuade Hinton that the likely outcome is to eliminate Ms Patrick from our enquiries…"

"Hinton can demonstrate that she wasn't influenced by the establishment, Arabella can get back to working the constituency."

"And then the spotlight will turn on Bazza…"

FIFTY-NINE

The meeting with Hinton had been arranged surprisingly quickly. Bloomfield didn't need to be at his persuasive best, as she had clearly reached her own decision. She needed to be able to show any future enquiry that she had clean hands.

"All right. I accept that Arabella Patrick has some questions to answer about Kerry Franklin, but you two have gone against my express instructions by continuing to talk to Tedesco and Davey and you have used police resources when doing so. So please don't think that there will no consequences."

As they drove back to Devon, Tagg doing the actual driving as the junior officer, Bloomfield sought to allay his colleague's fears.

"Jools, she's out to save her own skin. She can't condone what we did, but trust me, any issues for us will disappear, however this pans out."

"I really hope you're right, sir."

*

"Good morning, Ms Patrick. How are you this fine morning?"

The easy charm of the clerk to the chambers of Sir Maxwell Patrick, QC, MP was entirely wasted on Sir Maxwell's daughter.

"Frank. I need to speak to Daddy. It's urgent."

"As luck would have it, he's in chambers this morning preparing for a conference."

"I don't care if he's preparing to meet royalty – put me through. Now!"

It was a full minute before she heard her father's leathery tones booming down the receiver.

"Bella dear, I know you'll be joining me on the green benches soon but don't be rude to Frank. He's practically family."

"Okay, okay. Look, go online and look at today's *Rhyminster Journal*. It's libellous! That old milch cow of a reporter, Julie, is saying that I was part of a conspiracy to rig the vote. Can you get me an injunction or something?"

Before her father could get a word in, her mobile rang. Looking at the caller display and seeing Flick's name, she told Sir Patrick to call her when he had a plan.

"Flick. It's about the *Journal*, I assume."

"What? No, far worse than that. I have it on the best authority that the police are going to interview you."

"About the election?"

"If only. They want to know more about the sodding tower. Tedesco and his moll have dug up some real evidence, and Jackie Hinton can't help you this time. You are on your own."

Over at Minster Precincts Lynne was rescuing Tedesco from Sally's latest *Children in Need*-themed monologue, practically dragging him into the meeting room.

"You are very hyper today. Too much exercise, I reckon."

"Listen! Jools just messaged me. Hinton is reopening the investigation – and they're starting with Arabella."

Restraining himself from punching the air and shouting 'Get in!', behaviour he habitually restricted to Argyle matches, the kindly private detective just smiled and gave Barker a stroke.

SIXTY

She'd only discussed what had actually happened with her husband. Crime wasn't Crispin's area of expertise, but he knew enough to be able to confidently advise his wife that, if the truth ever came out, she'd be up to her neck in excrement.

Granted, she probably wouldn't face a murder charge. When she wandered over to the cathedral on that bright August afternoon the intention of killing another was far from her thoughts.

How would her father put it? *Actus reus,* but an absence of *mens rea.* Or, she may have done the deed, but she hadn't planned it.

But would she get away with involuntary manslaughter? She was defending herself against Kerry, but did she use reasonable force? If she was being completely honest it had been very easy to fend her off; she wasn't armed, and the tour guide seemed too frightened to do more than just shove her a bit.

As Crispin put it, her real problem was the fact that she had deliberately left Kerry in a precarious position and had been reckless as to the consequences, making things far worse by consistently lying about her role in her death ever since she had given her initial statement when she got down from the tower.

And now Jackie Hinton had let slip to Flick Gallant that there had been a witness.

Was it that boring little man with the whiny accent who had been going on about park-and-ride schemes? Or that weaselly geek with the Morrison's bag? The thought of him was almost enough to make her retch.

Crispin was up in town and so the Porsche was lying idle in the garage at Stannary House. She needed to think fast. And that meant driving faster.

*

Arabella Patrick wasn't at home to visitors when DS Tagg and DC Lovell called round, so they invited themselves in to wait for her, to the simmering displeasure of Mrs Bellhatchet, the cleaner and general factotum.

"We'll give it half an hour if we may? And could you call your employer? It's very important…"

While the CID duo kicked their heels the object of their investigation was speeding down the M5 with her sound system on full blast.

Arabella Patrick's playlist couldn't have been more different from that of John Tedesco.

It featured selections from *Carmina Burana*, Wagner and, from the popular end of the spectrum, Meatloaf and Queen.

As she sped out of Devon her plan crystallised. *There's no other way*, she thought to herself as she turned off the motorway and drove into Taunton Deane Services.

Once she was safely parked, she Googled Rhyminster Cathedral on her phone and then called the reception desk.

"Hello, my name is Alice Brewer. I was wondering, do you have a tower tour today?"

Having booked for that afternoon she wandered into the services. It was full of ugly tattooed misshapes. *At least I won't need to canvass dreadful people like this at the election anymore*, she thought to herself as she scuttled past Subway and KFC.

Delving further into this circle of hell, she was relieved to find that there was a Sunglasses Hut outlet, where she bought some hideous but effective eyewear, and a crappy 'Souvenirs of Somerset' section, where she snapped up the longest scarf she could find, which featured images of Cheddar Gorge and Weston-super-Mare. A notepad and biro completed her purchases.

*

After twenty minutes, Tagg decided that time was up. Their presence had served its purpose in putting the wind up the gruesome Mrs Bellhatchet, and she began to suspect that Arabella had been tipped off: Hinton via Gallant was her best bet.

*

"Don't worry, you will be fine. Once you get going, you'll enjoy it. The training will just kick in."

Jock Barton's words of comfort were addressed to Mike Wooldridge, who was about to lead his first tower tour.

Wooldridge, like so many of the volunteers at the cathedral, was a retired teacher. He'd been a deputy head at a comprehensive in Newton Abbot, so the prospect of a small group of hardy pensioners didn't faze him.

"Let me see who we've got for you today," said Barton, studying the printout of the tour group.

"We've got nine for you this afternoon. Mr and Mrs Rosson from Northern Ireland, a group of four walkers doing the South-West Coast Path, the obligatory American couple – these two are from North Carolina – and the usual last-minute local. Alice Brewer, who lives in the Close, apparently."

SIXTY-ONE

He couldn't concentrate on his other cases and, as Sally looked as if she was about to badger him about her wretched charity work at any moment, Tedesco decided that he needed another wander around the cathedral to reboot his day.

As he entered the Close, the afternoon gloom began to assume the form of an almost physical presence which threatened to seep into his very being.

"John, I'd been wondering how you were. I'm at a bit of a loose end until evensong. I was heading across to the refectory. Care to join me?"

Canon Wilfred, the saintly precentor, had the uncanny habit of suddenly appearing when Tedesco was in a dark or doubtful place, not unlike the angel who looked out for James Stewart in *It's a Wonderful Life*.

Although music was the basis of his professional life as a cathedral musician, Wilf Drake knew better than to discuss it with Tedesco.

During the early part of their friendship, they had tried to influence each other's tastes and the sensitive cleric could never forget Tedesco's crestfallen face when Wilf gave his verdict on the music of Clifford T Ward: "Interesting. All in three/four time."

This was something that irritated the songwriter-obsessed detective. Professional musicians always focused on technical things like time signatures and key changes, and thus completely missed what the right combination of music and lyrics meant to fans like him: emotion, empathy, melodies they could hum.

It was a bit like how he felt about cars. He loved the reassuring sound and feel of his Lancia but had zero interest in what lay under the bonnet. That was why he employed Jan Webber at Rhyme Autos.

The two old friends ordered a pot of Minster Blend tea and found a table discreetly sited behind a stone column.

"You looked as though you were carrying the world on your shoulders, John. Is it Sorcha? It's coming up to the anniversary, isn't it?"

Tedesco, looking uncharacteristically perplexed, responded, "What? No, it isn't Sorcha, thanks for asking. I'm on tenterhooks, actually."

"You look it. Would it help to talk?"

"I know this won't go any further. The police are reopening the file on Kerry Franklin."

"So, it wasn't an accident? You and Lynne never really thought it was, did you?"

*

Arabella screeched out of the car park at the services, just avoiding a collision with an Eddie Stobart HGV as she failed to check her wing mirror whilst rejoining the motorway.

As 'Bat Out of Hell' segued with a shameless lack of subtlety into 'We Are the Champions', she began to have second thoughts. She could cope with prison – she had survived her boarding schools, after all. But she couldn't survive the humiliation.

The putative MP being called in for questioning. The TV cameras, the social media shitstorm, followed by the inevitable arrest and conviction despite Daddy's best efforts. And when she got out, the pointing fingers, the wagging tongues. No more hunt balls, no more Verbier.

No one would really miss her, least of all Crispin and Flick. They were welcome to each other. She'd known about their affair for months.

*

Mike Wooldridge seemed self-consciously over-confident as he gave his introductory briefing to his charges.

Eight of the group had been on time but, typically, the token local had been late.

To the palpable irritation of the grim-faced couple from Ulster, Wooldridge had given Alice Brewer an extra five minutes. Then, just before he was about to begin without her, an exotic creature wrapped in a shawl emerged from the mist. The shawl, or maybe it was a long scarf, incongruously featured a view of the pier at Weston-super-Mare and she was wearing huge Hollywood sunglasses. She resembled a pound-shop version of Joan or Jackie Collins. What on earth was she doing rocking up in Rhyminster on a grey afternoon?

The latecomer gave no apology for her tardiness and seemed to pay little attention to the safety briefing, prompting

Wooldridge to ask her to listen as he went through it a second time.

*

While Bloomfield was trying to organise patrols at the key motorway junctions – there being no sight of Arabella at her known haunts and having ascertained that both Crispin and Sir Maxwell were conveniently busy in court – Tedesco and Drake were quietly finishing their tea, oblivious to what was about to happen.

"I'd better wander back to Minster Precincts before Sally sends out a search party," said the private detective.

"You that way, me this way," said the canon precentor, confident that Tedesco would appreciate the allusion to *Loves Labours Lost*.

The cathedral and its people had done it again. He felt settled, calm, ready for the latest revelations.

Sorcha, as ever, had been presciently right. He could never leave Rhyminster. The cathedral was his lodestar, his campanile, his sense of permanence.

He was rudely shocked back to reality by the sound of voices. "Look out!"

"What the fuck is that! Someone's jumped!"

Tedesco looked up just in time to see another body landing with a sickening thud on Cathedral Green.

SIXTY-TWO

'Alice Brewer' was pronounced dead at the scene. Once the glasses had been removed the corpse was rapidly re-identified as being that of Arabella Patrick.

Before she jumped, she had carefully secreted a letter in the inside pocket of her coat.

The note was never made public, but it contained an admission that she had abandoned Kerry to her fate and had been, in her words, 'totally relaxed' about letting Alan Meer take the blame.

Several days later, Tedesco and Davey went to the Kingfisher for supper. This was becoming an end of case ritual, a chance to reflect on what they had been through away from the office and the cathedral.

"Lynne, one thing sticks out for me. The symmetry of this case. Do you see what I mean?"

"Obviously. It began and ended with someone jumping off the cathedral. Do you think they will ever allow the public up there again?"

"Not for a long time. And I feel for that tour guide, Mike. He's beating himself up about it, but it sounds as though there was nothing he could have done. It wasn't just the tower I was thinking of when I mentioned symmetry. Poor Angela Meer was left to drown by Kathleen."

"And Kerry was left to fall by Arabella. I get it. The difference is that Arabella would eventually have been convicted if she hadn't taken matters into her own hands."

"Fair enough, but I wouldn't have wished Kathleen Meer's bitter, crabbed little life on anyone."

Lynne took a sip of Merlot and then she leaned in towards her companion.

"Jools told me about the suicide note," she whispered. "It wasn't just an admission. Arabella mentioned that Hinton had ignored evidence in order to protect her, egged on by the chief constable and, of course, Felicity Gallant. It was only when Julie leaked the memo about the botched election and the attempt to rig any rerun that Hinton started to listen to Bloomfield."

"But now Arabella has shafted her from the grave."

"And it gets better. The note also contained lurid disclosures about Crispin and Flick Gallant."

"Are you trying to put me off my delicious Lyme Bay mackerel, Mrs Davey?"

"It isn't a pretty image, I grant you. What will happen to the local party, do you think? Will they choose Bazza by default?"

"Not if Lady Fiona has anything to do with it. Or Sir Vere, for that matter."

"John, I know that Arabella was a pretty repellent character, but Bazza was the real villain here, surely?"

"We will never know. I am convinced that it was he who put Kerry up to her half-hearted attempt to eliminate Arabella, but any chance of proving that died with her."

"What about when Kerry's estate gets wound up? The bank statements might make for interesting reading."

"What are you thinking? Some suspicious payments from Barry Gulliver? I doubt it. If he was going to pay Kerry for shoving Arabella off the cathedral, he'd want her to fulfil her part of the bargain first. The guy is a typical Yorkshireman, after all."

"And so now he's free to pursue women with impunity, I suppose."

"I'm not so sure. My gut tells me that Barry Gulliver will be presenting himself as a new man, a champion of family values. He might even find God."

Lynne giggled. "You really are an old cynic. Come on, one for the road, then I'll call Mickey Hunn to get us home in one piece."

*

The ever-smiling Mickey dropped Lynne off in Water Lane before driving round the Close to St Budeaux Place.

Once inside, Tedesco checked on Barker, who was peacefully curled up asleep in his basket, then poured himself a generous glass of claret, got out his casebook, took up his ink pen and carefully inscribed one word on the final page.

Fin.

Faced with the agonising choice of a suitable track to mark the moment he went for the Beatles, a classic slice of McCartney.

He removed *Revolver* from its sleeve with reverential care, as if he was preparing the vessels for holy communion, then dropped the needle on the track, silently dedicating it to Kerry: 'For No One'.

As the two and a half minutes or so of perfection ended, Tedesco reflected that for Barry Gulliver it wasn't so much a case of *fin*, but *a continuer*.

The North Canonry, one month later.

Tedesco could sense the expectant buzz in the air as he and Barker made their familiar way to the residence of the Bishop of Rhyminster.

It was a bit like the walk through the parkland surrounding Argyle's ground on a matchday, or the feeling he got as an orchestra tuned up before a concert.

The main door was welcomingly open, and they were warmly greeted by Hilary, who commandeered Barker for some as yet unspecified duties before pointing the dog's master in the direction of the impromptu bar area.

Tedesco was delighted to find that the barman was Jos Elsted, who had provided the wine for the evening.

"Ah, John. I was hoping you would be here. I've got something interesting from the Languedoc that I'd appreciate your opinion on."

As he took his generously filled glass with him into the noisy main room, he saw Lynne in the centre of a group of *Searchlight* reporters, laughing merrily at something or other as Duncan Chivers looked on with evident devotion.

He didn't mind. He genuinely liked Chivers, who was one the few men he knew who remotely approached being good enough for his colleague. But he had to admit to how he was feeling, and he didn't need any prompting from his internal soundtrack to tell him that he was a jealous guy.

"Mr T!"

It was, of course, the agency's esteemed PA, Sally Munks, dressed for the occasion like a rustic extra from a Hardy adaptation.

"Can I tempt you with a vegan sausage roll?"

"Oh, go on then. I assume there is a carnivorous alternative somewhere?"

"You are so funny out of the office! Lynne seems to be enjoying herself, doesn't she?"

Next up was a clearly tipsy Julie Stringer, who wanted his 'take' on the real reason for the Bishop's resignation and if he had heard any whispers about his successor.

"Do you think it will be a woman this time? Or will they go like for like?"

"Julie, I admire your zeal, but can you stop being a reporter for just one evening? Or would it drive you insane?"

As Julie went in search of more garrulous and indiscreet interviewees, Tedesco noticed that Sir Vere Alston was standing on his own, so he made a beeline for him.

"How are you this evening, Sir Vere?"

"You are a good fellow, Tedesco. Do you know, no one has asked me how I am since the dreadful business last month. Frankly, it's been sheer hell. The party is in turmoil, Flick Gallant is under some sort of investigation, Foster has been suspended and that lout Gulliver and his crew are demanding that he is selected as the candidate by default."

"That would be terrible. I'm afraid that I could never vote for him."

"Neither, in all conscience, could I," whispered the

Knight of the Shires. "Lady Fiona thinks I should announce that I will postpone my retirement."

Further discussion of local politics would have to wait as Robert Dwyer, Lord Bishop of Rhyminster, was bringing the room to order by the traditional 'spoon on glass' method.

Joined by Hilary, who was accompanied by Barker, the bishop began by welcoming the guests.

"Hilary and I wanted our special friends to be with us tonight, both human and canine."

Barker wagged his tail appreciatively, to 'oohs' and 'aahs' from the other guests.

"So, representing the clergy, we have Dean Dan and his wife Jo – who many of you will know as your fitness instructor – Canon Wilf, and my interim successor, the suffragan bishop of Dartmoor."

Pete Leiper was Bishop Bob's de facto deputy, and he would be minding the shop while the interminable process of discernment went on. A new bishop wasn't expected to be announced for at least nine months, to allow for an episcopal gestation period.

"Representing the media – and may I say, genuinely, that the south-west is superbly served by its local TV and newspapers – we have Vicki Thomas, Duncan Chivers and Nicky Tedesco from the BBC, and Frank Uglow and Julie Stringer from the *Journal*." He paused for a couple of seconds.

"Shall we have a toast now? To local journalism!"

Once the hubbub had subsided, he continued by welcoming the Derringtons – "Our exemplary member of parliament, Sir Vere Alston,"– and then he added some generous words about Tedesco – "A lawyer and my friend, famed for his devotion to his clients, who, in partnership

304

with Lynne, continues to serve our cathedral community in more ways than he will ever know."

Hilary elbowed him, with zero subtlety.

"And as the bishop's wife has reminded me, there are some real heroes to be saluted. Firstly, the group of volunteers who have produced and served the wonderful food we are sharing."

This prompted several loud hear hears, before Bishop Bob added a generous tribute to Jos Elsted.

"Now to more serious matters. My retirement."

This announcement brought forth a chorus of well-meant booing, stopped in its tracks by the precentor, who led the room in a chorus of 'For He's a Jolly Good ellow'.

The bishop called for order.

"That's quite enough! I do have some words to say, and I want to make sure that there is plenty of time for some Christian fellowship, otherwise known as carousing, before the evening ends. Firstly, I know that there have been rumours about our reasons for leaving. So in no particular order, I can confirm that I have not lost my faith, fallen out with the archbishop, or given up on the Church of England, endlessly frustrating organisation that it is. I will be seventy next year, and I just want to spend time with Hilary, my grandchildren, and my books. Very boring, I know. Jos has promised that he will deliver to our new home in Yorkshire, and we hope you will all visit.

"That isn't to say that we won't miss you all, or this house, which has been a true home for the family. And we will miss the diocese of Rhyminster. I have often said it, but it repays repetition. This diocese is one of God's little miracles. And finally. There are three women in my life who have enabled me to carry out this work."

"I say, bishop!" Julie interjected.

"Thank you, Ms Stringer. The first of these is obviously Hilary. She has been with me through the good times and when life has become more challenging, showing me love and providing me with a deep well of common sense. Then there is Amanda, our esteemed diocesan secretary, recently referred to in the *Church Times* as the Church of England's answer to Nicola Sturgeon. I think it's the power heels!

"Amanda, you deserve all the praise that comes your way, but I hope that you will stay and help my successor to bed in. And finally, the sainted Barbara. I'm the third bishop to benefit from the legend that is Mrs Battershill. I pray that my retirement doesn't give her any ideas."

At that moment Sally Munks and two of the other servers emerged with three huge bouquets for the three women, before Bishop Bob handed the floor to the diocesan secretary.

Once Amanda Leonard had presented various gifts from the parishes to Bob and Hilary, the carousing could restart. Tedesco thought he would go in search of Lynne, but then saw that his sister was walking purposefully towards him.

"How's it hanging, bro?"

"Have I just stumbled into a rap video? I'm hangin' tough, sis, if you want to know."

"Look, I'd love to talk about Arabella Patrick – you knew all along, didn't you – but I'm getting worried about you."

"I wouldn't say I knew all along, but…"

"Classic John Tedesco avoidance! I saw your sad little face when you spotted Lynne and Duncan."

His kindly expression seemed to crumple under the weight of his loneliness.

"Is it that obvious?"

"Mmm. You are exasperating, you know that? I will never really understand your relationship, tendresse or whatever you dressed it up as, but you have to move on from Sorcha. We all hoped that you and Liz might get together; however, everyone knows that you and Lynne are made for each other."

Tedesco looked across and saw that Chivers had his arm round his colleague.

"If you don't act soon, it will be too late," was his sister's parting shot.

*

He glanced at his watch, not wanting to be the first or last to leave.

Hilary noticed this.

"You can't think of leaving us yet, Barker is busy hoovering up the crumbs! And Bob wants a word before you go."

Tedesco looked on as the border terrier swept up the remains of the canapes, and then he endured a tedious ten minutes with the rather too earnest Bishop Pete before Bob came to his rescue.

"Thanks for waiting, John. I wanted to thank you in person, not just for supporting me and Dan and the cathedral through the dreadful events of the last year, but for all the advice you gave me as diocesan registrar. You were a superb legal adviser. And Hilary and I have already got a spare bed for you in Helmsley. I know you get a nosebleed anywhere north of Exeter, but you will love it there. Promise you'll visit soon?"

He promised. Actually, a break would do him good. The Dwyers were moving to what looked like an idyllic spot close to the North Yorkshire moors and he'd Googled it. Helmsley had a castle and a micro-brewery as well as some great walking country on its doorstep. Bishop Bob had suggested a walk to Rievaulx Abbey, which looked stunning.

Once Hilary could bear to be parted from Barker, and once he had extricated himself from his sister's embrace, he found his coat, put Barker on his lead and then the two of them wandered back home through the moonlit Close.

"What next for Rhyminster, old friend? We're going to miss our bishop and his lovely wife."

The border terrier looked up at him adoringly and Tedesco bent down to stroke him.

Acknowledgments

To Lucinda, who thought she had married an even-tempered solicitor, but woke up one morning to find that she was living with a temperamental writer, words are never enough to convey my thanks, and to everyone at Salisbury Cathedral and at Godwins Solicitors in Winchester for continued friendship and support.

These stories are not detailed police procedurals – Bloomfield is to Tedesco as Hastings is to Poirot – so please forgive any technical inaccuracies or mistakes, which are mine alone.

Finally, I hope that this novel will inspire readers to go up cathedral towers, rather than be frightened off.

I have climbed up countless steep and narrow stairs in the interests of research, and have always been amply rewarded by the view, whether scanning the Liverpool skyline for glimpses of Anfield and Goodison Park or looking down at the peerless English beauty of my adopted home city of Salisbury.

So, take a break from hulling strawberries, ironing your newspaper, black-leading the grate or whatever and book a tower tour. You won't regret it.

This book is printed on paper from sustainable sources managed under the Forest Stewardship Council (FSC) scheme.

It has been printed in the UK to reduce transportation miles and their impact upon the environment.

For every new title that Matador publishes, we plant a tree to offset CO_2, partnering with the More Trees scheme.

For more about how Matador offsets its environmental impact, see www.troubador.co.uk/about/